When Lyla awoke, Jade was leaning over her, stroking her brow. "Mm-m," Lyla murmured groggily. She pulled Jade to her and kissed her deeply on the mouth. "Take these clothes off."

"No time," Jade said. "It's after ten. I've got to go." She rolled her tongue tip over Lyla's lips.

"We have to stop meeting like this," Lyla gurgled.

"Like hell." Jade kissed her again. "Get up, we've got to fix the bed."

"Next time I'm not going to fall asleep," Lyla said.

"That's what you always say."

"It's your fault. You sap my energy."

Jade laughed. "Luckily, it'll be regenerated by next week."

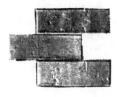

WED
NES
DAY
Nights

CAMARIN
GRAE

The Naiad Press, Inc.
1994

Printed in the United States of America on acid-free paper
First Edition

Edited by Ann Klauda and Katherine V. Forrest
Cover design by Pat Tong and Bonnie Liss
    (Phoenix Graphics)
Typeset by Sandi Stancil

Library of Congress Cataloging-in-Publication Data

Grae, Camarin.
   Wednesday nights / by Camarin Grae.
        p.   cm.
   ISBN 1-56280-060-4
   I. Title.
PS3557.R125W4   1994
813'.54—dc20
                                                          93-47337
                                                               CIP

Books by Camarin Grae

Winged Dancer
Paz
Soul Snatcher
The Secret in the Bird
Edgewise
Slick
Stranded
Wednesday Nights

CHAPTER 1

Lyla Bradshaw sensed someone watching her. She kept walking. *I'm getting paranoid,* she thought, looking around, seeing no one, *the Wednesday night jitters.* She got to the building, rang the doorbell, and Jade buzzed her in.

Soon they were naked. Lyla held Jade's wrists against the mattress, moistening when Jade moaned lustily beneath her. Jade was submissive now. Writhing. Lyla entered her. Both women were trembling. Lyla pulled her finger part way out, slowly, loving the slipperiness of it. Then in again to the warm, moist chamber. Using her whole hand, she started thrusting vigorously. Jade screamed when the first climax came. Lyla loved the sound.

An hour later, there was pillow talk and wine, and Lyla dozed off as she always did.

"Yeah, hello," Hank Lester said into the phone.

"Lennox Rug calling. We're having a special on wall-to-wall carpeting and —"

"Carpet your ass, lady," Hank said. He slammed down the receiver.

Sally chuckled.

Fifteen minutes later, Hank's phone rang again.

"Don't answer it," Sally said.

Hank tossed the newspaper aside and grabbed the phone. "Yeah?"

"Mr. Henry Lester?"

"Yeah, who're you?"

"I'm calling from Ames Enterprises. You haven't picked up your prize yet, and we're wondering if you're planning to come and get it?"

"What prize you talking about, lady?"

"Your Panasonic VCR, sir. From the *Ames Aims to Please* raffle."

"You serious?"

"You're Henry Lester of Twenty-five Forty West Roscoe Street?"

"Yeah, that's right."

"Didn't you receive your notification card? Saying that you won?"

"You mean . . . yeah, I did get something in the mail a while back. It didn't say I won; it said I was a finalist or something. I figured it for a scam."

"It's no scam. Your name was drawn. You've won the VCR. You should have received notification to come and pick it up."

"You conning me? I didn't even enter no raffle."

"Well, someone entered your name, sir. Apparently, for some reason, you didn't receive the card saying you're a winner."

Hank scratched his head. "So, what's the catch? What

2

do I have to do to get this VCR, go and visit some swampland in Florida?"

"It's a raffle, sir, not a promotion. Your VCR is right here in Chicago. All you have to do is come and pick it up. I'm sorry you didn't receive the mail notice. It should have come two weeks ago. Today's the last day for you to claim the prize. We're located at Nineteen Thirty-four West Fullerton. Ames Enterprises, second floor, just left of the stairwell. You have until nine-fifteen tonight."

Hank glanced at his watch. "I can be there in five minutes," he said.

"Please bring some identification with you."

Hank grabbed a pencil from the table and wrote the address on the newspaper. "I'm not sure I believe this," he said.

"I'll be here until nine-fifteen, Mr. Lester. It's up to you."

He hung up the phone. "Get this, Sally. Some chick says I won a VCR. Some raffle or something."

Sally laughed. "Yeah, right."

Hank put on his heavy construction boots and his blue jeans jacket. He tore off the corner of the newspaper where he'd written the address. "I'm gonna go check it out. You wanna come along?"

"On a wild goose chase? I got better things to do."

He found a parking place a few doors from the address the woman had given him. It was a run-down building on the south side of the street. He climbed the stairs to the second floor. The corridor was deserted. He found the *Ames Enterprises* sign and knocked on the door.

"Who is it?"

"Hank Lester."

"Come on in, it's open," a cheerful, female voice called.

The only light in the office was from a desk lamp. There were several chairs, a table, shelves stacked with papers and boxes.

"Have a seat, I'll be right with you," the voice said from an adjoining room.

Hank sat in the padded plastic chair across from the desk. He stretched out his legs and crossed his arms,

3

wondering what the chances were of his walking out of here with a VCR.

The door on his right opened. Hank turned his head and stared into the barrel of a thirty-eight caliber revolver.

When Lyla awoke, Jade was leaning over her, stroking her brow. "Mm-m," Lyla murmured groggily. She pulled Jade to her and kissed her deeply on the mouth. "Take these clothes off."

"No time," Jade said. "It's after ten. Benjameanie's coming to my place tonight. I've got to go." She rolled her tongue tip over Lyla's lips.

"We have to stop meeting like this," Lyla gurgled.

"Like hell." Jade kissed her again. "Get up, we've got to fix the bed."

"Next time I'm not going to fall asleep," Lyla said.

"That's what you always say."

"It's your fault. You sap my energy."

Jade laughed. "Luckily, it'll be regenerated by next week."

"Candace mentioned how good my mood's been since last summer." Lyla stroked Jade's leg. "It's true, you know. We make Candace happy, too."

"Everyone's happy." Jade smoothed her palm around Lyla's bare breast. "The happy foursome. Except Benny's not so happy. I think she thinks I'm having an affair."

"That woman is lacking in basic trust," Lyla said.

Candace was watching TV when Lyla got home. "Hi, hon," Candace called. "How was class?"

"Exhausting," Lyla said. "What are you watching?"

"Some dumb movie. You hungry? There's strawberry shortcake."

Lyla got their cake. They ate it in front of the TV, side by side on the sofa. The movie *was* dumb, a made-for-TV romance. Lyla kissed her partner's round cheek. "I love you, woman."

CHAPTER 2

The topic at the staff meeting was *transference*. Emily Granser, the director of the clinic, traced the concept from Freud's original notion of clients *transferring* onto the therapist feelings they had for their parents, to the modifications made by the ego analysts and by the object relations and self-psychology theorists. Then the group discussed examples from their own cases.

"What about that client of yours, Lyla?" one of the psychologists said. "The man who told you he was in love with you, and then dropped out of treatment when you wouldn't see him outside the therapy? You mentioned that he reactivated. Are you working on the transference stuff?"

"Ivan Dorley," Lyla said. "He made the appointment but then never came."

"I had a client once who tried to *become* me," another therapist said. "She started dressing like me and talking like me. One day I ran into her in the supermarket. After that, she started buying the same foods she'd seen in my shopping cart. She used to spy on me, too. It was creepy."

Heads nodded around the table.

"That one ended well, though," the therapist said, and proceeded to talk about how the therapy had evolved, with the client finally making significant progress in solidifying her own identity.

"One of my ex-clients used to stand outside my office, watching me through the window," a social worker said. "He even followed me home a couple times."

"How did you handle that?" one of the interns asked.

"What would you suggest?" the social worker responded.

Some lively discussion followed, and Lyla thought again what a good decision it had been to join this group. The staff worked well together and was often stimulating and supportive toward each other. Lyla was the only lesbian working at the clinic, but not the only feminist. Even their part-time psychiatrist was learning.

Although she hadn't intended it, Lyla had become the clinic's primary resource for counseling rape victims. It started because of her volunteer work at WICCA, a rape crisis line. Lyla's expertise in the area had grown to the point where she sometimes spoke and often presented workshops on the topic of rape and the rape culture. Working with rape survivors was painful, but as she frequently told Candace after a draining day, "The gratifications are worth it, right?"

On her way home from work that day, Lyla stopped at the supermarket to pick up French bread and romaine

7

lettuce for the Caesar salads she and Candace loved. In the produce section someone poked her arm.

"They let anyone into this store," the woman said.

Lyla looked coolly at her. "Right, even you," she retorted. "Long time, Reggie."

"You need a haircut."

Lyla shrugged. "You always did like my hair short."

"And you never gave a fuck what I liked."

Lyla felt the familiar old frustration and anger. She turned and examined some apples.

"So how's Candy? Sweet and tubby as ever?" Reggie said.

Lyla placed several delicious apples in her cart. "We don't need to have this conversation."

Reggie laughed. "You still have a rod up your ass."

"You're still angry and rude."

"You used to love it."

"Not that part of you."

"You used to beg me to eat you out."

Lyla walked away, pushing the shopping cart. Reggie followed. "So are you still making TV appearances? I haven't seen you on the tube since last fall when you said the cure for rape was to convince men that women aren't pussy little pushovers for them to conquer. That is what you said, isn't it?"

"Something like that."

"So have you made any more TV appearances?"

"That was my one and only," Lyla said. She maneuvered down the aisle toward the breads.

"Ah, nostalgia. That's what you used to call me."

Lyla glared at her. "Reggie, it's been five years for Christ's sake! Let it go."

"Don't flatter yourself, it's long gone, *Liarla*. You're barely a dim memory to me now."

"Good."

"I've got better things to think about."

"Good." Lyla squeezed a loaf of French bread. She put it into her cart. "I never lied to you."

Reggie guffawed. She looked at Lyla disdainfully, shaking her head. "I've got no time for this. Places to go, people to see. Stay out of trouble, huh?" And she was gone.

Lyla caught a glimpse of her a few minutes later in one of the checkout lines. They ignored each other.

On the drive home, Lyla thought about how the relationship with Reggie Hirtz had evolved — the excitement in the beginning, Reggie's energy and intensity, her cocky air of self-assuredness that intrigued and amused Lyla. The aggressive lovemaking. But it hadn't taken too long for Lyla to realize how troubled Reggie was, and how angry and possessive. Lyla had pulled back; Reggie had pushed forward more insistently. Lyla knew it wasn't going to work. Reggie tried everything to make her stay. The ending had been ugly, and Reggie obviously was still bitter.

At home in the kitchen, Lyla told Candace about the encounter. "She's worse than she ever was," Lyla said. "So full of anger and hate. I think she'll always hate me."

"That narcissistic injury you gave her," Candace said.

Lyla smiled. "The way you talk. You'd think you were married to a *psycho*therapist. I don't think Reggie will ever let it heal."

"Maybe I should do all the grocery shopping from now on," Candace said. "Well, at least she never did any of the vengeful things she threatened."

"I bet she's still plotting."

Candace kissed her partner's neck. "How does an omelette sound?"

"Num."

They prepared the meal together. Candace talked about the new hire at her office and how funny he was. "He has three dogs; one's a Siberian huskie." She added grated cheese to the eggs. "He put their pictures up on his wall."

"Kinky," said Lyla.

"Speaking of dogs, guess who I saw when I was walking Gal? Jim Julian. He pretended not to see me again. I think he knows about us."

"Maybe so."

As they were clearing the table, Lyla reached around

Candace from the rear and gave her breast a gentle squeeze.

Candace turned and kissed her partner tenderly. Lyla stroked Candace's back beneath the T-shirt, then her front.

Candace pulled her toward the corner of the room. "The blinds are open."

"Oh, heavens, what will the neighbors say?" She kissed Candace's eyelids. "Are the blinds open in the bedroom?"

"I don't think so," Candace said coyly. "Come, let's go find out." Candace took her hand and led her upstairs.

When they came back down, Candace finished cleaning up the kitchen, then took the newspaper and settled into her recliner chair. After talking on the phone for a while, Lyla picked up the novel she'd been reading, a sappy lesbian love story which she was enjoying immensely.

"I'll be damned," Candace said. "Listen to this."

Lyla looked up from her book. Candace could never read the newspaper without sharing tidbits of the news with Lyla. Lyla didn't mind.

"A man was found dead in an office building on Fullerton. He had the word *RAPIST* tattooed on his forehead."

"Really?" Lyla said. "How did he die?"

"It doesn't say. It happened to two other guys, too. Some months ago. They were also tattooed but they weren't killed. All three of the men had been tried and acquitted of rape." Candace looked at her partner. "How about that, Lyla? Somebody's out there getting rapists."

"Amazing," Lyla said. "I wonder who could be behind it."

"Maybe Reggie and her gang," Candace offered. "That's what they advocate, isn't it?"

"Castration," Lyla said, "by the state."

"Maybe they've decided they'd rather do it themselves. Or maybe rape survivors are getting together and making their own justice."

"Let me read that when you're done, will you?" Lyla said.

Lyla tried to continue reading her novel, but she couldn't concentrate. Her thoughts were on her friend, Bella, who'd been brutally assaulted and raped the previous summer and had ended up dying from the injuries. The words on the pages blurred before her tear-filled eyes.

The next day, Lyla had a therapy session with Angela Smith, one of her rape survivor clients. The aftermath, as well as the rape itself, had been extremely traumatic. Angela had suffered through the ordeal at the hospital and the questioning by the police; she'd looked at endless mug shots; she'd dealt with the nightmares, the insomnia, the anxiety that had caused her to constrict her life. The symptoms had lasted for months, but she was almost over them now. She no longer jumped at every sound; her sleep was back to normal. But her rapist was still out there, and that made her uneasy, she had told Lyla many times.

In today's session, Angela mentioned the tattooings, wondering if the one who died had been her rapist, hoping so, guiltily feeling gratified that "those animals were being punished," and that one of them had been stopped permanently from ever raping again.

"Maybe more of them will be branded and killed," Angela said, "and the killings will just go on and on until they're all dead, until there are no more rapists left."

Although the sex was as hot as ever the following Wednesday, Lyla sensed that something was troubling Jade. She seemed a little distracted, not quite her usual raunchy, rambunctious self.

11

"Something on your mind?" Lyla asked as they lay in Vicky's bed sipping their wine.

Jade sighed. "The lean, mean, Benny machine. She's at it again."

"What this time? Another jealous rage?"

"No. Scarier. She's being subtle, calm. That's not like Benny. She's making these sort of veiled allusions, like she knows I'm seeing someone, but she's choosing not to confront it directly."

"That certainly isn't like the Benny you've described."

"It gives me the creeps. Like she's plotting something. You know what it reminds me of? What she did to that asshole, Leon, I told you about."

"The guy who messed with your car and who you —" Lyla wrinkled her nose.

"Yeah, the one we sprayed with that stinky chemical. Benny knew what we were going to do to him. She and I saw him in Walgreens soon after he'd written that lezzie crap on our cars and let the air out of our tires. I ignored him, but Benny had to make a crack. 'So, macho boy,' she said, 'you here to buy some Air Wick?' "

Lyla chuckled.

"The other day she told me to enjoy myself while I could. When I asked her what that was supposed to mean, she said, 'All bad things do come to an end, even Wednesday nights.' "

"Is she opposed to gambling?"

Jade laughed.

"So she doesn't believe you play poker on Wednesday nights. But if she thought you were . . . uh . . . doing what you're doing, she'd be a bit more direct, don't you think?"

"That's what's so creepy about it. If she knew I was with a lover, she'd have a fit. She'd call me every name in the book and threaten to break your neck."

Lyla cradled her neck in her hands.

"She'd follow me here to Vicky's and lay into both of us."

"Really? Has she ever been violent?"

"Not with me," Jade said. "She wouldn't dare. But I heard she did get a little rough with a lover once."

12

"Hmm-mm."

"Are you scared?" She stroked Lyla's chin. "I'll protect you."

"Hey, I'm the butch," Lyla said, and she moved atop Jade, covering Jade's lips with her own, kissing her deeply.

CHAPTER 3

It was Tuesday, the first day of June. The air was balmy and so was Lyla's mood as she drove home from work. She was thinking about how good her life was. Candace was a treasure — a dear, giving, warm, accepting, perfect partner for her. Jade was a delight — exciting, funny, mysterious, and the sexiest woman Lyla had ever known. Her work was challenging and gratifying. Her friends were varied and plentiful. Her parents were more than merely good-enough. Her health was excellent, her dog was adorable, her house was charming, her car was reliable. She couldn't seem to stop the list and began to laugh aloud. She looked around the car for something wooden to knock on.

Candace was already home and had dinner started when Lyla arrived at their old, two-story, Victorian house.

"Hi, loved one," Lyla said, giving her partner a warm hug and kissing her softly on the lips.

"Mm-m, you're in a good mood," Candace cooed. She was wearing jeans, her favorite red sweatshirt, and soft leather slippers.

"How could I not be with a sweetie like you? Mm-m, whatever's cooking smells delicious. Shall I do a salad?"

The two women finished preparing the meal. They had worked side by side in this kitchen many times before in the three years they'd owned the house. *Domestic bliss,* Lyla often said.

At the dining room table, they ate and talked while the stereo played Cris Williamson in the background.

"The National Alliance of Women had one of their *Fight Back* rallies in the Loop today," Candace said. "They think tattooing rapists isn't a bad idea."

"N.A.W. is supporting that? I'm surprised," Lyla said. "Don't tell me they advocate killing them, too."

"No. Just the tattoos."

"It's not a new idea," Lyla said. "Women have been talking about it for years."

After the meal, they were in the middle of a game of backgammon when the doorbell rang. Two men stood on the porch. Lyla looked at them quizzically through the window of the locked door.

"Police," one of the men said, showing a badge.

"Oh?" Lyla opened the door. "What's up?"

"Are you Lyla Bradshaw?"

"Yes."

They moved into the hallway. "We have a warrant for your arrest," the shorter of the two said. He was wearing a shapeless tan jacket, no necktie.

"My arrest?" Lyla felt herself getting hot. "What for?"

"Traffic Division. Outstanding parking violations," the other cop said. He was tall with a pock-marked face.

"Impossible," Lyla said, her mind flashing to Reggie. "I don't have any unpaid parking tickets."

15

The shorter one handed her a piece of paper. Lyla skimmed it. The violations had occurred five years earlier, on Reggie's old Pontiac. "It's a mistake," she said. "I sold that car before the tickets were issued."

"You can tell your story down at the police station," the pock-faced one said. "You have to come with us now."

"But —"

"Come on, lady. It's a warrant. You have no choice."

"What's going on?" Candace came and stood next to Lyla.

"Those tickets Reggie got on the car I sold her. They want to arrest me for them."

"That's ridiculous," Candace said indignantly. "She's not responsible for those tickets."

"Ma'am," the shorter officer said impatiently. "The vehicle is registered to Lyla Bradshaw. Under the law she's responsible for any parking violations no matter who was driving."

"I sold her the car, license plates and all," Lyla said. "That was my mistake." She looked at Candace. "I guess I have to go with them." She grabbed her blazer off the hallway hook.

"Call Kate," Candace said. "She has the right to call her attorney," she said to the cops.

"From the police station," the taller cop said.

"I'm coming with you," Candace said.

"That's up to you, ma'am. We're taking her downtown, Eleventh and State." The officer took one of Lyla's arms and walked her to the door.

"I'll call Kate," Candace said. She watched as the two police officers took her partner to their car and drove away.

The sign on the door said, *Interrogation Room 3.* Lyla sat across the table from Detective Carel Lopez. Another plainclothes officer stood near the door.

"I'd like to ask you a few questions," Carel said. "First, I need to remind you of your rights." She recited each of them, checked that Lyla understood, then said, "Maybe if you and I just talk awhile, we could clear it up quickly."

"My attorney's already been called," Lyla said, "but hopefully, I won't need her. It's ridiculous, really. You see, the car that got those tickets — it used to be mine, but five, maybe six years ago, I sold it to a friend of mine. I did get notices of the violations, but my friend said she'd taken care of it. She said she'd paid the fines. She was responsible. If she didn't pay the fines, then she's the one you should be talking to."

"All right," Carel said. "We'll check that out. Jake," she said to the other officer, passing a sheet of paper to him. "Get someone to run this again. See if the fines have been paid."

Jake left the room.

"You seem to be making a pretty big deal out of some parking tickets," Lyla said, looking at her ink-stained fingers. They had taken her fingerprints and photographed her.

"Eight hundred dollars worth," Carel Lopez said, "but actually, there is another concern we have." She looked at Lyla closely for several seconds. "We got a report that your car was at the scene of a recent crime."

"The Pontiac? I told you that's not my car. It hasn't been for five years." Lyla wondered what kind of trouble Reggie was in.

"No, not that car. The Honda."

Lyla stared at her.

"You do own a nineteen ninety-one Honda Accord, don't you?"

Lyla nodded.

"A white one?"

"That's right. What crime?"

"It occurred a couple weeks ago, on Wednesday, May nineteenth. Do you happen to recall where you were that evening, between nine and ten o'clock?"

A Wednesday. Of course Lyla knew where she'd been. "What crime are you talking about? Who saw my car? Where was it seen?"

17

Carel Lopez smiled. Her teeth were perfectly straight and brilliant white. Lyla realized she was strikingly attractive. "Let me ask the questions, all right?" the detective said. "That's what your taxes pay me for. So can you account for your time on Wednesday evening, May nineteenth?"

"Yes, as a matter of fact, I can," Lyla said, "but I don't see why I should until I hear what you're suggesting I did. Am I being accused of something? There are a lot of white Honda Accords in this city."

"With tag N-I-K sixty-three?"

Lyla said nothing.

"That is your licence plate number, isn't it?"

"Yes, but —"

"We have a positive identification by a witness. The car and a description of you."

Jake returned and remained standing by the door. Lyla thought of telling the same story she told Candace about her Wednesday nights. Of course, it could easily be checked. "I was with a friend that night. She can verify it. Now will you please tell me what this is all about?"

"What's your friend's name?"

"I don't see any reason to bring anyone else into this unless you tell me what it's about."

The detective looked directly into Lyla's eyes. "Have you ever been raped, Dr. Bradshaw?" She asked the question matter-of-factly, but Lyla thought she saw something in the officer's eyes, compassion maybe, or was it pity?

"Hey, what is this?" Lyla snapped. "Does this have something to do with my work with rape victims?"

"It might. You tell me."

"I have no idea what you're talking about." Lyla realized she was perspiring. "I think I *do* need my lawyer," she said.

"All right. In the meantime, we have to lock you up. We'll resume the questioning when your attorney arrives."

"Questions about whether I've been raped? Why do you ask that?"

"You really hate rapists, don't you, Dr. Bradshaw?"

18

"Well, they sure as hell aren't my favorite people. What are you getting at?"

Carel Lopez looked at Jake, then back at Lyla. "You said you want your attorney present. Are you retracting that? Shall we talk some more?"

Lyla hesitated. "Can I check with my friend? She should be here at the police station. Can I talk with her and see if my attorney's on the way?"

"Jake, could you check that out? Candace Dunn, right? See if she's at the desk area. See if she reached the lawyer."

As soon as Jake left, Carel looked pointedly at Lyla. "Anything you want to say?"

"This is too weird. No, I suppose I shouldn't be talking to you at all, but I don't know why. I haven't done anything."

"The witness I mentioned is here at the station. Would you mind having her take a look at you? Maybe she'll say it definitely wasn't you she saw."

"Fine," Lyla said. "Bring her in. Maybe I'll finally find out what the fuck is going on." She almost laughed, thinking of Candace's observation that she only *talked dirty* when she was really upset. *Well, I have a right to be upset,* she thought.

"We can't do it that way," Carel said. "We need to see if she can pick you out from a group of other women who look similar to you. For your own protection."

"A lineup, you mean?"

"That's right."

Lyla ran her fingers through the edges of her curly hair. "I'm not a criminal," she said, more to herself than to the detective.

"There's nothing to it," Carel said. "Shall we set it up?"

"What if I refuse?"

"Then we'll do it later. After you consult with your attorney. You will have to do it eventually."

Jake was in the room again. "You might as well get it over with," he said to Lyla. "Your friend, Miss Dunn, left a message for your lawyer."

"Can I talk with Candace?"

"Sure," Carel said. "After the lineup."

They took her to a windowless room to wait. A uniformed police officer stayed with her. He didn't speak. Gradually the room began to fill until there were four women besides Lyla — all Caucasians with brown, curly hair. Their ages seemed to range from late twenties to early forties, their heights were within several inches of Lyla's five and a half feet. Lyla didn't think any of them looked at all like her. Were they prisoners, she wondered, people accused of crimes? Did they know what they were accused of? Three uniformed officers were now in the room. One of them told the women to line up single file in front of the side door. He gave them each a rubber mask, a ghoulish version of the Frankenstein monster.

"Put on the masks," the officer told the women.

"What's the idea?" Lyla asked.

He didn't answer. Lyla slipped the mask over her face and adjusted the elastic. The heat of her own breath inside the mask made her feel even weaker than she already was. She was third in line.

The cop opened the door, telling the first woman to go all the way to the end of the platform, stand under the number 1 and face the mirror. The rest of the women were told to follow and stand under their numbers.

The bright light in the lineup room made Lyla squint. She stood between two other masked, curly-haired women, feeling utterly humiliated. Above her head was the number 3. She could see herself reflected in the tinted mirror wall in front of them. She looked ridiculous in the mask. Her shoulders were slumped. She straightened them.

"Number three, take a step forward," a voice said. It was coming through an amplifier somewhere. Lyla stepped forward. "Turn to your left." She turned and waited. "Now, to your right." Lyla obeyed, the feeling of humiliation deepening. *It will be over soon,* she told herself soothingly. *They'll apologize for their stupid mistake and Candace will take me home. We'll have some of the vanilla pudding that's in the fridge, and we'll sit in front of the TV and hold each other.*

"Take the masks off," the officer said. Again he had Lyla turn to the left and right.

"All right, ladies, that's it."

The five women trooped back into the next room. The officer named Jake was there. He took Lyla's arm. "Back to interrogation," he said.

"So what happened?" Lyla asked. He didn't answer.

In Interrogation Room Three, Detective Lopez was at the table again. "Sit," she told Lyla. "We got one positive I.D. and two tentatives."

"This is absurd." Lyla was having trouble getting air.

"We got an anonymous phone call that your car — tag number N-I-K sixty-three — was seen parked on Fullerton Avenue, near Damen, at nine-twenty-five p.m. on May nineteenth."

"Impossible."

"We get a lot of tips like that. Most of them come to nothing. We ran the tag number, came up with your name. No record. No arrests. We figured this was nothing, but we asked around anyway. Turns out that someone else also saw your car on Fullerton that night. And then another witness saw it at another crime scene, on Montrose Avenue, near Ashland. That was Wednesday, February tenth."

Lyla shook her head.

"At the May nineteenth occurrence, you were seen running out of the building at Nineteen Thirty-four West Fullerton by our witness who gave the positive I.D. She saw you get into your car and drive away. You seemed to be in quite a hurry."

"I don't know what you're talking about."

"The witness watched from her apartment window."

Lyla took deep breaths. "What are you getting at? So someone who looks like me came out of a building and drove away in a car like mine. What crime are you talking about?"

21

"Here," Carel said, handing her a box of tissues. "You're perspiring."

Lyla wiped her forehead.

"According to the witness, you were wearing a blazer similar to that one, with the sleeves rolled up like that. And you had on a big silver bracelet."

Lyla looked at her bracelet. Silver and turquoise. It was a gift from Candace, bought in Arizona when Candace had taken a trip with her parents. And her sleeves. Lyla liked her arms bare so she always pushed or rolled up the sleeves of her shirts and jackets.

"It wasn't me." Lyla's hands were trembling.

"Our witness just said it was."

"Your witness is crazy."

"Two of the victims were also at the lineup. They said you seemed more like the perpetrator than any of the others. Of course, they hadn't seen your face."

"Victims? What crime are you accusing me of?"

Carel looked at her, tilting her head. "Homicide," she said.

Lyla's eyes widened.

"And assault, with a hypodermic needle and with a tattoo gun."

Lyla felt faint. "You mean . . . you think . . . ?"

"Your spree of vengeance is over, Dr. Bradshaw. Why don't you tell me about it?"

"The tattooings . . . the men who . . ."

"That's right. The courts let them go, but that isn't right, is it? They were rapists and yet they were free to rape again. That's why you did it, isn't it?"

"No, no!"

"It's not? Then why? Did one of them rape you? Or someone you know? Is that what made you do it?"

"This is beyond belief," Lyla said, the absurdity of it calming her. She laughed hollowly. "The parking tickets were bad enough, but . . . you can't be serious. Listen, I can prove exactly where I was on May nineteenth. There's someone who will vouch for me. Why the hell would anyone . . . why would they identify me? Why would someone say they saw my car when it wasn't there? They must have gotten the plate number wrong, that's it. Did you check similar numbers? N-I-K sixty-two or M-I-K or any similar ones?"

"What's your alibi's name?"

Lyla hesitated. She wasn't sure what to do. "I'm done talking," she said at last. "I'll say no more until my lawyer's here."

Detective Lopez rose. "The arraignment will be in the morning. You'll be formally charged then. When your attorney comes, the prosecutor will want to question you."

A uniformed officer took Lyla to the lockup. She was alone in a small cell with a coverless toilet and tiny sink. She sat on the thin mattress of the metal bed, her mind spinning. *How could this be happening? Mistaken identity, that's the only explanation. Coincidence. A car like mine with a similar license plate number. Someone who looks like me.* She chewed her lip nervously. *But so many coincidences. Maybe someone's trying to make it look like it was me, to lay the blame on me. But why? Who would want to do that to me? Maybe someone who saw me on TV that time, talking about rape. I'd be the perfect one to blame, wouldn't I? It could look believable that I'd be motivated to do something to rapists. Yes, that must be it.*

She paced the cell, her thoughts tumbling over each other, until she was told her attorney was there. They took Lyla to a room similar to the interrogation room. Kate Ralla was at the table.

"They briefed me on the charges and the evidence," Kate said.

"Is Candace still here?"

"Yes, she's out front."

"They wouldn't let me see her."

"They apparently used the traffic offenses to get you down here for the lineup," Kate said. "I wish you hadn't agreed to it, but that's water under the bridge now. A woman named Laura Falk places you at the scene of the May nineteenth homicide. It was at night and she was

23

some distance from where she claims to have seen you, so we might be able to shake her I.D. The two guys who were tattooed and survived were at the lineup, too. Because of the mask, their I.D.'s will mean nothing."

"Kate, they're saying I killed that guy." Suddenly Lyla was sobbing, tears streaming down her face.

Kate handed her a tissue. "Just try to relax. You need to talk to me, Lyla."

Lyla took several deep breaths. She blew her nose. "Is this all a dream?"

"More like a nightmare, kiddo. So what do you know about it? What can you tell me?"

"What do I know? I know I was playing backgammon and then suddenly I'm dragged to the police station because of Reggie's tickets but then they start talking about rape and do I hate rapists and then they make me stand in a lineup and put on a Frankenstein mask." She took a deep breath. "I was with Jade McGrath on Wednesday night, Kate. All we have to do is get Jade to tell them. Oh God, will Candace have to know that part?"

"Slow down, Lyla. What Wednesday night are you talking about?" Kate looked at the papers in front of her. "The first tattooing took place on December thirtieth, last year. The next was February tenth, and the last one, the homicide, was May nineteenth."

"May nineteenth was a Wednesday, right?"

"All the incidents took place on Wednesday nights."

"I was with Jade McGrath." Lyla started feeling panicky again. "How could they possibly think it's me?"

"Here's what they got, Lyla. A woman named Sarah Silverman claims to have seen a parked white Honda, plate number N-I-K six three, in front of a mostly unoccupied office building on Montrose near Ashland. The woman lives in the area and suspected that drug dealing was going on in the building. She kept track of people she saw come and go. You were on her list, your car, that is, for February tenth."

"So they think I'm dealing drugs, too?"

"No, just drugging and killing rapists," Kate said. "A woman named Marianne Newman claims she saw a car like yours parked on the north side of Fullerton, near Damen, on May nineteenth. She works the night shift at a factory in the neighborhood. Said she'd gotten sick that night and had left work early. She noticed a ninety-one, white Honda Accord parked on the north side of the street. She saw a woman get out of the car and walk east." Kate looked at her notes. "The next one's the worst. Laura Falk, the one who identified you in the lineup. She lives at Nineteen-Thirty-nine West Fullerton, across the street from the building where Henry Lester's body was found. On May nineteenth at around nine-thirty p.m., she claims that from her apartment window she saw a woman run out of the building across the street, get into a white compact car and drive away. The license plate started with N-I-K."

"It wasn't me. I was with Jade. We were together in Vicky's apartment all evening."

"Good."

"And the other nights, too. Every Wednesday night."

"What do you mean?"

"Every Wednesday night for the past ten months, I was with Jade McGrath."

Kate nodded. "I see. Just the two of you, right?"

"Right?"

"From what time to what time?"

"Seven to ten-thirty."

"Always seven to ten-thirty?"

"Like clockwork. The clockwork love affair. I'd have dinner with Jessie Luce, then she'd go to dance class and I'd go to meet Jade."

"Did anyone besides Jade ever see you between those hours, especially on the Wednesdays we're worried about?"

"Someone could have seen me coming or going, but between seven and ten-thirty, I was alone with Jade."

"And whose apartment was it? Vicky something, you said."

"Vicky Kranz. She's a friend of Jade's. I've never met her."

"Did anyone ever telephone while you and Jade were there?"

"It rang sometimes. We didn't pick it up. The machine got it."

"I see. And where would your car be while you were in Vicky's apartment with Jade?"

"Parked on the street. Usually within a block or so of the apartment."

"But it wouldn't be parked in the same place every time?"

"No. It's a congested area, parking is tight."

"Well, maybe we can find someone who remembers your car being there during the time the crimes were committed."

Lyla nodded, but didn't think that possibility was very likely. "Won't it be enough that Jade verifies we were together?"

"It'll help, but we need more." Kate looked at Lyla's worried face. "Don't worry, we'll find it. Tell me about your rape work. I know you work with rape survivors, both on the crisis line and as therapy clients. Did you ever advocate tattooing rapists' foreheads, or any other violence against them? Were you a part of any group that does so advocate?"

"Like LUSAR?"

"Ah, yes, I've heard of them — Lesbians . . . something . . . Against Rape."

"Lesbians United to Stop All Rape," Lyla said.

"Are you a part of that?"

"God, no. Reggie Hirtz's involvement in it was one of the reasons we split."

"Ah, well that's good. So you opposed this group."

"I opposed some of their tactics and goals. But not all of them. Reggie got a lot more involved in it after we broke up. That was over five years ago."

"But you never made statements to the effect that rapists should be tattooed or killed or castrated or anything like that."

"Certainly not publicly."

"Privately?"

"No. Well, I might have talked about the tattooing

idea. And I've had discussions about the castration possibility. I oppose it. If they can't get their dicks up they'll just use a broom handle or something. Rape is primarily a crime of violence, as you know, not lust."

"You sound angry. You don't want to come across as an avid rapist-hater."

"Get serious, Kate. Tell me you don't hate them."

"That's not the point, Lyla. I'm thinking of a jury."

"A jury? Oh, shit. You mean there's going to be a trial?"

"Not if I can help it. I hope to stop this thing before it goes any further, but we need more than we've got so far."

"Do you think someone's trying to frame me?"

"Do you?"

"It crossed my mind. I have no idea who."

"What about Reggie Hirtz? You don't exactly hold a warm place in her heart, from what I've heard, and she's part of LUSAR."

"Reggie can be pretty obnoxious and aggressive, but she'd never . . . she wouldn't kill anyone, Kate."

"The death of Henry Lester may have been unintentional," Kate said. "The other two victims have brain damage, probably from airplane glue they were forced to inhale. Would Reggie Hirtz drug and tattoo someone she thought was a rapist?"

Lyla shrugged. "Maybe. I hope not."

"We'll have to check her out. Now, think some more, Lyla. What else comes to mind? Did you watch TV at Vicky's? Some show you remember that could help establish what you were doing those Wednesday nights?" She half-smiled. "I mean, what else you were doing."

"We had music on."

"Radio?"

"Stereo."

"Did a salesperson or any kind of solicitor ever come to the door? Or anyone at all?"

"The doorbell rang once. A few months ago."

"And?"

27

"We didn't answer it. Do you think I'm terrible, Kate? Betraying Candace."

"I'm not thinking about that."

Lyla didn't want to think about it either. "Can people get fake license plates made?" she asked.

"I suppose. That would fit the frame-up theory. I want you to make a list of all the people who might have some reason to frame you. Anyone you can think of who might have something against you — ex-lovers in addition to Reggie Hirtz, neighbors you don't get along with — anyone you can think of. And also add anyone who might want rapists branded and brain-damaged or dead, and who would see you as a good person to lay the blame on because of your work with rape victims."

"That could be anybody," Lyla said. "I was interviewed on television last year. Anybody could have known I work with rape survivors."

"Make the list," Kate said. "And keep thinking about those Wednesday nights. Maybe you went out to a grocery store one of those nights. Maybe you did pick up the phone once. It may not have seemed important then, but it sure as hell is now."

"All right," Lyla said. She stared at the table. "What happens next?"

"The arraignment's tomorrow morning at ten. The prosecutor will talk to you now; I'll be present. Then tomorrow he'll present the evidence against you and ask that you be bound over. I'll fight it, of course, but I think he'll succeed. I'll try to get bail for you, but given that it's homicide, that may not be possible. I'll push the doubtfulness of the eyewitnesses' identification. I'll talk about your standing in the community, blah, blah, blah. Failing that, I'll demand a preliminary hearing before it goes to a grand jury. That'll give me another shot at getting bail. In the meantime, I'll talk with Jade McGrath. Write down her address and phone number."

"Are you saying I might have to stay in jail? That maybe there won't be bail and . . ." She wrote down Jade's phone number and address and handed the paper to Kate. Her eyes were tear-filled.

"We're talking Class A felony," Kate said. "All I've got so far is Jade McGrath. As soon as I'm done here, I'll try to contact her. I'm going to get the prosecutor now. He's going to ask you a lot of questions. I'll tell you which ones to answer and which ones not to."

CHAPTER 4

Lyla barely slept that night. In the morning her head felt heavy, and her eyes swollen. They had refused to let her see Candace. After Kate left, Lyla had been taken to her cell. *Such a horrible mistake,* she thought over and over. Her hands were shaking as she worked on the list Kate had asked for.

Someone came with a breakfast tray. Lyla could manage only the coffee and a few bites of toast. Kate arrived with fresh clothes for Lyla, slacks and a beige blazer and crisp white blouse. Lyla handed Kate her list.

"This is a good start," Kate said. "An ex-patient, the husband of an ex-patient, the boyfriend of a present patient, a neighbor, and an ex-lover."

"But I know it wasn't Reggie," Lyla said. "The most likely one is Larry Hunt. He blames me for his wife divorcing him." Lyla buttoned her blouse. "How did it go with Jade?"

"Once she recovered from the shock, she confirmed everything you told me. She did mention one thing you didn't, though — that she made phone calls on some of those Wednesday nights. You were asleep, I guess. One of the calls was to her mother in Bloomington, Indiana. Of course, that doesn't really help you. Did you ever make any calls, Lyla? Try to remember."

"I remember. I didn't use the phone at all. I only did one thing at Vicky's apartment."

"Sometimes you napped."

"Yes, sometimes I napped. Did you talk with Candace?"

"She'll be in the courtroom."

"Does she know about . . . ?"

"She kept talking about your Wednesday night dance classes, kept pushing me to talk to your teacher."

"So, you told her where I really was those nights."

"I put her off. I told her I'd be checking everything. Then she said she'd call the dance studio herself. I told her not to get involved with the investigation, that she could mess it up."

"I'd rather tell her myself."

"But she got suspicious."

"I see. So, then you told her."

"Only after arguing with her awhile more. She'd have found out anyway, Lyla. She'd have to. If she'd called the dance studio and learned you didn't go to classes, it could have been worse for her."

"I suppose."

Kate glanced over some papers she'd taken from her briefcase. "I'm pleading you *not guilty,* of course. Right?"

Lyla looked at her. "Of course," she said.

Kate put papers in front of Lyla. "Sign these," she said, "so Candace can get access to your money for the bail."

Lyla signed.

"I'll argue mistaken identity by Laura Falk," Kate said. "It was dark, she was a distance away from where

31

she saw the person come out of the building. I'll also cite the high rate of distortion and error by eyewitnesses. I'll say that you spent that Wednesday evening with Jade McGrath as you did every Wednesday, and that McGrath is prepared to testify to that fact. I'll argue that your upstanding character, your lack of any criminal record, or any history of violence or advocacy of violence, makes the prosecutor's claim that you committed the assaults, one of which resulted in homicide, untenable. Then I'll push for bail based on the fact that your guilt is far from evident and the presumption of same is not great."

Lyla tried to listen, but her head was buzzing.

"Do you have any rich relatives, by chance?"

Lyla didn't answer. She was slumped in her chair.

"Lyla, come on. You have to keep your spirits up. Keep focused, huh? We've got quite a fight ahead of us, so don't wimp out."

Much of the arraignment was a blur to Lyla. Everything happened so quickly. Several times she caught glimpses of Candace sitting in the spectators' section, looking gaunt and frightened. As Lyla stood before the round-faced judge, he read the names of the man she was accused of killing and the two she was accused of assaulting, the means used to commit the crimes, the tattooing, and the dates on which the crimes occurred.

Then the prosecutor spoke. He had on the same sandy brown suit he'd worn the day before when he'd questioned Lyla. He acted as if he had no doubt of Lyla's guilt as he cited the evidence against her.

Then it was Kate's turn. She referred to Lyla as Dr. Bradshaw and talked about Lyla's dedication to helping people by psychotherapy and consciousness raising and how violent acts and irresponsible activism had always been anathema to her. She spoke of Lyla's good reputation and her upright character. Then she talked about Jade McGrath who would testify that she was with Lyla on the evenings of the assaults.

The judge said something which Lyla couldn't make out. Kate responded; the prosecutor interrupted her, talking about this being a capital offense and bail being inappropriate. Kate argued for a while, then both she and the prosecutor stepped back from the bench. The judge looked through papers. Everything was quiet except for the buzzing in Lyla's head.

Finally the judge spoke. "The defendant is to be held without bail." That was all Lyla heard. He said more but the buzzing had gotten too loud. She was afraid she was going to faint. There was something about a grand jury. Then Kate said something, and then it was over. Lyla was taken away by a police officer. She didn't even have another chance to look at Candace.

Kate came to her a short time later. "That didn't go very well," she said, "so I'm giving it another shot. I've requested a preliminary hearing. It will take place tomorrow, before a different judge. Keep working on that list, Lyla. And give me details about each of the people."

"He said no bail," Lyla said numbly. "That means I have to stay in jail."

"One more night," Kate said. "With luck, tomorrow's judge won't be such a hard ass. I'll try to come up with some more arguments for allowing bail. Hang tough, kiddo. I've got to go now; I have lots to do."

"Can I see Candace?"

"Not here. Either you'll be out tomorrow or you'll see her at Cook County."

"Cook County Jail?" Lyla felt stomach-sinking dread. "Is that where they're going to send me?"

"Try to be optimistic. If all goes well, you'll be home tomorrow. Candace says she has thirty-some thousand in CDs. She's prepared to cash them in the moment we get the good news."

"Her inheritance. I can't let her —"

"Yes you can. You'll pay her back."

"Will it cost that much?"

"You'll need to pay ten percent of whatever the judge sets as the bail figure. I'll try to keep it down. It'll probably end up being at least a couple hundred thou'."

33

Lyla looked exasperated. "But you told the judge about Jade. Wasn't the fucker listening?"

Kate put her hand on Lyla's arm. "The judge thought the prosecutor had enough evidence to hold you, Lyla. I told you that's what would probably happen. Our main goal right now is to get bail for you. Now I'm going to go work on that, okay? I'll see you tomorrow morning."

Lyla nodded. "Tell Candace I miss her."

"I'm sure you do."

For the first time in many months, Lyla spent a passionless Wednesday night. She slept fitfully. Her dreams were nightmares and the nightmares continued when she awoke.

There was one bit of good news the next day. The judge allowed bail. One million dollars. Lyla was handcuffed and taken by paddy wagon to the women's division of Cook County Jail. In a semi-trance state, she endured the humiliation of the transport and the processing into the jail. She did what they told her, all in a fog. Another night passed, this time in a cell with three other inmates. Lyla barely registered their presence. They left her alone.

In the morning she was taken by a female guard through a long, cell-filled corridor and down some stairs. "In there," the guard said. "Number eight."

Lyla saw a line of prisoners in booths. She went to number eight. Candace sat on the other side of the window. Seeing the woman she had loved deeply for the last five years, Lyla began to cry. At first she just stared at Candace, then started to say something. Candace gestured to the phone intercom. Lyla picked it up.

"Oh, Candace. It's so good to see you. It makes me feel real again. Thank you for coming, hon. I feel . . . it's like . . . like culture shock. Like I'm on another planet or something. This isn't anything that could ever happen to me. I . . . I don't think I'm handling it too well."

"Not many people could," Candace said soothingly. "We'll get you out of here."

Lyla nodded. Her lip was quivering, then her expression changed suddenly, from fear and defeat, to anger. "Someone's doing this to me," she said, her voice hoarse, almost a whisper.

"Yes," Candace said. "That's the only explanation. We'll find out who, Lyla. Maybe it's one of the people you told Kate about. Kate wants to hire a private investigator."

"Whoever did it obviously knew how I spent Wednesday nights. They probably followed me."

Candace's eyes brimmed with tears.

"Oh, Candace, you must hate me. I don't even know why you're here. I . . . oh, shit."

Candace blinked and tears trickled down her cheeks.

"Do you want to hear about it?" Lyla asked. "About Jade?"

"If you want."

"I don't love her, Candace. I never did. It was never more than . . . than Wednesday nights."

Candace nodded. "Hot sex."

"Yes. Jade is . . . there were never any strings. It was a game, really, for both of us. It had nothing to do with my love for you. Nothing at all."

"I see."

Lyla shook her head. "I'm really paying for it," she said.

"We'll find the killer," Candace responded.

"Kate believes I didn't do it, doesn't she? She knows I couldn't possibly have —"

"Of course," Candace said.

"She believes I was framed?"

"Yes, we all do. We'll find out who did it, Lyla. The grand jury investigation doesn't take place for two more weeks. Kate hopes that by then we'll know who did it and you won't be indicted. She's going to talk with that woman who identified you. Oh, by the way, they searched the house. They took your computer and printer and all your disks. They also took all the pills from the medicine cabinet, even the aspirins."

"Great. Anything else?"

"Your gray tweed blazer and ... that pair of handcuffs. That's all. The place was a mess after they left."

"This must be horrible for you, hon. You're ... you're going to stand by me?"

"Of course I am."

"I need you to. But ... aren't you mad at me — about Jade?"

"Yes, of course I am. But I'd sure as hell rather that we can prove you were having sex with your no-strings-attached lover on Wednesday nights instead of out drugging and killing people."

Lyla's head slumped. Her eyes were closed. "My life is over," she said.

"Lyla, cut that out! Don't defeat yourself. I talked to your folks. They can raise ten or fifteen thousand."

"Oh, my poor parents. They know about it then?"

"I called them. I wanted them to hear it from me rather than read it in the newspapers."

"It's in the newspapers? That I've been charged with ... with murder?"

"Yes. I tried to reach your sister but —"

"She's in Colorado. I wonder if she knows. God, the last time I talked to her we had that fight."

"Kate's going to bring some more papers for you to sign so she can get your money from your accounts."

Lyla nodded. "There goes our trip to Hawaii," she said, giving a weak laugh.

"No way," Candace responded. "That's where we're going as soon as this is over."

"The bond money's non-refundable," Lyla said. "Didn't Kate tell you that?"

"Yes. We'll find a way."

"You know what I think happened. I think someone took my car those nights. She followed me. She knew where I was on Wednesday nights and she took my car and made sure it was seen. She got a wig to make herself look like me. But I think more likely it was a man. A man wearing a wig. Somehow he got a key to my car."

"Kate said it's possible that the witness who identified you in the lineup is part of the frame."

"I thought of that. And the other ones, the ones who said they saw my car and gave the plate number. Who are they, Candace? Has Kate found out yet? Are they connected with each other in any way?"

"The May nineteenth one lives in the neighborhood where the murder took place. On Fullerton."

"She's lying about seeing me," Lyla blurted. "They're all lying."

"Yes, they could be. Or else, like you said, maybe someone disguised herself — or himself — to look like you."

"Yes, and took my car." Lyla sighed. "Oh God, hon, it all sounds so ridiculous."

Neither woman spoke for a while. "Is it pretty bad in there?" Candace said at last.

Lyla just looked at her.

"Oh, hon, I'm so sorry."

Lyla sighed deeply. "How's Gal?" she said, trying to sound more cheerful. "Does she miss me? Are you mixing the dry dog food with the wet? Will I ever see her again?"

"We'll get you out, Lyla. They just can't convict you for crimes you didn't do."

Lyla laughed hollowly. "A lot of things are happening that can't happen," she said. "Will you call Emily for me?"

"I already did. She's behind you a hundred percent. And she said of course she's holding your job, even if this drags on for a while."

"It'll be rough on some of my patients. Even if by some miracle you raise a hundred thousand for the bail, I still won't be able to ... I don't think I'll be much good as a therapist until this is cleared up. It could take a long time. Oh, Candace, say this isn't happening."

"Oh, love, how I wish I could."

"And I know how terrible it is for you, too. All of it.

What a way to find about about . . . about my having a sexual affair. Oh, shit. Candace, I'm so sorry about that. I never wanted to hurt you. Never, ever."

"It's okay, kinky girl. I know you like things that I'm not into sexually. I also know that you and I have a great relationship. To tell the truth, I thought you might have an adventure some day. I wasn't completely shocked."

"I love you," Lyla whispered into the phone, looking into Candace's eyes.

"I know, my love."

Over the next few days, Candace went each afternoon to see Lyla. She had just returned from a visit and was sitting at the dining room table staring at the pile of newspapers. *Rape Crisis Worker Held for Vengeance Spree on Accused Rapists,* one of the headlines read. One article talked about the mixed public reactions. An organization had already formed to raise money for Lyla's defense, but other women's groups and many individuals were condemning the assaults as vigilantism. There was also something about a letter that had been sent to each of the victims, and that other men who'd been acquitted of rape charges had received the same letter. Candace wondered what that was about.

The phone rang.

"Her bail's been paid," Kate said.

"Fantastic! Who did it? Feminist groups? They raised the money that quickly?"

"It was one group," Kate said. "They're called Kwo-femazonians. Ever hear of them?"

"Yes, of course. Lyla's sister, Leslie, is part of that. The group is based in Colorado."

"Lyla didn't mention them as a possible money source."

"I'm sure it never crossed her mind," Candace said.

"She thinks they're weird. She's not very happy with her sister's involvement with them."

"Well, blood came through. It's too late to get Lyla out tonight, but we can go pick her up tomorrow morning. I'll stop by for you."

"The earlier the better," Candace said excitedly.

CHAPTER 5

"Do your Colorado friends believe she's innocent?" Candace asked. She and Lyla's sister were sitting on the back porch. Lyla was in the shower, where she'd gone the moment she'd gotten home from Cook County Jail.

"Most of them," Leslie answered. Leslie was two years younger than Lyla, and two inches shorter. She had the same narrow face and curly hair as her sister, but her eyes were much darker. "Because they believed me when I told them about the sort of person Lyla is. Some aren't sure; they can understand how a woman who works with rape survivors day after day might be driven to desperate acts."

"But even they okayed putting up the money?"

Lyla joined her sister and Candace, taking the chair

with a good view of the backyard. The tulips were in bloom.

"The money came from the Kwo-femazon Feminist Fund," Leslie said. "It was their decision. A close friend of mine is a member of the board. She told me the vote was unanimous."

"Was it your idea?" Lyla asked, toweling her hair, "for your group to put up the bond money?"

"Yes. I filled out the application, and then spoke at their meeting."

"Kwo-am love you," Lyla said, her eyes teary.

Leslie smiled. "And us all," she said. "They want you to visit the commune."

"I can't leave the state," Lyla said bitterly. "If I do, the bail will be revoked. They tried to make it so I couldn't drive a car either, but Kate got them to drop that."

"Not drive a car? What was the purpose of that supposed to be?"

Lyla shrugged. "Maybe the prosecutor figured I'd have a hard time drugging and tattooing more rapists if I had to use public transportation."

"Reggie would be happy to chauffeur you," Candace quipped.

Leslie frowned. "Do you still see Reggie?"

"Not if I can help it," Lyla said. "I ran into her at the grocery store recently. And I saw her at a Halloween party last year. It wasn't pleasant either time."

"You're much better off without her," Leslie said. "She was never right for you. Not like Candace. I think you two are perfect for each other."

Lyla looked guiltily at Candace.

"Don't tell me you're having problems," Leslie said.

"Are we?" Lyla asked her partner.

Candace shook her head. "Our only problem right now is finding out who's trying to destroy you," she said.

"I was with a woman named Jade McGrath on the nights of the tattooings," Lyla said to Leslie. "Alone. Just the two of us."

"You mean you and she were . . ."

"Yes." Lyla stared out the window. "I'm some shit, huh?"

Leslie looked at Candace.

"She's a shit," Candace said. "Do you think I should dump her?"

"I don't know." Leslie looked uncomfortable. "Is it serious? I mean with this other woman . . . does it threaten —"

"No," Lyla said.

"So is it over now?" Leslie asked.

"Leslie, enough already," Candace said. "She's an intrusive little twit, isn't she?" Candace said to Lyla.

"Very. Always nosing into other people's affairs."

Leslie chuckled.

"I mean other people's *business*. You know what I mean," Lyla said, flustered.

"Well, at any rate," Leslie said, "this Jade character is your alibi, then. So didn't she tell the police?"

"Of course," Lyla said. "They think she's lying to protect me."

The telephone rang. Candace went inside, then returned and told Lyla it was someone from the *Bradshaw Defense Fund*. "She wants to talk with you. She's calling from Minneapolis."

The caller identified herself as Lisa Cronbach. "We're behind you all the way," she told Lyla. She explained that her group had already raised fifteen hundred dollars, and that the donations were pouring in. "We need to make arrangements to get the money to you."

"I can't tell you how much I appreciate this," Lyla said.

"Well, there's a mutual advantage. Your case is riling people up about rape and that's exactly what we need. It's probably scaring the shit out of any creep who's thinking about raping someone."

"I suppose so," Lyla said. "Should I put you in touch with my lawyer? That's probably the best way to proceed." Lyla gave the caller Kate Ralla's phone number and then thanked her wholeheartedly. "And thank all the donors for me, will you? Maybe I can thank them myself at some point."

"Maybe so," Lisa replied. "Most of the money we got so far is from our own community here in Minneapolis. If I'm right, though, we'll be hearing from women all over the country."

"That's great," Lyla said.

"You're a hero to a lot of people."

Lyla didn't respond.

"I know you can't talk about the case now, but someday I'd really like to hear about it."

When Lyla returned to the porch, she sank heavily into her chair. "They think I did it," she said.

"What!" Candace said. "Is that what she told you?"

"In effect. Maybe I shouldn't accept their money."

No one spoke for a while. Finally Lyla said, "I guess it makes sense, in a way. They think I've acted out their fantasy. Got some revenge for all the women who've been raped or who live in fear of it."

"Which means all of us," Candace said. "Yes, you're right, I've been reading about it in the paper. A lot of women are delighted that someone finally took some action."

"Well, somebody else is their hero, not me," Lyla said.

"I think we should use the money to hire a private investigator," Candace said.

"Good idea," Leslie said. "I wonder where the investigator would start."

"With Lyla's list of suspects, I would think," Candace responded.

"Who's on the list?"

"Regina Hirtz, for one," Candace replied.

Leslie's jaw dropped. She looked at her sister. "You think it was Reggie?"

"No."

"I do," Candace said. "I thought so even before Lyla was arrested."

"You're kidding!" Leslie said.

"It's just because Candace hates Reggie's guts," Lyla said. "You remember what a total asshole Reggie was when I first started seeing Candace."

"Yeah, but..." Leslie was still looking at Candace. "You really think so?"

"If I were investigating the case, I'd sure as heck want to know where Regina Hirtz was those Wednesday nights," Candace said.

"Who else is on your list?" Leslie asked.

"The ex-husband of a former patient of mine. Some of my ex-patients themselves. That creates a problem in terms of confidentiality. If an investigator questions them, he or she will have to reveal the reason, I suppose. That would be great — *Your ex-therapist believes you wiped out some brain cells of a couple of people and murdered a third, and that you're making it look like your therapist did it.*"

"Maybe the investigator could be a bit more subtle," Candace said.

"Maybe another tattooing will take place," Leslie offered. "Then the cops will have to get their feet from off your back, Lyla. Just make sure you're with a crowd every Wednesday until this thing's over."

"There won't be any more tattooings," Lyla said. "It's clear I'm being framed, so whoever did it would be a fool to strike again now."

"I suppose." Leslie looked at her sister questioningly. "You really have ex-patients who might do this to you?"

"It's possible. I see quite a mix of people at the clinic. Some of them are pretty seriously disturbed. There's one I terminated with years ago. He was in and out of psychotic episodes, but mostly controlled on meds. I wasn't very helpful to him, but he had a positive transference, thought I was Ms. Wonderful. He didn't want the therapy to end. I'd been seeing him for months and he wasn't making any progress with me. My work with him was really a waste of time; he needed skills training more than psychotherapy. I switched him to every other week, then to monthly appointments. By that time he was living with his parents in Winnetka. I connected him with a psychiatrist out there, and a day hospital program. After we terminated for good, he started writing me letters. They were weird."

"Threatening?" Leslie asked.

"No, more on the seductive side. Rambling and partially incoherent, but full of sexual content. Suggestive. Then last year I found a magazine rack on the front porch. There was a note. He'd made the magazine rack himself, just for me, it said. He said he was in love with me, couldn't get me out of his mind, stuff like that. That was the first time he was so blatant. He pleaded for me to write to him."

"Did you?"

"No."

"Did you keep his letters?" Leslie asked.

"Yes. They're in his file at the clinic."

"So, he feels rejected by you."

"I'm sure. And he's certainly capable of violence. He had periodic rage episodes. He'd get in fights in bars. Once he killed a neighbor's cat for shitting in his yard."

"And he knew you worked with rape victims?"

"I never talked about that with him, but my office bookshelves are full of books on rape. And he might have seen me on that TV show or seen the news clips of it."

"If those witnesses are telling the truth, is it possible that he could have dressed himself to look like you? I mean, he's not six-foot-five or something, two-hundred and fifty pounds?"

"He's probably a couple inches taller than I am. Thin. I think he could have disguised himself." Lyla pictured Eric Hefner. It had been painfully difficult working with him. "He was fascinated by violence," she said. "He also had a history of substance abuse."

"It sounds like you think he's the one," Candace said.

"I think he could be. I wrote this all out for Kate. She said she'll check into it. There are others, too. The former husband of one of my ex-patients, for instance. He used to beat her. He blames me for her divorcing him."

Leslie nodded pensively. "Is there anything we could do? Do some checking ourselves?"

The phone rang again. This time Lyla answered it.

"Kate Ralla told me you were released," the caller said. "Is this a bitch or what? How're you doing, Lyla?"

"A lot better now than a few hours ago. How about you, Jade? I hear the police have been giving you a rough time."

"They've stopped for now. At first they were saying I'm covering up for you, then they shifted to accusing me of being your accomplice. It's all so crazy. I would have visited you at Cook County but Kate advised against it. If it's been a nightmare for me, it must have been a week from hell for you." She paused. "Kate told me Candace knows about us. How is she taking it?"

"She's sticking by me."

"I figured she would."

"I should have told her from the beginning."

"So you've said, but then you —"

"Right. Things were so good all the way around, I figured why make waves, why upset her."

"What she didn't know wouldn't hurt her. And it wouldn't have, Lyla. It was a good choice at the time. Who could have predicted something like this would happen?"

Both women were silent. Finally Jade said, "I guess there won't be any more of our *Wednesday nights*." She laughed hollowly. "I knew it would end, but . . . shit."

"I haven't had a sexual thought since the cops first came to my door."

"I know what you mean," Jade said.

"Not you, Jade! I don't believe it. You'd probably have an orgasm sitting in the electric chair."

"That's not funny."

"Gallows humor."

"We'll find out who did the assaults and is framing you. Kate has me trying to think of any enemies of mine, or anyone who'd want to destroy us . . . or you. You won't believe who keeps coming to my mind."

"Benny."

"Hah! So you've thought of her, too? I feel guilty even considering it. As jealous and possessive and outrageous

46

as Benny can be, she does have her limits. Even if she *had* found out I was seeing you, she certainly wouldn't murder anyone over it. Even rapists."

"Murder may not have been the intent," Lyla said. "That could have been accidental."

"Which makes little difference to the legal system."

"I know. *Had* Benny found out about us?" Lyla asked.

"Before the police mess? She's playing it like she hadn't, but I'm not so sure. She took it real calm when I told her what I was really doing on my Wednesday poker nights."

"I figured you'd have to tell."

"The police questioned her, too, so I had no choice. She said she understands my appetites, and isn't surprised. And she's been real supportive about my problems with the police."

"That doesn't sound like Benny."

"I know. She's keeping her distance, though. We haven't touched each other since the trouble began."

"I keep thinking about what you told me a couple of weeks ago. That she was acting odd and had made some crack about you enjoying your Wednesday nights while you could."

"I know. I keep thinking about that, too."

"So, where was *she* on the tattoo Wednesdays?"

"One of the cops actually asked her that — the woman, Detective Lopez. You know the one?"

"Yes," Lyla said. "So, what did Benny answer?"

"She says she was at some friend's house on May nineteenth. That she remembers because that was the day of the big Convention Hall fire. It doesn't matter, though. I don't really believe she could have messed up those rapists like that. She's not that vicious."

"I suppose not."

"She did do a number one time on a woman a lover of hers was seeing. Did I ever tell you about that?"

"She called the woman's boss and outed her."

"Right. That was after she ice-picked the tires on the woman's car."

"You didn't tell me that part."

47

"Benny definitely has a violent streak. She beat up her brother so bad one time he had to have stitches."

"Jesus!"

"She's no saint."

"No," Lyla said. "In fact you're beginning to convince me she might be the killer. Was she ever raped?"

"That policewoman asked her that, too."

"Really? That's good to hear. It means I might not be their only suspect. So *has* Benny ever been raped?"

"Are you kidding? She'd tear the balls off any guy who tried."

"Maybe now," Lyla said, "but maybe not when she was a lot younger. It could have happened a long time ago."

"Benny was always butch."

"God, Jade, I just realized what I'm doing. I'm doing the same thing to Benny that the cops are doing to me."

"You're doing what you have to do, Lyla. Someone is trying to have you take the rap for crimes they committed, so of course you have to look into even the remotest possibilities."

"It couldn't be a woman."

"Yes, it could. We just don't want it to be."

"Candace thinks it might be my ex — Reggie Hirtz."

"You were involved with Reggie Hirtz? You never told me that."

"I never told you lots of things."

"I know her. She's a piece of work. Part of that radical lesbian separatist group, the ones who ..." Jade stopped talking.

"Right," Lyla said. "Lesbians United to Stop All Rape. Candace thinks they did the assaults and Reggie volunteered me to take the credit."

"This is too crazy. Benny thinks the cops ought to go after Leon James. He's the dyke-basher we sprayed with stink juice. She thinks he's homophobic and crazy enough to attack a bunch of rapists just to blame it on some dykes."

"Oh yeah? But why me? I don't even know the guy."

"Maybe he knows you know me."

"The list of suspects grows ridiculous," Lyla said.

"Mine includes two ex-patients, the husband of an ex-patient, the boyfriend of a present patient, a neighbor, and an ex-lover."

"Patients who weren't happy with the therapy, huh? Boy, that'd be a bit extreme, wouldn't it?"

"This whole thing is a bit extreme."

"True. Who's the neighbor?"

"Jim Julian. We used to play backgammon together. Then one day he came on to me. He got really crushed when I told him I wasn't interested."

"Is he a serious possibility?"

"No. But he's as serious as most of the rest of them. Unfortunately, the only person there's any evidence against is me. Be careful crossing streets, Jade. You're all I have at this point."

"And I don't seem to be nearly enough. The cops got pretty nasty with me, Lyla, trying to make me admit I was covering up for you. Damn, I wish we'd had a *ménage à trois* one of those tattoo nights."

"You suggested it one time, remember?"

"I remember. You said it was too kinky."

"I wish I hadn't been so uptight."

"Maybe some other time," Jade said, chuckling. "Lyla, seriously, let me know if there's anything I can do. I suppose there's no way we can get together now, alone, I mean, but . . . well, anyway, let me know, all right?"

"I'll let you know," Lyla said. "Just stay healthy and close by."

"Will do," Jade said.

CHAPTER 6

In the days immediately following her release from jail, Lyla heard from nearly everyone she knew. They phoned, they sent notes, some came to her house. They offered support, asking if there was anything they could do. They assured her that the truth would be found out and she would be cleared. Her parents were frantic and wanted to come from Pittsburgh to be with her. Lyla told them maybe later. Lyla spoke with Emily Granser, the director of the clinic, and also several of her colleagues. And, of course, she had frequent conversations with her attorney, Kate Ralla.

On Friday afternoon, three days after her release, Lyla arrived at a ten-story office building near McClurg Court and rode the elevator to the third floor. The sign on the office door said, *Fedor and Fedor, Private Investigators.*

Patrice Fedor answered the door herself. She was an athletic-looking woman who appeared to be around Lyla's age, thirty-five. Kate had arranged the meeting, as she had the previous day when Lyla had interviewed another investigator, a man named Robert Mallory. Lyla had found Mallory condescending and arrogant, and by the end of their conversation, felt sure he believed she was guilty. She told him she didn't think he was right for the case.

Patrice directed her to an easy chair.

"Who's the other Fedor?" Lyla asked.

"My brother," the investigator answered, taking the chair opposite Lyla. "We consult with each other on all our cases. It helps keep us objective."

"Kate Ralla told you about my situation?"

"The basics, and I've read the newspaper accounts. I'd like to hear the story from you." She reached over to her desk and grabbed a notebook.

Lyla took a deep breath. "I was arrested on June first. The police had gotten an anonymous call on May twentieth, the day after the last incident, the one where the guy died."

Lyla told the investigator about the police witnesses and what each of them claimed, including the fact that one of them had picked her out at a lineup.

"The cops kept asking me what computer I used to print the Ames Enterprises letters. Apparently each of the men that got tattooed had been sent a letter saying he was a finalist and could win a VCR. That's how the tattooer lured the victims to the different offices for the tattooing. A number of other men who'd been acquitted of rape got the same letter."

"Yes, that was in the newspaper," Patrice said.

"The police took my computer and printer. They also checked the ones at the clinic where I work. None of them matched."

Lyla explained to the investigator how she, in fact,

had spent her Wednesday nights. After that, she briefly described each person on her list of possible suspects.

"Do you know any of the men who were assaulted?" Patrice asked.

"No."

"Do you have an extra car key?"

"Yes, Candace has it. She keeps it with her own keys."

After asking a few more questions, Patrice leaned back in her chair. "I've heard enough now to know that I would be willing to take the case." She told Lyla what her fees would be, and said she was ready to begin immediately.

"From what you know at this point, do you think it's just a series of coincidences," Lyla asked, "or do you think someone is trying to frame me?"

"My guess would be the latter," Patrice responded. "If you decide to hire me, I'll want to know everything you can think of about each of those people on your list."

"I *would* like you to take the case," Lyla said. "I think you believe me, and I think you'll do everything you can to find out who's doing this to me."

"Good." Patrice smiled for the first time, and Lyla detected the warmth beneath the investigator's crisp demeanor. "Then let's begin. First, I want to know exactly how you spent the nights of the assaults, the more details the better."

They continued talking for another two hours. Lyla remembered that there had been one Wednesday night since the tattooing began that she had not spent with Jade. "I was sick with the flu," she said. "I called Jade and cancelled. It was sometime in February. I was sick for two days, didn't go to work. One of those nights a friend of Candace's dropped by. She could verify that I was home," Lyla said excitedly, "and so can Candace."

Patrice wrote as Lyla spoke. "The friend's name?"

"Sharon Groch," Lyla said. "God, I hope it was February tenth."

"The night of the second incident. If that's when you

52

were sick, it would certainly help. The clinic where you work will have a record of your missed days, I assume."

"Yes, and I can also check my own appointment book. I'll do that as soon as I get home." Lyla made a note on the pad of paper Patrice had given her.

"Were there any Wednesday nights that you didn't drive?" Patrice asked. "Perhaps your car was in for repairs one of those days?"

Lyla shook her head. "No, I always had my car. Wait, that isn't true. There was one night that I drove Candace's car. Her back seat was full of painting supplies, cans and rollers and drop cloths. She had plans to go out with a bunch of friends that night and needed the back seat. Rather than clean out her car, she asked if we could switch cars. I drove her car to work that day, then used it that night to meet Jade."

"When was this?"

"During the holidays. That's when Candace was doing the painting for a friend. And then that night she went to a play. It was probably sometime in late December."

"December thirtieth, if we're lucky," Patrice said. "You're doing real well, Lyla. Tell me more about the naps you took Wednesday nights. Did you always have wine before you slept?"

Lyla nodded. "It was part of our ritual."

"And Jade always served the wine, bringing it to you in the bedroom, right?"

"Right."

"And you said sometimes she would nap with you and sometimes she wouldn't. But she was always there when you woke up except that one time when she came back from the drugstore at about ten o'clock. Is that correct?"

"Correct."

The questioning continued. Patrice asked Lyla if she'd ever noticed any neighbors around Vicky's apartment. She asked about the times Lyla had the feeling she was being watched. Lyla wasn't able to come up with anything helpful. Patrice wrote down Jade's phone number, then switched to questions about Lyla's list of possible suspects.

"I'm just grasping at straws with this list," Lyla said. "Kate insisted I do it. I don't think the killer is anyone I know."

"I'll be checking other possibilities," Patrice said, "but for now I want to hear about the people on your list. Start with Reggie Hirtz."

Lyla told the investigator every relevant fact she could think of about Reggie and her organization, LUSAR. Patrice took notes. When there seemed to be no more information Lyla could give, Patrice said, "She and her group are definitely worth checking out. Maybe I'll join LUSAR." She asked for a physical description of Reggie and wrote down what Lyla said. "Can you get a photograph of her for me?" Lyla said she could. "All right," Patrice said, "let's move on." She checked her notes. "Eric Hefner. Tell me about him."

"A very disturbed man," Lyla said. She talked about her ex-patient's psychopathology, their lack of progress in therapy, his declaration of love for Lyla, his history of violence.

"I sure wouldn't rule him out," Patrice said when Lyla finished. "I'll need his address in Winnetka and the name of the psychiatrist he's seeing there."

"The psychiatrist won't talk with you, you know," Lyla said, "not about a patient."

"You are," Patrice responded.

"That's different. I talked with Kate about it. In a situation like mine, I'm free to break therapist-patient confidentiality with my attorney, to the extent and within the limits that it's necessary to build my defense. By extension, that applies to an investigator working with my attorney."

Patrice nodded. "I'll still want the psychiatrist's name." She smiled. "I have my ways."

Lyla laughed. "I bet you do."

"And, of course, Kate can subpoena him if it becomes necessary. What about the other ex-patient?"

"Ivan Dorley. I think of him mainly because he recently made an appointment with me, but then no-showed. He'd dropped out of therapy over a year ago."

Lyla told the investigator about her work with Ivan and how he felt rejected by her when she wouldn't see him outside the therapy.

Patrice wrote as she listened. "Okay, tell me about the wife-beater now."

"Larry Hunt," Lyla said, "the husband of my patient, Louisa. He physically abused her. After I'd worked with Louisa for several months, she felt ready to make the break. She moved out of their apartment and went to stay with a cousin in Elmhurst. Larry wasn't about to let go easily. He cajoled and badgered her to come back to him. She refused. She filed for divorce. Larry then wanted to have a joint therapy session. Louisa reluctantly agreed to it. I thought maybe the meeting would help him accept that the marriage was over. Louisa made her position very clear when the three of us met. She had stuck it out as long as she could, but no longer saw any hope for the marriage, no longer wanted it. It wasn't just the violence, she said, but their general incompatibility.

"I can still picture his face when he glared at me and said, 'It's your fault! You did this to her! You're the one who turned her against me!' His eyes were full of hate. He said Louisa had always listened to reason until she started coming to see me."

"Did you feel frightened?"

"Somewhat."

"I can see why. And then?"

"I continued working with Louisa. The divorce was finalized a few months later, but Larry still didn't stop harassing her. She finally decided to move to another state. New Mexico."

"When was that?"

"Last November."

"Hmm," Patrice said. "A month before the assaults started. Interesting."

"I got a Christmas card from her. She said she was doing fine. Had found an apartment and a job. No mention of Larry."

"Do you have an address on him?"

"As far as I know he's still at the apartment where

he and Louisa used to live. We have the address at the clinic."

"Anything else you know about him? His job? Where he hangs out?"

"He's a mechanic, but I don't know where he works. Louisa used to talk about his dune buggy, one of those trucks with the huge wheels. He drives it on the sand dunes in Michigan. Louisa hated the thing. They used to fight about it."

Patrice nodded. "This guy sounds like a live one, Lyla. Prone to violence. Blaming you for his losing his wife. Him, I definitely want to check out. Get that address to me right away."

Lyla made a note on her pad of paper.

"All right, who's next? Or are you getting tired? Do you want to stop for now?"

"I'm fine," Lyla said. "Let's see, we've already talked about Reggie, Eric Hefner, Ivan Dorley, Larry Hunt. That leaves Benny, Aldo Pranza, and Jim Julian. There's also that guy, Leon, that Jade mentioned, but you can talk to her about him."

"So what about this Jim Julian? He's your neighbor, right? You and he were friends for a while, and then he got mad at you. Tell me more."

"He's an introverted guy," Lyla said. "Limited social skills, kind of on the nerdy side. I met him the summer before last. He owns a house a few doors down from me, across the alley. One day I was working in my backyard and he came down the alley and stopped to talk. I ended up going with him to take a look at his garden. He was very proud of it. After that day he'd show up just about every time I was in my yard. He gave me a lot of gardening tips. One day I mentioned that I play backgammon and he got all excited, told me it was his favorite game, that he and his mother played all the time. I got the impression that he was quite tied to his mother. *Momma's boy,* Candace called him.

"So Jim and I would play backgammon from time to time on my picnic table. He played a very aggressive game, which surprised me. Most of the time he won. I

56

remember telling him once that he was too good for me. That got a little weird because he said he was thinking the same thing about me, that I was too good for him, but he didn't mean backgammon. He talked about my being a professional, a doctor and all, and that he hadn't even finished college. He said I probably thought he was a real loser. Obviously his self-esteem was pretty low. I did what I could to bolster him up. Candace warned me not to be too nice to him or he'd get ideas."

"Was she right?" Patrice Fedor asked.

"Unfortunately, yes. A few months after we met, he asked me if I had a boyfriend. I told him no and that I wasn't looking for one. He got real sympathetic, assuming I'd been hurt. He said he knew what that was like but that he'd never hurt me. He talked about how *fond* of me he was. Then he asked me to go out to dinner with him. It got real uncomfortable. I told him I liked my life the way it was, and that I didn't want to date anyone. The pain on his face was . . . well, raw. It was painful to see. Next to being rejected, there's not much I dislike more than rejecting someone."

Patrice nodded. "And then?"

"We had very little contact after that. I'd run into him occasionally when I was walking my dog. Once he asked if I'd like to play backgammon with him in his house. And he made a few other attempts to get together. Of course, I declined each time. He seemed to handle it okay. The last time we had a conversation — that was well over a year ago — he said if I ever changed my mind and wanted to play backgammon or anything, to let him know. After that, he'd just say hi to me if our paths crossed."

"Did he seem angry?"

"No, not then. But later — I believe it was around last fall sometime — he did. He'd look right through me if he saw me, not say a word."

"Hmm. Do you think he found out you and Candace are lovers?"

Lyla shrugged. "I don't know."

"Maybe his crush on you turned to hatred," Patrice suggested.

"Could be," Lyla said. "That's why he's on the list."

"Well, I'd say he belongs there," Patrice said. "What does he do for a living?"

"Cashes in the CDs from his dead father."

"He doesn't work?"

"Part-time. Office work at a real estate place on Lincoln Avenue. At least, that's what he was doing when we were on talking terms. Boy Friday stuff. Gopher, typist. Oh, yeah, and he made signs for their windows. He's had some training as a graphic designer."

Patrice had Lyla give her the exact location of the real estate office, then asked if there was any more about Jim.

"Not that I can think of," Lyla said.

"OK, next?"

"Aldo Pranza," Lyla said. "He may be more capable of the assaults than anyone else I've mentioned. Maybe we should have started with him."

"He's the one whose girlfriend was raped."

"It sent him into a macho rage. I guess he's over it now. Angela says he's almost back to normal, at least in regard to the anger. But there've been other changes in him since Angela's rape. Angela was worried for a while that he was having an affair. He'd cancel plans with her, not giving much of an explanation. Wasn't as available as he used to be. He seemed secretive, preoccupied."

"Sounds like something was going on with him. But Angela decided it wasn't another woman?"

"He's been more committed to her than ever. They're talking about marriage."

"She's still your patient, right?"

Lyla sighed. "I don't have any patients at the moment," she said bitterly. "But, yes, Angela was still seeing me when all this started, and she wants to wait until I come back." Lyla shook her head, feeling terrible frustration. "I contacted all my patients. Some agreed to transfer to different therapists; some chose to wait, hoping I'll be back working soon. I hope they're right."

"So do I," Patrice said.

Lyla could see that the investigator really meant it.

"I'm finding out firsthand now what it feels like to be a victim," Lyla said. "It sucks."

"It sure does," Patrice responded. "I think we've covered enough for today. I have plenty to start with. I'll need a photograph of you, several actually. Recent ones. And one of Jade if you have it."

"I'll get them to you," Lyla said, "and I'll call you after I check those dates."

Patrice crossed her fingers. "We're going to be needing some good luck," she said.

When Lyla left Patrice Fedor's office, she was feeling almost good — truly hopeful for the first time since the ordeal had begun. The moment she got home, she went to her appointment book. Her heart was pounding as she flipped the pages. She found February tenth. "Shit!"

"What's the matter, hon?" Candace stood behind her.

Lyla flipped more pages until she came to February seventeenth. She kept flipping. "Damn, here it is. I was sick on February twenty-fourth."

"What are you . . . oh, I know," Candace said. "You were hoping —"

"When did you go to that play, hon? You know, that day we switched cars. It was soon after Christmas, wasn't it? What was the date?"

"Was that a Wednesday?" Candace asked eagerly. "Oh, God, let it be December thirtieth. Let me think. Let me think." She paced the room. "Was it the day before New Year's Eve? I have no idea. Maybe Paula will remember."

She ran for the phone. After speaking briefly to Paula, she put her hand over the mouthpiece. "She's getting her checkbook. She wrote me a check that day for her ticket to the play."

Lyla held her breath.

"Oh," Candace said dully. "Thanks, Paula." She turned to Lyla and shook her head. "It was January sixth."

"Fuck!"

Candace put her arms around Lyla. Lyla's shoulders

were shaking. "We'll come up with something, hon. Come on, come to the sofa and tell me how it went with Patrice Fedor."

As she talked about Patrice, Lyla began to feel less discouraged.

"Did she tell you what she's going to do?" Candace asked.

"Figure out who's framing me," Lyla said. "And nail the fucker."

CHAPTER 7

Patrice Fedor entered the Dog's Bark Bar and Grill and took a stool at the bar. She wore tight black cotton pants and a low-cut polyester blouse. "A Bud Lite," she told the bartender.

Her eyes flicked over the dozen or so people in the room and fixed on a lean, muscular man in his thirties, dressed in jeans and a red T-shirt. Over the past few days, she had asked around about Larry Hunt, the suspect who blamed Lyla for his wife divorcing him. Patrice learned that this bar and the Star Bowl bowling alley were two of his haunts. When her beer arrived, she carried it to the end of the bar and took a stool next to the man.

"I know I know you," she said.

He looked her up and down, a half-smile on his smooth, tanned face.

"Seriously," she said. "It's not a line. We definitely met somewhere. What's your name?"

"Larry. And yours?"

"Lil Diamond," Patrice said. She glanced around the bar. A man and woman sat silently at a table. Someone in a plaid shirt clanged at a video machine. She looked back at Larry. "Can I buy you a drink?"

He raised his eyebrows. "Sure, I could handle another beer."

Patrice could tell he'd already *handled* quite a few. She hoped that would make him talkative. She ordered the drink, looked him over some more, and then said, "I remember now. It was at the Star Bowl on Montrose Avenue. That's where I saw you before."

"Could be. When was this?"

"Last month. It was my friend's birthday. May nineteenth. A Wednesday. We sang happy birthday to her and you joined in. Do you remember?"

Larry looked pointedly at her. Was he thinking about how he actually had spent that night, Patrice wondered, murdering Henry Lester? Or was he just trying to remember?

"It wasn't me," he said.

Patrice opened her purse and slapped a bill on the bar. "I'll bet you twenty bucks I'm right."

Larry looked at the money then back at Patrice. He took out his wallet and laid two tens on top of Patrice's twenty. "You lose. I wasn't even in Chicago that night. That's the day I left for Michigan. I was in Silver Lake at the Motel Six." He took a huge swallow of beer. "From Wednesday until Sunday. I took some vacation time to go dune buggy riding."

"Damn!" Patrice said. "You must have a twin out there somewhere, Larry." She pushed the money toward him. Too glib, she thought. Sounds like an alibi to me.

* * * * *

In her car, Patrice wiped off the heavy lipstick, and slipped a light sweatshirt over her low-cut blouse. When she got to her Lincoln Park apartment, she called the Motel Six in Silver Lake, Michigan.

"This is WBBT Grand Rapids' Magic Date Contest!" Patrice declared. "You and one of your patrons could be winners!"

She explained that her radio station was calling Michigan motels looking for one which had a guest registered the night of May nineteenth whose initials were L. H. "If you had one," she said, "both you and L. H. can be winners. Do you have your registration book handy?"

There was a pause. "L. H., you say. Yeah, I got one."

"Fantastic! What's the name?"

"Well, uh . . . oh, I guess I can tell you that. I know the guy. Comes here all the time. Name is Larry Hunt. He's from Chicago."

"He's a winner! Did he arrive at your motel on the nineteenth?"

"Yep. He stayed four nights. Got in late on the nineteenth. Woke me up."

"How late, sir?"

"Oh, two or three in the morning, it must have been. That doesn't matter, does it? We still win, don't we?"

"Well, I don't think a couple of hours should make any difference. I'll check and get back to you," Patrice said. "Be sure not to tell Larry Hunt about the contest, okay? We want to surprise him."

"Yeah, sure," the proprietor said, "I won't tell."

CHAPTER 8

As soon as Lyla heard the voice, she wished she hadn't answered the phone.

"I didn't think you had it in you, Bradshaw," Reggie said. "Tattooing is definitely the way to go. I've been advocating it for years. But I never thought of brain damage. Did you learn to do lobotomies in graduate school?"

"Cute, Reg," Lyla said. "You're as sensitive as ever."

Reggie laughed. "Okay, okay, I'm sorry. I know you've been having a rough time. I hear they had you at Cook County. Anyway, the reason I'm calling is to extend an invitation to you. We'd like you to come to our LUSAR brunch as our guest."

Lyla resisted her impulse to slam down the phone. "I'm not interested in your *loser* group," she said sharply.

"Hey, don't knock your supporters, woman. We're all behind you on this. They're calling you the Joan of Arc of radical feminism."

"Maiming and killing people has nothing to do with feminism, Regina. And I had nothing to do with what happened to those rapists."

"Right, right, I understand. But do you have any idea how things have started popping since you hit the headlines? We're doing an action tomorrow night, and because of you, we'll have a hundred people instead of just a dozen. We're picketing Steven Gendlin's advertising firm. You know who he is, don't you? The guy who rapes women who come to him for job interviews."

"I heard about him," Lyla said.

"Well, the charges against him have been dropped. The criminal justice system blew it again. Now it's our turn. Maybe we should tattoo his forehead. Heh-heh-heh. Hey, that would help your defense, wouldn't it?"

"Reggie, stop being disgusting. This isn't funny. I'm fighting for my life, for God's sake."

"I'm not laughing," Reggie said. "I know it's not funny. So what about coming to the brunch? Everyone would love to meet you."

"Tell your friends I'm not their hero. I'm not their goddamn fantasy avenger."

"You're a hero whether you did the actions or not, Bradshaw. We've gotten over thirty new members since the cops arrested you. And it's not just happening in Chicago. Haven't you been reading the papers? People are coming out of the woodwork to rally around you and this issue. There's a fund-raiser being planned for you here in Chicago. Did you know about that?"

"No."

"Somebody will be calling you. Are the cops tapping your phone? There's a lot you should know about what's been going on. And a few things I'd like to hear from you. Why don't we meet somewhere?"

Lyla felt like telling her to take a flying leap. But then she thought maybe she'd learn something that could help her case. She wasn't ruling out the possibility that LUSAR was behind the assaults. "All right," she said.

As soon as she hung up, Lyla called Kate Ralla's office. "Hi, Rhonda, this is Lyla Bradshaw. Is Kate free?"

"She will be in a minute," the secretary said. "Someone's just leaving. How're you doing, Lyla?"

"Hanging in," Lyla said.

"Well, personally I can't believe they're actually planning to prosecute you. If you were guilty, you sure would have provided yourself with a better alibi. Oh, she's free now. I'll put you through."

"What's up, kiddo?" Kate said.

Lyla told her attorney about the planned meeting with Reggie.

"Not a good idea," Kate responded. "Let Patrice Fedor do the investigating. You could do more harm than good."

"I thought you might say that, but I can't just sit and do nothing, Kate. Maybe I'll learn something from Reggie that will help."

"Patrice's working on that. She's already infiltrated LUSAR. She'll be at a demonstration they're doing tomorrow night. You should stay out of it, Lyla. Besides, Reggie has an alibi for May nineteenth. Several of her LUSAR friends say they were with her. I thought you didn't see Reggie as a serious suspect, anyway."

"I didn't want to," Lyla said, "but to tell the truth, I'm not sure. What I called for is to ask if you have suggestions about how I should proceed with her. I was thinking I might talk about Jade and see if I can get Reggie to slip, maybe acknowledge that she knew about Jade and my meetings at Vicky's."

"That might help if you could do it, but you could also blow it by tipping her off that she's a suspect."

"I'll be careful. So, do you have any suggestions?"

"Don't tell her we have an investigator working on the case. Don't tell her we think you were framed. Don't tell her anything. Don't talk about the case. That's my advice."

"I've got your point. Okay, she'll be here soon. I'll let you know how it goes."

They went to a restaurant on Diversey Avenue. Lyla ordered iced tea; Reggie ordered a meal.

"You know, I used to sort of hate you, Lyla, but I don't anymore," Reggie said. She smiled magnanimously. "I've forgiven you. Everything feels different now. Yeah, I've finally really let go."

"Good for you, Reg."

"Try not to be sarcastic, huh? Remember, you're the one who dumped me."

"You're the one who was impossible to be with."

"You were seeing other women."

"Only after I told you it was over with us."

"That I have trouble believing."

"Jesus Christ, Reggie. Let's not rehash it, huh? It's dead, all right?"

"Right, as dead as that rapist. Did you tell Candace it was over with her before you started seeing Jade?"

Lyla felt immediate guilt, then anger, then a rush of excitement. She looked Reggie coolly in the eye. "What are you talking about?" she said. "Who's Jade?"

Reggie laughed heartily. "Your thing with Jade McGrath is public knowledge, my friend."

"Oh? How so? I didn't see anything about it in the newspapers."

"It's sure on the grapevine. The gossip started way before you were arrested. I've known for months."

"Known what?" Lyla demanded. "And where did you hear it?"

"I never reveal my sources." Reggie grinned. "We figured you and Jade were just fucking, but I guess that's not all you two did together." Reggie leaned close to Lyla.

"Just between us, Lyla, did you and Jade mean to kill that one? Or did you just intend to do the brain damage and tattoos? If you don't want to answer, that's okay."

Lyla held Reggie's eyes. "What exactly was the grapevine saying about me and Jade?"

"Oh not much, really." Reggie leaned back again. "Just that Jade's friend, Vicky Kranz, taught aerobics on Wednesday nights and that Jade had keys to Vicky's apartment."

Lyla shook her head. "It's so hard to have any privacy in this community." She tried to sound light.

"Well, Vicky happened to mention it confidentially to a friend, who happened to mention it to Tessa. You know Tessa — my main squeeze. You met her at that Halloween party."

"Yes, I remember her."

"She's the best thing that ever happened to me, Lyla. A terrific person. Very loyal. She's one of the original organizers of LUSAR, you know. She remembers you, too. Says you didn't seem like my type."

"She's right."

Reggie laughed. "That was quite a wild party last Halloween, wasn't it? Tessa never did get her wallet back. She lost it there. Or someone stole it, more likely."

"Really? I lost . . ." Lyla almost literally bit her tongue. Until that moment, she had forgotten that she'd lost a spare key to her car at that party. The key was in a tiny leather pouch which she'd had in her pocket. Since Candace had driven them home that night, Lyla hadn't realized she'd lost the key until the following day.

"You lost what?"

"Uh . . . my watch. A couple months ago. At Found and Out."

"Too bad. I hope it wasn't a Rolex. Speaking of big bucks, money has been pouring into LUSAR since the news broke about the rapist tattooings. We're thinking of organizing a Guardian Angels-type brigade. You know, to patrol high-risk areas to escort women to their cars and things. That's part of the prevention side of what we want to do. I'm more involved in the *outing* side — outing rapists. Picketing is just a mild example. We really are thinking of going the forehead tattooing route." Reggie ran her finger across her brow, smiling.

Lyla stared at her coldly.

"I'm serious," Reggie said. "Of course, before we start doing it, we'll do a big publicity push about it, telling people what it's about and assuring them the evidence against the men who get the tattoo will be indisputable. It will be, too. Like it was with your guys. We'll make sure only the guilty get the *mark of the rapist*. We plan to skip the brain damage and killing part." She looked at Lyla. "So, what do you think?"

"I think you're sick."

"I feel fine," Reggie said. "You do have a good lawyer, don't you, Lyla? Kate Ralla, I heard. One of us, right? Will she be able to get you off? I'd hate to think of you spending years in prison. Of course, if you did get convicted, you'd be a celebrity there. Your name will go down in herstory, Lyla. A true martyr."

Lyla was feeling immensely disgusted. "Did LUSAR know any of the three who got tattooed?" she asked.

"Nah." Reggie took a bite of her Polish sausage. "There are so many rapists. Those three were new to us." She chewed and swallowed. "Is there anything I can do to help with your defense? Character witness or anything? I could testify to your non-violent nature. I wish I could provide an alibi for you. Of course, you have Jade."

"Maybe you could help me find the real killer," Lyla said.

"Yeah, someone with a white Honda just like yours."

Lyla looked askance at her. "How would that help?"

"Your car was spotted at the scenes, wasn't it?"

"How did you know that?"

"How?" Reggie swallowed her mouthful of food. "The newspaper," she said. She took another bite. "Does your lawyer think the grand jury will indict you?"

Lyla's head was pounding. "It's not looking good," she said.

Reggie reached over and touched her hand. "Well, I'm on your side. I'll be rooting for you."

Lyla felt like throwing up.

"It's weird that it took something like this to finally get me over it," Reggie said. "I just don't feel the anger towards you anymore."

"Five years is a long time," Lyla said.

"Five years and three months. I've changed since then. And you sure as hell have. You're certainly making your mark. The number of rapes has dropped incredibly, did you know that? The boys are scared, Lyla."

"Reggie, do you actually believe I did it?"

Reggie smiled, shrugging her shoulders. "What can I say?"

"I had nothing to do with what happened to those men. Causing damage to someone's brain and murdering is absolutely unthinkable to me."

"Hey, no need," Reggie said, holding up her hands. "I'm not the jury."

It was hard for Lyla to read Reggie. It always had been. Was she playing with her, knowing full well who the culprit really was, or did she actually believe Lyla was guilty? "Have you ever been to Vicky's apartment?" Lyla tried.

"No, I'm into monogamy these days."

"Very funny. I mean do you know Vicky?"

"Only by reputation."

"She lives on Aldine, east of Broadway." Lyla watched for a reaction to the lie.

"Oh? Lousy neighborhood. No place to park. I'm living on Wilson now, not far from you. I drive past your house every once in a while on my way to Osco's. Your place is looking good; I like the new siding. Once I saw Gal out in the backyard and I stopped to say hi. She went crazy. Pissed all over the sidewalk. I guess she misses me."

"Yeah, and I guess she'll miss me if I get sent to prison." Lyla's eyes teared. She couldn't prevent it. She looked away from Reggie.

"Prison is a big price to pay," Reggie said solemnly. "I truly do hope that never happens, Lyla. You've been through enough already. This has got to be one hell of an experience."

Lyla blinked back her tears.

"At least they let you out on bail," Reggie said. "So, what about coming to the LUSAR get-together? People know you can't talk about the case, so no one will expect that. They just want to meet you, maybe get your opinion of some of our plans. You might as well enjoy the attention."

"Yeah, while I can, huh? When you first joined this group and started telling me what they were into, I told you I thought they were a fringy bunch of extremists — advocating the death penalty for rapists, or castration. I assume that's still their position?"

"Of course."

"And I told you two wrongs don't make a right."

"And I said how original of you."

"I still believe what I said," Lyla said. "I don't share your group's goals."

Reggie laughed heartily. "All right, all right, I get it. You shouldn't be seen with us. It wouldn't look good for your case. You're right, I should have thought of that."

"You know, you never told me why you joined LUSAR in the first place. I asked you, but you never really gave me an answer. You'd never been an activist before then. Why this group? Why this cause?"

"Oh, come on. I have to tell *you* why I want to stop rapists?"

"I mean your personal reasons."

"Because I'm a woman. Because every single woman lives in fear of being raped. I can't believe you're asking me this."

"There are many causes that affect women's lives. Why this one for you?"

"Stop playing psychologist."

"Did it happen to you? I know there were lots of things about yourself that you never told me. Was that one of them? Were you raped?"

Reggie didn't answer. She stared at her empty plate.

"Was it a long time ago?" Lyla said gently. "When you were an adolescent?"

Reggie shook her head. Lyla waited. "It wasn't me,"

71

Reggie said at last. "Two women I love were raped." She looked at Lyla, her eyes red. "Casey was one of them."

"Your sister."

"When she was seventeen. Her prom date. She had nothing to do with men for a good two years after that. I was hoping she never would." Reggie chuckled weakly. "Her husband's a good guy, though. Casey's doing okay. Actually, I think her rape had more of a long-term effect on me than it did on her. I can still remember her telling me about it. She was so emotionally injured, so disillusioned."

"You were there for her," Lyla said.

"I did what I could. She wouldn't tell anyone else, and she wouldn't let me tell anyone. Our parents still don't know. I wanted her to press charges but she wouldn't hear of it. I came very close to going after the guy myself. She stopped me, made me promise I wouldn't."

"So you both just held it in."

"The first time I told anyone was at my first LUSAR meeting."

"I see."

Reggie was twisting her paper napkin into a tight rope. "And the other one was a close friend of mine. Someone you don't know. It happened last year. The guy broke into her apartment." Reggie's jaw was clenched. "Son of a bitch beat her black and blue. She still has nightmares. They never caught him, of course." Reggie looked Lyla in the eye. "She hopes he was one of the three."

Lyla nodded. "I wish you could have told me about your sister five years ago. It would have helped me understand."

"It wouldn't have made any difference," Reggie said, her mood obviously shifting. "My involvement with LUSAR isn't why you broke with me. Don't you remember what you told me? That you couldn't breathe. You felt *constricted* by me, that was your word. Like I was suffocating you. That had nothing to do with LUSAR."

"True," Lyla said. "I did feel that way. But when you started talking that radical hate stuff, that iced the cake."

Reggie leaned back in the booth. "Well, as you've said yourself, Lyla, all that is part of the dead past. Gone and very close to being buried now." She smiled. "We had some good times though, you and I. Those are the memories we should keep. That's where I'm at now." She shook her head. "It's weird that I told you about my sister."

"I'm glad you did."

"You're sounding like a therapist again."

Lyla shrugged.

Reggie picked up the check. "My treat," she said.

CHAPTER 9

Candace took a sip of her drink as she watched Lyla place a tray of cut raw vegetables on the picnic table. "I like coming home and being waited on hand and foot," she said. "So did anything else happen today?"

Lyla took a carrot stick. "Jade called."

"Ah, yesterday Reggie, today Jade. Never a dull moment."

"She wants to get together to talk about the case."

Candace looked at her partner stonily.

"I think it's a good idea," Lyla said, scooping up some dip. "Maybe between us we'll remember something new that could help." She looked sincerely at Candace. "You know there's absolutely no danger of anything happening."

Candace shrugged.

"But in any case," Lyla said, "I think you should be there, too. Maybe she could come here, to the house."

"I don't want her at the house," Candace said firmly.

"All right."

"I try to think of her as just a sexual plaything that you had some fun with, like a fantastic vibrator or something."

Lyla nodded. "That's close."

"I hope so. If I thought you two had more than that . . ."

"We didn't."

"Well, I'm not ready to meet her."

"That's fine."

"But I don't want you to be alone with her."

Lyla put her carrot down. "How would it be if Leslie were there?"

"That would help," Candace said. "Lyla, if you ever feel the need again, you know, to go get . . . to act out that part of you, to have that kind of a sexual thing again, with Jade or with anyone else, I want you to tell me, all right?"

"All right, but it's not going to happen again."

"It won't be easy for me, but I'd rather know."

Lyla nodded understandingly. "I'd planned to tell you as soon as it started with Jade. I should have. But . . . Candace, it was so separate from us, like . . . like going to a masseuse or having gourmet meals or —"

Candace looked askance at her.

"Well, sort of like that. Anyway, there won't be any more. It's not worth it. It's too upsetting for you and you mean more to me than . . . than whatever kicks I got out of . . . out of being with Jade. You're much more important to me than a sexual fling."

"Ten months is an awfully long fling."

"Yes, but it was still a fling. It was compartmentalized, Candace. You're in my soul. She was just some momentary . . . gratification."

Candace was quiet for a while. "You seem to enjoy our sex life."

75

"I love our sex life," Lyla said sincerely.

"But it's not enough for you. I'm too *vanilla*, as they say."

Lyla smiled lovingly. "Vanilla is my favorite flavor. It's rich and creamy and very, very satisfying. The other is ... yes, my taste for a little S and M is there, but it's not central, Candace. I told you how I feel. I'm intrigued but I'm not driven. I don't *have* to act it out."

"Good."

"I think for me," Lyla continued, "that kind of sex — sex with power games — can't be there with someone I love. It's not about love or commitment or sharing a life. For me, it's an aside."

"Like gourmet food, huh?"

Lyla smiled. "I am very deeply in love with you."

"I don't want you having sex with anyone else, whether she's an *aside* or not."

"I know." Lyla was quiet, thinking. "Maybe I should get into therapy," she said, "see if I can get past that SM part of me, even though it's just a small part."

"Would it feel like a loss if you did get past it?" Candace asked.

"Not really," Lyla said. "It would be like giving up fatty foods."

Candace rolled her eyes.

"And it's terribly politically incorrect, anyway, the power-over thing. I guess there are a number of reasons why I should explore what it's about for me." She sighed. "Maybe I will," she said. Her eyes became teary.

"Right. After you're free. After we have our lives back." Candace began to cry. "Oh, God, everything is turned upside down."

Lyla held her and cried with her.

The next day Lyla went to Patrice Fedor's office. Again they sat across from each other in easy chairs.

"Would you like to hear about the men you're accused of assaulting?" Patrice asked. "I read the court records."

"All right," Lyla said, not sure she really did.

"I'll do them chronologically, in order of the assaults." She glanced at her notes. "The first was Lawrence Thomas. Thirty-one-year-old African-American. A cab driver. On June fourteenth, last year, he met a Julia Stenson at a singles bar called Mutti's."

As Lyla listened to the story, she felt heavy-hearted. "I've heard similar cases," she said, "though never with a screwdriver as the weapon."

"It worked as well as a knife," Patrice said. "At the trial, Thomas had witnesses who swore he was with them at the time of the rape. Julia swore it was Thomas. Unfortunately, she got the color of his car wrong. The defense attorney really played that up. As you know, Thomas was acquitted."

"So it goes," Lyla said.

"I spoke with a couple of Julia's friends. No one connected with her seems a likely candidate for having done the tattoo assaults. For a while, I thought her brother might be a possibility, but then I found out he was in Europe at the time Lawrence Thomas was assaulted."

"How is she doing?" Lyla asked. "The survivor."

"Julia? Surviving," Patrice said. "She wasn't unhappy to hear that Thomas can't put a sentence together anymore."

"They say he'll never recover," Lyla said. "Permanent aphasia."

Patrice nodded. "Ready for number two?"

"Go ahead."

"Tony Anastopoulos. He's a twenty-eight-year-old hospital orderly. Born in Greece. He met Jeanine Forrester at a dinner dance where she'd come with her girlfriend, Christina Tetrinas. After the dance, Tony invited Jeanine to his apartment."

Patrice recited the facts of the rape, and then of the trial. "The defense argued that Jeanine had willingly had sex with Tony, then because he spurned her afterwards, she claimed rape."

"Not a surprising defense in such cases," Lyla said.

"It obviously worked," Patrice responded. "I talked with Jeanine's friend, Christina. Told her I was a writer doing a story on the effects of rape on the victim's friends and family. She talked pretty openly with me."

"And?"

"And, nothing. She knows Jeanine and her family well. No likely avengers among them."

"Too bad," Lyla said. "We're getting nowhere fast."

"There's an interesting footnote to this one," Patrice said. "A LUSAR member told me someone from the group had interviewed Jeanine after the acquittal. She was absolutely convinced that Jeanine's story was true."

"It probably was," Lyla said. "So LUSAR knew about that case. That *is* interesting. I talked with Reggie the other day. She's acting as if she thinks I'm the killer, and as if she's proud of me. There was nothing in the newspapers about my car being seen at any of the crime scenes, was there? I read all the articles and didn't see anything."

"No, I don't think that was in the papers," Patrice said. "Unfortunately, the business about the Ames Enterprises letters was."

"Well, Reggie knew about my car. And I also remembered while talking to her that I'd lost my car key at a Halloween party. Reggie was at that party. She could have gotten the key."

Patrice was making notes.

"And Reggie knew about my Wednesday nights with Jade. She knew we met at Vicky Kranz's apartment."

"She told you this?"

"Said she'd learned it through the grapevine — before I was arrested. She also told me that her sister had been raped as a teenager and, recently, a close friend of hers was raped."

"Well, well," Patrice said. "I'll definitely have to get to know Ms. Reggie Hirtz better. Since I'm now a LUSAR member, that shouldn't be difficult. Anything else about her?"

"Just that she was different towards me. Not nearly

as hostile as she used to be. She said she'd finally let go of her anger."

"Because she's gotten even with you now, huh?" Patrice said.

"That thought certainly crossed my mind."

"She and LUSAR have risen on my list," Patrice said. "They're using each other as their alibis, you know."

"Yes, you told me." Lyla gestured toward Patrice's papers. "What about the last rapist, the one who died?"

"Henry Lester," Patrice said. "This one's really nasty. The woman he raped was Ruth Tremaine, a fifty-five-year-old widow. He broke into her home on March sixth, last year. It was brutal." Patrice gave some of the details. "Her son, James, found her the next morning, tied to her bed."

Lyla shook her head.

"Lester also robbed her," Patrice said. "Stole a silver candelabra, among other things. From the police mug shots, Ruth picked out Henry Lester, a twenty-seven-year-old construction worker. He had two convictions for breaking and entering and burglary. The police got a search warrant. At Lester's apartment, they found a silver candelabra. They arrested Lester and Ruth Tremaine identified him in a lineup. Unfortunately, the candelabra somehow disappeared before Ruth was able to identify it.

"Also, Ruth didn't make a good witness. She cried most of the time she was testifying. When asked to identify her assailant, she was hesitant, saying he'd looked so different before. He'd been unshaven and slovenly dressed during the rape, and, of course, was cleaned up in court. Also, Ruth testified that the rape occurred in the middle of the night, whereas Lester's girlfriend swore he was at her place that night, from midnight on. The defense argued mistaken identity, and the jury apparently bought it."

"Poor woman. I bet she still hasn't recovered."

"I'll be talking with her soon, and also her son. If Lester's death was intentional, it's possible that Lester was the one the killer was really after, and that the other two were just a cover."

The door opened. A man with a thick mustache entered the office. "Sorry, I forgot something. I'll be out in a second." He went to the desk in the far corner.

Both women watched as he picked up an address book and slipped it into his pocket. "Sorry for the interruption," he said, and he left.

"My brother," Patrice said.

"I figured. Have you told him about my case?"

Patrice nodded. "He thinks it's Jade."

Lyla rolled her eyes. "Some detective."

"I did some checking on Larry Hunt," Patrice said. She told Lyla about her talk with Larry at the Dog's Bark bar and then the phone call to the Michigan Motel Six. "Larry could have killed Henry Lester and still have arrived in Silver Lake late that night. So we've got motive — his belief that you caused his divorce — and opportunity," Patrice said, "not to mention his propensity for violence."

"I suppose he could have followed me from the clinic," Lyla said, "and found out about my Wednesday nights."

Patrice nodded. "I may stop in at the Dog's Bark again. And I've got other leads I'm working on."

Lyla sighed. "I hope something pays off."

"We still have five days before the grand jury convenes," Patrice said. "No telling what might be under the next rock."

CHAPTER 10

On Wednesday night, Lyla and Leslie met with Jade at a restaurant on Belmont Avenue. Lyla made a half-hearted joke about the choice of meeting nights, but no one found it amusing, including her.

"The cops searched my apartment," Jade said.

Lyla nodded disgustedly. "Did they take anything?"

"Not that I could see. I watched the whole procedure. One of them was a total pig. He dangled my dildo in the air and said, 'Look what we have here, a dyke's best friend. Snap-on tool. Heh-heh-heh.' Then he told some stupid homophobic joke."

"You have a dildo?" Leslie said.

Lyla and Jade stared at her.

"I haven't had a good night's sleep since this began," Jade said.

"Me neither," Lyla responded.

"I've been thinking of getting some sleeping pills. How do you stand it, Lyla? I know it's ten times worse for you. I can't concentrate at work. I painted a customer's living room the wrong color and had to do the whole job over. Have you been going to work?"

"I'm on a leave of absence."

Jade nodded. "And I'm sure I'm being followed. There's probably some plainclothes cop outside this restaurant right now. Are they following you?"

"I don't think so."

"I hate it. You know they think you and I were in on it together."

"I know. What about those phone calls you made to your mother from Vicky's?" Lyla asked.

"Wrong nights," Jade said. "Damn the luck." She took a sip of her coffee. "I feel like I'm in prison already, like they're watching my every move."

"This is terrible. It's so unfair," Leslie said.

"That was great, what you did," Jade said to her, "raising the bail money for Lyla."

"We figured it was a worthy cause," Leslie responded. She was close to tears. "Now we have to find out who's framing Lyla. Lyla says your friend, Benny, is a possibility."

"She appears not to be my friend anymore," Jade said. "I haven't heard from her in days."

"Fair-weather friend, huh? Or, do you think it's her guilty conscience?" Lyla asked.

"She says she needs time to deal with my betrayal."

"You believe it?" Leslie asked.

"I'm not sure. Like I was telling Lyla, Benny's reaction to this whole thing is out of character for her. She's the possessive, jealous type. She's been too cool about this situation. Supportive and understanding at first, now distancing herself from me. No raging at me, no recriminations."

"Maybe she's involved with someone else," Leslie offered.

Jade laughed. "She has other lovers, all right. That's

82

the unspoken contract with Benny — she can, but her lovers can't. Your basic double standard."

"I didn't know that," Lyla said.

"Yeah, well it's true," Jade said. "I wish the cops would search *her* apartment."

"They'd find her dope," Lyla said. Her eyes suddenly widened. "They didn't —"

"No, they didn't find mine."

"You use marijuana?" Leslie said.

Lyla and Jade stared at her.

"I got rid of it when this poop first hit the blades," Jade said.

"Smart," Lyla said.

"Anyway, no matter how this all turns out, as far as I'm concerned, Benny and I are history."

"And you and Lyla?" Leslie asked.

"Leslie!" Lyla said.

"I'm just asking."

Jade was laughing. "So what about *your* love life?"

"I'm celibate," Leslie stated.

It was Lyla's turn to laugh.

"For the past two months," Leslie responded defensively.

"Yeast infection?" Lyla asked.

"I wish I had a lesbian sister," Jade said.

"You have lots of lesbian sisters," Leslie responded seriously.

"This one's a piece of work," Jade said to Lyla.

Lyla smiled. "Isn't she great?"

Jade eyed Leslie assessingly. "Not bad," she said. "So, tell me, Lyla's kid sister, are you going to the concert Friday?"

"Holly Near? I was thinking about it."

"I've got an extra ticket. What do you say?"

Leslie shrugged. "Sure, why not?"

Lyla wasn't particularly liking this. "I invited you to go with us," she said to Leslie.

"Now, now," Jade said. "Leslie's a grownup. I bet she bossed you around when you were kids," she said to Leslie.

"She tried."

"I still boss my little sister around, but she needs it," Jade said. "I'm glad to hear you're going out and about, Lyla. It's no good to just stay home and worry. Tell me what the private eye you hired has found out."

"She just gave me an update today." Lyla told Jade what Patrice had been doing and what she'd learned.

"I have an appointment with her tomorrow," Jade said. "She seems very interested in Benny."

"She'll help you remember things you didn't know you knew," Lyla said.

Jade nodded. "There *will* be a happy ending to all this, won't there?"

"I'm staking my life on it," Lyla responded.

On Friday evening, Lyla and Candace went to the concert. As Holly Near sang of world peace and nurturing the earth, Lyla had moments when she didn't even think about the case. During the intermission, Candace ran into some friends. Lyla told her she'd meet her back at their seats.

She went outside for some air and literally bumped into a woman. "Sorry," Lyla said. She stared at the women, momentarily disoriented, knowing she knew her, but not able to place her immediately. Then she did.

"Lopez," she said, flustered. The police detective also looked flustered.

Recovering her composure, Lyla smiled sardonically. "Fancy seeing you here," she said snidely, and started to walk away.

"If you haven't already, I think you should hire a private investigator," Carel Lopez said.

Lyla turned back. "Oh?" She stared at her. "Why do you advise that? I thought you were sure I'm the mad killer."

"I know you're not mad, and as far as your being a killer . . . well, I have my doubts. Strong ones, actually."

"That's good to hear," Lyla said. "So, what changed your mind?"

"Gut feeling. No one in the department agrees with me, though. I'm on my own with this."

"Well, you happen to be the only one in the department who's right." Lyla felt her lip quivering. "I had nothing to do with what happened to those men."

"I hope you didn't."

Lyla leaned against the brick wall. "I suppose I shouldn't be talking to you."

"I suppose *I* shouldn't be talking to *you*."

They both laughed. "You come here often?" Lyla asked.

Carel chuckled. "Holly Near concerts, you mean? Sure. Everyone comes to them. Now, Alix Dobkin would be another story."

"Closet case, huh?" Lyla smiled, feeling herself relaxing.

"I take the fifth," Carel said, returning the smile.

"Well," Lyla said, "I suppose we should go in. It's probably about to start." Carel began to move toward the door. "Any other advice before you go?" Lyla asked. "Besides the P.I.? We've already hired one, by the way."

"If you didn't do the assaults, then it has to be a frame-up," Carel said.

"Exactly."

"By someone who hates rapists and doesn't mind having you take the rap, or by someone who deeply despises *you*. Any idea who might want to do that to you?"

"I have a list of possibilities," Lyla said. "I've told the investigator about them. I'm not sure if I should tell you or not. I'll ask the investigator. Maybe she'll contact you."

"That's fine," Carel said. "I've already begun checking for connections between the tattooed guys and the women they were accused of raping. Henry Lester was a bad ass, and Tony Anastopoulos was no gem. Did you ever hear of either of them before the tattooings?"

Lyla shook her head. "This is beginning to feel like

Interrogation Room Three," she said. "You still aren't convinced I didn't do it, are you?"

"I'm keeping an open mind," Carel said. "There's an angle I'm working. In most rape cases, no one's ever charged. I'm talking about reported cases. And most rapes, as I'm sure you know, are never even reported. So it adds up to a multitude of traumatized and angry women out there, not to mention their angry husbands and boyfriends . . . and girlfriends. It could be that our perpetrator is some enraged rape survivor or the loved one of a rape survivor."

Lyla nodded. "That was what you were thinking about me when you asked if I'd been raped."

"Yes, it was. Anyway, this woman — or her husband or lover, or even her brother or father, maybe — decided to take matters into her or his own hands."

"Do you think the killing was intentional?"

"There's no way to know for sure, but my hunch is that the perp intended to do some damage, but not to go all the way. Getting revenge by branding and brain damaging as many rapists as possible until someone got arrested for the crimes. Until *you* got arrested. Then the deeds would have to stop."

"You and my investigator are thinking along the same track," Lyla said. "Only so far she's found zip from that angle. Are you thinking random rapists, or do you think one of the tattooed men raped your hypothetical perpetrator, or raped the perpetrator's girlfriend or sister or whatever?"

"Could be either way," Carel said. "I'm checking."

"And why do you think I was picked to take the blame?"

Carel smiled. "I watched a tape of that TV show you were on, and the news reports about it. You were good. Articulate about the causes of rape — *rape culture*, I believe were your words — rape reflecting the sex-role stereotypes carried to their most heinous extremes. And it was also apparent how pained you were by the pain of the victims. But most interesting to the murderer, I would imagine, was how angry you were. A controlled but

86

clearly intense anger at the rapists and at the criminal justice system that convicts so few of them. For those reasons, you make a perfect fall guy, Lyla."

Lyla nodded. "And to make it even better, I'm busy secluding myself with a secret lover every goddamn Wednesday night. I figure the killer followed me and knew how I spent those nights."

"That's what I figure."

Lyla smiled at Carel. "I'm glad to have you on my side," she said warmly.

"I'm not on *your* side," Carel responded sharply. "I'm on the side of truth."

"Same thing," Lyla said, not put off by Carel's gruffness. "If there's any way I can help you find the real *perp*, let me know."

"If your lawyer knew about this conversation, she wouldn't like it," Carel said.

"There's no way I can incriminate myself," Lyla retorted, "no matter what I tell you."

"No lawyer would agree with that, even if you're as innocent as Holly Near. Anyway, I have enough to go on at this point to keep me busy. If I do need more from you, I'll let you know. You can have your lawyer present, of course."

"She'll be glad to hear you're more interested in finding the guilty party than just getting a conviction," Lyla said.

Carel smiled sardonically. "I'm sure she will. She probably won't believe it, though, and will tell you to keep the hell away from me." Carel took her hands out of her pockets. "I'm going inside now," she said. "It would probably be better if you wait here awhile before you come in."

Lyla watched her stride briskly away.

CHAPTER 11

Lyla's arm and leg were wrapped around Candace. She kissed Candace's neck. "Have I told you lately that I love you?"

"Tell me once again it's true," Candace murmured, turning to face Lyla.

Lyla kissed her eyes and her lips. Candace kissed Lyla in return, deeply, as her hand stroked Lyla's thigh, then moved toward her crotch. Lyla slid herself into her lover's hand, moving rhythmically, her own hand finding Candace's breast.

The lovemaking was slow and tender and satisfying. Afterward, Lyla lay back on her pillow. "This is the most relaxed I've felt in weeks."

"You're beautiful when you're relaxed," Candace said, gently stroking Lyla's face.

"I'm glad we went to the concert last night."

Candace stretched and yawned. "Did you happen to notice Leslie? She was with some really fantastic-looking woman."

Lyla had hoped Candace would *not* notice. "I only had eyes for you," she said, pulling Candace to her.

"God, we're corny."

"I know."

They didn't get out of bed until nearly noon. Soon afterward, Jenny Wocjak, who lived down the alley, came over with a plate of cookies.

As Lyla and Candace sat in their kitchen chatting with their neighbor, Patrice Fedor was talking with a neighbor of Aldo Pranza. The neighbor told her he'd seen Aldo driving a white car several times, instead of his usual red one. He wasn't sure of the make. "One of those Jap cars, I think."

"Could it have been a Honda?"

"Possibly."

Next, Patrice questioned a co-worker of Aldo's, Peter VanOost, who everyone called *Dutch*.

"I figured Aldo was in some kind of trouble," Dutch said. "It doesn't surprise me."

"Why is that?" Patrice asked.

"I always thought he was crooked. The guy's a real jerkoff. When I seen him at the courthouse a few months back, I figured they'd caught up with him. But then he kept coming to work so I guess that meant he got off, right? Or is that what you're here asking questions about?"

"What courthouse?" Patrice asked.

"You know, the Criminal Court Building. I was there 'cause I witnessed a mugging. I seen Pranza goin' up the stairs. He didn't see me."

"You're sure it was Aldo Pranza?"

"Hey, I've known the guy eight years. What'd he do, stick up a Seven-Eleven? Or beat somebody up, maybe?"

"What makes you think that?"

"The guy's got criminal tendencies, I tell you. I know he likes to beat on people. He got mad at me one time 'cause I reported him to the foreman. Lazy son of a bitch expects me to cover for him. He got wind that I was the guy that snitched. Said he was gonna get me. He took his good old time about it, but then he ambushed me on my way home from work one day. Punched me a couple times in the face. Gave me a shiner. I never reported it. I hope you nail the bastard, whatever you're after him for. Good riddance to the bum."

"You think he might hold up a store?"

"He's got a gun."

"Oh?"

"Yeah, an automatic. I seen it in his locker at work. I know his lock combination. The jerk mumbles it out loud when he opens the lock. I went in his locker once looking for my leather jacket. Someone copped it and I figured Pranza's the type. Well, the jacket wasn't there, but there was a pistol. Also, one of those needle things . . . you know, a syringe. I guess he's a junkie, too, on top of being a general asshole. Hey, listen, you just make sure you don't tell him it was me that told you this stuff."

From Dutch's apartment, Patrice drove to Webster Street in the DePaul area. Somehow she hadn't expected a LUSAR member to live in yuppieville. After finally finding a parking place, she rang the bell at the only unrenovated building on the block. A muscular blond woman answered the door.

Health club addict, Patrice thought. "Mary Yates?" she said.

"You're Lil, right? I thought you weren't coming. You're late."

"Sorry," Patrice said.

Mary led her through the oak-floored hallway to a room that was set up as an office. It had a computer, printer, two desks, and wall shelves stacked with sundry papers.

"Have you done proofreading before?" Mary asked.

"I worked for a magazine a few years ago," Patrice said.

"Well, here's the copy that needs proofing." She handed Patrice a stack of papers. "It shouldn't take long." She sat at the computer and stared at the screen, Patrice apparently forgotten.

Patrice settled herself at a desk and began to read. The first article was about a man accused of raping two college students in Rogers Park. The charges had been dropped because of lack of evidence, but LUSAR thought there was plentiful evidence. They "targeted" him. He got so fed up with the harassment that he asked for a meeting. Several LUSAR members spelled it out: They would end the harassment if he would read all the literature on rape that they gave him, write a paper supporting the position that rape is a crime of aggression fostered by sexism, and then give a presentation on the topic to a local Moose meeting. He accepted. At the end of his "enlightenment," he claimed to have reached a true understanding of the dynamics of rape and said that his attitude was changed forever.

Patrice wondered if that were possible. She corrected the typos and spelling errors and went on to the next article.

Mary continued tapping away on her keyboard. Finally, she printed out what she'd been writing. "This is the last one," she said. "How're you doing?"

"I'm nearly done."

"I'm glad you're doing this," Mary said. "I'm no good at catching my own mistakes. So what made you decide to join LUSAR? The tattoo avenger?"

"Yes, but also from reading your newsletter," Patrice said. "Once I learned about LUSAR, I decided this was one organization I definitely wanted to support."

"Great. We've been getting lots of new members lately. You work for a computer company, you said?"

"Software development. I'm the office manager. One of the programmers who works there gave me your newsletter. A friend of hers knows Reggie Hirtz."

"Ah, Reggie. Yeah, she's been involved in LUSAR for years, way before I joined."

"My friend says Reggie's quite a character."

Mary laughed. "I won't argue with that."

"Very possessive of her lovers."

"Your friend must have heard about what happened with Carrie." Mary took a handful of peanuts from a glass bowl on the desk. "Have some," she told Patrice.

"What happened with Carrie?" Patrice asked, taking a couple of nuts.

"It was Carrie's friend, Mickey that got it," Mary said. "Carrie was Reggie's lover at the time, oh, two-three years ago. Reggie found out Carrie was seeing a woman named Mickey. She didn't like it. She got into Mickey's place somehow and tore it apart. Totally trashed it. Of course, they couldn't prove it was Reggie but everyone knows it was. She'd tell you herself if you asked, felt she was perfectly justified."

"She's got a violent streak, huh?"

"Reggie does not like her lovers to stray. She's the last person I'd get involved with. Much too dangerous. Let me see what you've got so far," Mary said, reaching for the pages Patrice had finished. She started reading. "Ah, good. Yeah, I always spell *intransigent* wrong, got a mental block or something. This is great. I really appreciate this, Lil. Have some more peanuts."

When Patrice got back to her office, there was a message from her fiance on her answering machine, and one from Lyla Bradshaw. She called Lyla first.

"Anything new?" Lyla asked.

Patrice told her what she'd learned about Aldo Pranza. "If this Dutch is telling the truth, it's pretty incriminating for your client's boyfriend. The syringe, the gun, being at the Criminal Court Building."

"And the car," Lyla said excitedly. "He might have gotten one like mine, and somehow gotten license plates with my number."

"Could be," Patrice said. "My next step is to go check out his locker."

"I'll keep my fingers crossed," Lyla said. "I have some news, too." She told the investigator about her encounter with Carel Lopez.

"Interesting," Patrice said. "I definitely *will* get in touch with her. You sound in a better mood."

"I am. A little. And the news about Pranza helps."

"He's not the only one I'm checking on," Patrice said. "Have you ever read one of the LUSAR newsletters?"

"Yuck."

"Fascinating stuff, Lyla. They do a lot of picketing of men they believe are rapists — at their jobs, their apartments, their hangouts, distributing flyers, warning women who relate to these men, painting *rapist* on the guys' cars."

"I've heard they do stuff like that." Lyla said.

"There was an article by your ex in one of the old newsletters. She had some choice things to say about rapists, including, quote, *These vermin should not be allowed to live,* end quote."

"Pretty incriminating," Lyla said.

"There's something else I learned about Reggie Hirtz. Several years ago, when she discovered her girlfriend-at-the-time had another lover, Reggie vandalized the lover's apartment. Apparently did extensive damage."

"I used to be afraid she'd do something like that to Candace."

"There's a lot of violence in that woman," Patrice said. "Despite her claim that she was with her LUSAR buddies on May nineteenth, I sure haven't ruled her out."

"I hope the one we're after turns out to be Aldo Pranza rather than Reggie," Lyla said.

"Unfortunately, it doesn't look like we're going to have anything solid on any of the suspects by Monday. But don't let it get you down if the grand jury indicts you, Lyla. With a little more time, I'll find the real killer."

"I'm counting on it," Lyla said. "Did you hear about the fund-raiser they're having for me tomorrow?"

"Yes. LUSAR is one of the sponsors."

"I've been asked to be there," Lyla said.

"I think you should stay away."

"Kate said the same thing."

"So take our advice, will you?"

Lyla said that she would.

As Lyla and Patrice talked on the phone, Detective Carel Lopez was sitting on an ancient overstuffed chair in Elizabeth Graham's figurine-cluttered apartment watching Elizabeth examine the photos.

"Oh, yes, I've seen these two many times," the elderly woman said. She pointed out the window. "Coming and going from that red building across the street. They looked like nice girls. They're not in trouble, are they?"

"That's what I'm trying to find out," Carel said. "Do you remember when you saw them?"

"In the evenings. Once a week for months, maybe even a year. But I haven't seen them lately. Has something happened to them?"

"Tell me about the times you did see them, Mrs. Graham."

"I see lots of things down there," Elizabeth said. She rocked slowly in her chair. "I sit here and watch TV and when something outside catches my eye, I take a look. These two girls always came on Wednesday nights. They'd arrive when I'd be watching *One Eyed Jack.* Silly show, but I like it. First one of them would come, then the other. And then they'd leave at around ten-thirty — near the end of the news. But not together. They'd always come and leave separately. They came week after week, and then they stopped. I must say I kind of wondered what happened to them."

"What time would they arrive?" Carel asked.

"This one always came first," Elizabeth said, holding up the photo of Jade. "Then about ten minutes later, the other one would show up. Always between seven and seven-thirty when *One Eyed Jack* was on. I figured they were friends with one of the tenants in that building and that they visited on Wednesdays. Maybe they were sisters and maybe they were visiting their mother. And then, I thought, maybe their mother died and that's why they don't come anymore. Is that what happened, officer?"

"No, they weren't visiting their mother," Carel said. "Would they come every Wednesday?"

"Oh, just about. It got so I'd watch for them. I think there were a few Wednesdays they missed."

"Any idea which ones?" Carel asked.

"Now that would be hard to say. Sometimes I fall asleep in my chair, you see."

"Did they miss any recently that you can recall? What about May nineteenth?" Carel said.

Elizabeth shook her head. "I really couldn't say."

"Did either of them ever leave early, before ten-thirty?"

"Well, I was going to mention that. Several times, one of them did come out early. She'd leave, but then she'd come back. And then she'd leave again at her usual time."

"Which one was that?" Carel asked.

"This one," Elizabeth said, pointing to Jade's picture.

"How long was she gone those times?"

"Oh, maybe an hour. It could have been longer."

"Do you remember the last time that happened? When she left for a while and then returned?"

"As a matter of fact, I do," Elizabeth said, clearly pleased with herself. "It was the night of the big fire."

"The Convention Hall fire?"

"Yes, they kept interrupting TV shows with bulletins about it and I remember seeing the darker-haired girl leaving the apartment that night and then coming back an hour or so later."

"It was definitely the night of the fire?"

"Yes, definitely."

"Thank you, Mrs. Graham," Carel said, retrieving the photos. "You've been very helpful."

"Well, I always like to cooperate with the police," Elizabeth Graham said.

CHAPTER 12

Lyla's anxiety escalated as the State's attorney summarized the case against her. She scanned the faces of the twenty-three men and women of the grand jury. All of them were watching the prosecutor, except one, a woman who was looking fixedly at Lyla. Lyla held the woman's eyes.

The first witness was a rail-thin nervous woman named Marianne Newman. She testified that she had been walking on the south side of Fullerton Avenue on May nineteenth at nine p.m. She noticed a white Honda parked on the north side of the street, facing west.

"A woman got out of the car and walked up the street," Marianne said. "I was interested in the car because I'd been thinking of buying a Honda. I didn't really pay much attention to the woman, but I know the car was a ninety-one Honda Accord."

"Do you recall what the woman looked like?" the State's attorney inquired.

"All I can tell you is that she had curly hair. And she seemed to be nicely dressed. Tailored clothes. Slacks, not a dress."

"What race was she?"

"She was white."

Lyla recalled her conversation with Patrice about Marianne Newman. *Credible,* was the word Patrice had used. Patrice had concluded that Marianne was not part of the frame-up.

The next witness was Sally Schuman, the girlfriend of Henry (Hank) Lester, the tattoo victim who had died from an injection of Seconal. Sally told of the letter from Ames Enterprises that Hank had received, then of the phone calls at Hank's apartment on the night of his murder, and Hank leaving to pick up the VCR he thought he'd won. She cried during her testimony.

Then Laura Falk took the stand. Laura gave her address as Nineteen Thirty-nine West Fullerton, which was directly across the street from the office building where Hank Lester's body had been found handcuffed to a radiator. On May nineteenth, she said, at around nine-thirty, she was looking out her apartment window and saw a woman come out of the building across the street.

"She was walking very fast," Laura said, "seemed to be in a big hurry. Then she got into a white car that was parked a few doors east. When she pulled away, the tires made a screeching sound."

"Can you describe the woman?" the prosecutor asked.

"She was Caucasian. Five-feet-seven or so. Curly hair, medium-length. She was wearing a blazer — I couldn't really tell the color, but it seemed to be tweed, and she had on dark pants, probably black. The sleeves of the jacket were pushed up, to here, just below her elbows. And she had on a metal bracelet of some kind. I noticed the bracelet because the light from the street light reflected from it and it caught my eye. She was carrying a gray pack on her shoulder."

"Is the woman you saw here in this courtroom?" the prosecutor asked.

Lyla's heart was pounding as Laura Falk looked at her.

"Yes she is."

"Will you point her out, please."

"That one," Laura Falk said, "the one with the curly hair sitting at the table."

"Let the record show that the witness indicated the accused, Lyla Bradshaw."

Lyla bit her lip to stop the tears.

After Laura Falk left the stand, the director of the Evanston Dance Studio took her place. Lyla could barely look at her. She testified that Lyla had not attended dance class since July of the previous year.

When Candace's turn came, it was almost more than Lyla could endure. Candace looked so vulnerable. After establishing who she was, the State's attorney got Candace to acknowledge that she had not been with Lyla the evenings of December thirtieth, February tenth, or May nineteenth, nor, in fact, on hardly any Wednesday evening for the past several years.

"Where had Lyla told you she was those evenings?" the prosecutor asked.

Candace's voice was controlled, but Lyla was fully aware how painful this was for her.

"She originally told me she was at dance class," Candace said, "but later she said that, starting last July, she was actually with . . . with a lover those nights, a woman named Jade McGrath."

"So your partner had lied to you about those nights, about what she was actually doing. Is that right?"

"She didn't want me to . . ."

"Yes or no? Did she lie?"

"Yes," Candace said.

"And she changed her story," the prosecutor said.

"First, she said she was at a dance class, but later she said she was with a lover. When did the story change? Was it after she was charged with murder?"

Candace nodded. "Yes, after," she said softly.

Candace did not look at Lyla during her testimony, but afterward caught Lyla's eye and gave her a weak smile as she left the room.

The next witness was Tony Anastopoulos. His forehead was bandaged. Tony testified that the previous January, he had received a letter from a place called Ames Enterprises stating that he was a finalist in a raffle and could win a VCR. On February tenth, he received a phone call saying he had won the VCR and should come and pick it up at Fourteen Forty-four West Montrose.

"She said I had to come that night. When I got there, she pulled a gun on me. She had a Frankenstein mask over her face. She made me put handcuffs on myself, on my wrists and ankles, and then she stuck me with a needle and I passed out. The next thing I knew, it was morning and I was handcuffed to the handle of a file cabinet. The police were there. Someone who works in the office had called them."

"What else happened to you that night?" the State's attorney asked.

Tony pointed to his forehead. "She tattooed my forehead. I'm still working on getting the damn thing removed."

"What sort of tattoo?"

"Just a word. One word," Tony replied. "Printed real large and sloppy."

"What was the word?"

"*Rapist*," Tony said, "but I'm no rapist. Some woman accused me once, but I was found not guilty because I never did it. I never raped anyone ever and I never would," he protested loudly.

"All right, all right," said the State's attorney. "We understand. Tell us, Mr. Anastopoulos, were there any other effects of the assault?"

"Yeah, there sure were. My memory's shot and it's hard for me to concentrate. She did something to my mind. I just can't pick up on things like I used to. They told me it's from airplane glue. They said I'll probably always be this way." He glared at Lyla as he spoke.

It wasn't me, Lyla wanted to scream.

"But you do remember what happened that night, the night of February tenth."

"Oh yes, I remember that fine. It's new things I have trouble with. Trying to learn new things and remember them, that's what I can't do so well anymore."

"You say the woman was wearing a Frankenstein mask. Did it cover her whole face?"

"Yes."

"So you couldn't see her face, but can you describe her otherwise?"

"Mostly she wouldn't let me look at her," the witness said. "And there wasn't much light in the room, but I know she had curly hair. I could see that all right. And she was wearing a women's suit jacket. And loafers. And nylon stockings."

When Tony Anastopoulos finished testifying, a man in his early thirties took the stand. The word *Rapist* could dimly be seen on the black skin of his forehead. When the State's attorney asked him his name, he stammered and perspired, but no words came out. He was asked his address and the same thing happened. His mouth moved, he strained, but he couldn't get the words out. The State's attorney dismissed him.

Next, a neurologist named Emil Borensky came to the stand. Borensky identified the previous witness as Lawrence Thomas and testified that Mr. Thomas was suffering from aphasia most likely induced by prolonged inhalation of toxic fumes from a glue such as the type used in constructing model airplanes.

Lyla felt sick to her stomach.

A police officer testified next, stating that Thomas had been found on December thirty-first handcuffed to a radiator in an office building on north Clark Street. He'd been in a stupor, and had the word *Rapist* tattooed on his forehead.

The next witness was a gray-haired woman who

stated that she lived on Montrose Avenue. She testified that on the evening of February tenth, she had noticed a woman come out of the old office building at Fourteen Forty-four West Montrose.

"She got into a white car and drove away. The license plate number was N-I-K six three," the witness said. "I wrote it down on my list. I was making a list of license plate numbers of people who went into that building at night. I thought there was drug dealing going on in there. I turned the list in to the police last month."

The final witness was a police officer who testified about the anonymous phone call received the day after the Lester killing. The officer testified that the caller said he'd seen the story about Lester in the paper and that a woman had driven away in a great hurry the night of the killing. Her license plate number was NIK-63.

When the proceedings finally ended, Lyla found Candace in the hall. As they embraced, photographers took their photos. Dozens of women jammed the corridor.

"Your supporters," Candace told Lyla.

Lyla's eyes swept the crowd. "Thanks for coming," she mumbled.

"You have our support."

"We're behind you, Dr. Bradshaw."

"Let's get out of here," Lyla said to Candace. "Kate will call when she hears the decision."

They moved through the crowd and got a cab. At home, Lyla drank coffee and tried to read a magazine, but mostly she just sat, waiting nervously, staring at the phone. When it rang, she jumped.

"As expected, they did indict you," Kate said. "But it changes nothing, Lyla. You're still free. The bail wasn't revoked."

"Was that a risk?" Lyla asked.

"A slight one. I didn't want to worry you about it. The trial won't be until mid-August, so we still have a couple of months."

When Lyla hung up, the tears came in a great flood. Candace held her.

CHAPTER 13

The scene of the infamous love affair, Carel thought as she scanned Vicky Kranz's apartment. She was annoyed that she felt a tinge of jealousy.

"Is it possible that on any of those Wednesday nights, you came home early for some reason?"

Vicky shook her head. "I wouldn't do that, Detective. I knew what was going on here."

"Or any Wednesdays when you didn't let them use the apartment?"

"Nope. Every Wednesday evening I taught my aerobics class, and every Wednesday night when I got home there were fresh sheets on the bed."

"And you never got home before eleven?"

"After class I'd go out with the other aerobics instructor. Usually to Venice Dance. Sometimes we'd go to her place to talk or to watch TV until it was time to go home. I cut this deal with Jade." Vicky gestured around the room. "Look at the great paint job. Jade did it."

"Are you good friends with her?" Carel asked.

"We were roommates in college. I know Jade fairly well, but I wouldn't say we're *good* friends. We still hang out sometimes. And we take karate classes together. But we're very different people."

"What sort of person is she?"

Vicky grinned. "An outlaw. Rules are made for Jade to break. She got kicked out of the dorm at the U. of I., down state. She got an apartment with some friends and got even wilder."

"What kind of wild?"

"Oh, nothing serious, really. A little drinking and carousing. A lot of mouth. Political activism, especially about gay and lesbian rights, but other stuff, too."

"Was she an outlaw sexually?"

Vicky looked askance at the detective. "Sure," she said. "Jade topped and bottomed out with the best of them." She laughed. "I probably shouldn't be telling you about this."

"So she was into S and M?"

"She never hid it. She'll tell anyone about it herself. All you have to do is ask. Political correctness arguments never made a dent with Jade on that topic. She tried to start a group, you know, an SM social circle. Didn't get many takers. She did meet Luce that way though."

"Luce?"

"The great love of Jade's life. Until Luce converted to True Feminism, that is, and learned power games are an abomination. After that, Luce dumped Jade and Jade went crazy. Really, almost literally."

"What exactly happened?" the detective asked.

Vicky took a swallow from her coffee mug. "Well, when they first met, both of them were heavily into the power stuff — domination and submission. That was Jade's *Judith* period." Vicky smiled. "She took the name Judith for some reason and insisted everyone call her that. Anyway, Jade was an aspiring novelist at the time. She needed free time to pursue her writing and Luce needed a sex slave, so they made an *agreement*. Luce would support her, let her live in her coach house apartment in exchange for ten hours a week of total submission to her. Then when Jade finally acknowledged that she was a piss-poor writer, she went back to work and the two of them switched roles."

"Jade supported Luce and —"

"No, not that part. The other. Jade became the top."

"I see. When did all this happen?"

Vicky drummed a finger on the wooden kitchen table. "Mm-m, I'm not sure. They were together for quite a while, but it ended oh ... maybe about two years ago. Sure you don't want some coffee or something?"

"No thanks."

"Luce took a course in Lesbian Philosophy at Northeastern University. That's when she learned the evil of her ways. She turned like an ex-smoker, you know, did a one-eighty, became a rabid anti-SM type. Jade was fit to be tied." Vicky laughed uproariously. "Fit to be tied," she repeated, choking on the words.

Carel smiled.

"Actually, Luce's conversion didn't come all that easily. Once her head was there, she had to work to get her feelings to catch up, I guess. That's what I heard anyway. Not from Luce, but from a mutual friend. She told me Luce got into therapy."

"To get over her ... tendencies."

"I guess. But Jade couldn't get over Luce. *Fatal attraction,*" Vicky said, widening her eyes and chortling. "Well, not actually that bad, but Jade kept pursuing Luce after Luce made it clear that she had seen the light, was a new woman, and there was no room for Jade in her life. Luce finally moved to San Francisco. I wouldn't be surprised if Jade still carries the torch for her, or at least the anger."

"Who was Luce's therapist, do you know?"

"I have no idea," Vicky said. "Why? You don't have the same problem, do you?"

Carel ignored the crack. "What's Luce's last name?"

"Reagan."

Carel wrote in her notebook. "Same spelling as the ex —"

"Yeah, like that old ex-actor."

"Do you know her phone number in San Francisco?"

"You're going to call her? Why?"

"Do you know the number?"

"You told me you're trying to find out who really messed up those rapists. You mean that, don't you? You don't think it was Jade or Lyla Bradshaw, do you?"

"Do you?"

"No way. Certainly not Jade. I don't know Lyla, but from what I hear she's a decent woman. And not a stupid one. She'd have to be retarded not to provide herself with a better alibi if she was the tattooer. Your killer's a man," Vicky said. "Bet on it."

CHAPTER 14

Ruth Tremaine's house was as neat and as dead as a straight pin. A picture of Jesus hung over the sofa. Ruth had been resistent at first to the meeting, but Patrice had appealed to her conscience.

"Well, I suppose we should try to help," she finally had said. "I'll make sure my son is here, too."

She had tea and muffins ready when Patrice got to her house. They'd been talking only a few minutes when the son arrived, a thin, anemic-looking man in his early thirties.

"This is Patrice Langdon," Ruth said, "the researcher I told you about. My son, Jamie," she said to Patrice.

Patrice and Jamie shook hands. Jamie took a stiff chair across from the stiff sofa where Patrice sat. "Exactly what kind of research are you doing?" he asked, scrutinizing her.

"I told you, Jamie," the mother said. "It's about crisis intervention. Miss Langdon thinks learning more about my crisis can help other people cope with theirs. Did I get that right?" she asked Patrice.

"Yes," Patrice said. "My work is in the area of traumatic stress. I'm specifically interested in the long-term emotional effects of violent crimes on victims and their loved ones."

Jamie's eyes narrowed. "I don't think it's a good idea for you to do this, Ma. It'll just upset you."

"Yes, it probably will, dear, but I think we have a duty to do it anyway. It's to help others. She's going to ask you questions, too, so just cooperate. Go ahead, Miss."

"This is a bad idea," the son said.

"Shush, Jamie," the mother said. "I gave my word so we're going to do it."

He looked sullenly at Patrice. "What do you want to know?"

"The way I like to start," Patrice said, opening her notebook, "is to have the victim him or herself tell me about the aftereffects of the experience on each of the family members, beginning with the period about one month after the traumatic event. And then I ask each person to talk about his or her own reactions. In your case, the attack was sixteen months ago. Can you tell me, Mrs. Tremaine, how Jamie was coping with what happened one month afterwards?"

"Oh, it was still terrible for him. Wasn't it, dear? You were still steaming mad."

"I can't see how this is going to help anyone," Jamie said.

"He's very private," Ruth said to Patrice. "Miss Langdon doesn't use people's names, Jamie. Now you just sit there quietly while it's my turn to answer." She looked at Patrice. "One month after would make it early April, last year. Let's see. Jamie was still staying here with me then. Right after the attack, he'd put up the bars on all the windows. But he still didn't want me home alone at night. I was glad for it. Later, though, by summertime, I told him to go back home. He lives close by, you see, less than a mile from here."

"What was his mood like during that period?" Patrice asked.

"Depressed. Yes, I'd have to say he was quite depressed."

Jamie glared at Patrice. "This is none of your business."

"Jamie, go to the family room now. Go watch TV until it's your turn."

"I want to stay, Ma."

"Jamie!" The word came out as a high-pitched growl.

Jamie stood and left the room without a look at Patrice or *Ma*.

"He's very high-strung," Mrs. Tremaine said, when the sound of the TV could be heard from the other room. "Always has been. But he's a good boy." She smiled contentedly. "He's never strayed. Never let me down. Nor I him. I don't know what he'd do without me, nor me without him since my second husband died. I could always count on Jamie. But after the attack, well, I was afraid Jamie was going to have a nervous breakdown. As terrible as it was for me — that lowlife didn't just rape me, you know . . . he was . . . brutal . . . hit me and tied me and said terrible things to me." Ruth's eyes welled with tears.

"You worried that your son might have a nervous breakdown?" Patrice said, hoping to distract Ruth from memories of the attack itself, feeling bad that she had to put her through this.

"That was the worst part, seeing what it did to Jamie. He blamed himself, you see. Thought he should have been able to protect me somehow. The whole time he was putting those bars up on the windows, I'd hear him muttering, 'I should have done this sooner, I should have done this sooner.' Then when that horrible creature, Henry Lester, was arrested, Jamie wanted to go down to the jailhouse and tear the man's eyes out. 'I want to cut him. I want to take an axe to him. Shoot him in the knees, then shoot him in the face.' He'd go on and on like that, pacing the floor. The court will do it," I told Jamie. "Calm down," I'd say, "it'll be taken care of."

"But it wasn't," Patrice said.

Ruth shook her head disgustedly. "I'll never understand how the jury could have let that monster go. Jamie wanted to get them, too — the jurors. Find out who each of them was and go and dynamite their houses. And the police, losing the candelabra. How could they do that? How could they be so careless?"

"I don't know," Patrice said.

"Jamie has never done a violent thing in his life," Ruth continued. "And before the attack, he never talked about hurting anyone either. He's very religious, you know. We're Christians. Vengeance is for the Lord, I told him." Ruth wiped her eyes with a handkerchief she pulled from her sleeve. "The trial ended in October," she continued. "By Christmas time, Jamie seemed okay again. Not quite his usual self, but not so angry anymore. Quieter than he used to be. A little more inward, but I think he found peace."

"I see," Patrice said. "And then Lester was killed. How did that affect Jamie?"

Ruth stared at the thin, steel-gray carpet, then looked at Patrice. "He took it quietly," she said. "Didn't have much to say. I have to admit, I was elated when I heard the news. That's not a very Christian way to feel but I hope the Lord forgives me. Lester was an evil man. The devil had driven him to do great evil, and then his misdirected life was over. Who knows how many others he'd raped and beaten and robbed." She shuddered visibly. "It's best that he's gone."

"But your son didn't react very strongly to Lester's death?"

"He's the one who told me about it. He showed me the newspaper article. Handed it to me like a gift and said, 'He's dead, Ma.' That's all he said. Then he watched me as I read about it. I'm sure he saw in my eyes what I felt. I couldn't conceal it."

"Your reaction's certainly understandable," Patrice said.

"How did Jamie react to what had happened to the other rapists? Being tattooed and brain damaged?"

"We never talked about that," Ruth said. "Well, that's not exactly true. I brought it up once, but Jamie went inside himself like he sometimes does. I didn't bring it up again."

"You know, I discovered an interesting thing," Patrice said, "in talking to the other women who'd been raped by those other two men. Both of the women said that on the nights each of the three tattooings had taken place, they'd had unusually pleasant evenings. One went to a dinner party and had one of the best times she'd ever had. That was on the night of the first tattooing. The night of the second one, her boyfriend proposed to her. The night of Lester's killing, she had a particularly enjoyable evening with her parents and brother."

"Now isn't that something," Ruth said.

"And it was the same for the other woman," Patrice said. "She had unusually pleasant times those nights. What about you? Were those evenings especially enjoyable for you?"

"Why I don't know," Ruth said. "The only date I know is May nineteenth, the night Lester was killed." Her eyes lit up. "My sister had called that night. I remember because I called her the next night, after I heard the news about Lester, and she was surprised at first to hear from me again so soon. I had enjoyed that conversation with her the night before, the night Lester met his end. Yes, what a very pleasant evening that was."

"Was your son with you that night?"

"No," Ruth said. "We watched *Star Trail* separately that Wednesday. We never miss it. Sometimes he comes here to watch it, but mostly he watches it at his house and then we talk about it the next day. The police asked me about that, about whether Jamie and I were together on May nineteenth. I had to check the TV schedule to make sure. That night, we watched *Star Trail* separately."

"Then talked about it the next day?"

"Yes, Jamie called in the morning. That was the episode where they found the abandoned baby. I remember how upset Jamie was that a mother could just desert her child like that."

"And both of you always watch that show, every Wednesday?"

Ruth nodded. "It's one of our favorites. Do you like it?"

"I don't believe I've ever seen it," Patrice said. "What time is it on?"

"Nine until ten."

"Do you ever tape it and then watch it later?"

"No, never. To tell the truth, I hardly ever use that video machine Jamie got me. Just to watch rental movies from time to time. I told Jamie he should just take the machine to his house, but he says he wants me to have it."

"Does he have one of his own?"

Ruth shook her head. "I'm thinking of getting him one for his birthday," she whispered. "He'll be thirty-two in August."

Patrice nodded and smiled. "So that evening was particularly enjoyable for you," she said. "Talking to your sister, and watching your show. And how about February tenth? That was the night of the second tattooing. Do you remember how you spent that evening?"

"Oh, that was so long ago. I couldn't really say. I watched *Star Trail,* of course. The policewoman asked me about that night, too. I wasn't able to remember." Ruth looked disappointed with herself.

"That's all right," Patrice said.

"Wait a minute. I'm remembering something. Yes, February sixth was the day of the big church breakfast. Jamie went with me. I remember we talked about movies at the breakfast, me and Jamie and Emily Devlin and her husband, Ralph. They were talking about *Home Alone,* said they'd rented it at the video store and it was very good. Jamie said he'd rent it for us. Yes, and a few days later he did. It could have been Wednesday that we watched it," she said excitedly. "We could have watched it before *Star Trail* came on. I know it wasn't Thursday because that's Bible study night. I believe it was

Wednesday," she said, looking very pleased. "You can check with Jamie. If that was the night, then it was a very pleasant one. The movie was good and then we sat and had a nice talk about a trip we'd taken several years ago, to California. And we ate popcorn. I remember feeling very happy that night. We stayed up talking until almost midnight, which is very late for me, because we were having such a good time. Just like the other people you talked to." She looked delighted.

"Interesting," Patrice said, making notes. She then asked Ruth about the night of the first tattooing, December thirtieth, but Ruth could not recall how the evening had gone for her, although she was certain she had spent nine to ten watching *Star Trail*.

"I'd like to talk with your son now, if that's all right," Patrice said.

"Of course. Ja-a-amie!" Ruth called.

He came as far as the doorway. "I'd prefer not to be part of this," he said.

"All right," Patrice said pleasantly. "I don't want to impose on you. We'll just skip it then. I've already bothered you two enough. You've been very helpful, Mrs. Tremaine."

"I'm sure Jamie won't mind answering your questions once he gets started," Ruth said. "Tell her how I was a month after the attack, Jamie."

Jamie glared at Patrice.

"Really, it's all right," Patrice said. "I have enough." She rose and Ruth walked her toward the door. When she was about to exit, Patrice turned back. "Maybe just one question for you, Jamie."

"He'll answer it," Ruth assured her.

Patrice explained about the other two rape victims she'd talked with both having had pleasant times on the nights of the tattooings.

"The night they got Lester, I talked to Aunt Freda, remember?" Ruth said to her son. "I told you about it the next morning when you called to talk about *Star Trail*. That was the abandoned baby episode."

"Yes, I remember," Jamie said.

"And wasn't it a Wednesday night last February, during the week after the church breakfast, that we watched that rental movie — *Home Alone*?" Ruth asked.

Jamie stared at the stark white wall of the hallway, apparently trying to recall. "Yes," he said. "I know it wasn't Monday or Tuesday because I was with Cousin Trudy those nights."

"Helping her put up the new wallpaper," Ruth said. "And it wasn't Thursday."

"It was Wednesday," Jamie said.

"So it was," Ruth said, looking pleased. "And you and I had a very enjoyable time that night. We had popcorn." She smiled at Patrice. "The Lord works in mysterious ways," she said. "I can't help thinking He was guiding the avenger."

CHAPTER 15

Carel reached Luce Reagan at ten o'clock in the evening. She told her who she was and that she was investigating a Chicago homicide.

"The tattooed rapists, right?" Luce said.

"Do you know anything about it?" Carel asked.

"Just what I read in the papers — that you people think it was Dr. Bradshaw."

"Do you know Lyla Bradshaw?" Carel asked.

"Yes." There was a short pause. "She was my therapist. I'll tell you this — there's no way on earth she could have done what you're accusing her of."

"How well do you know her?"

"As well as one knows her therapist."

"Did you ever have contact with her outside the therapy? A personal relationship of any kind?"

"No."

"What about Jade McGrath?" Carel said. "You were romantically involved with her?"

"That's a euphemistic way of putting it. Yes, we were *involved* at one time. We're not on good terms now."

"You're the one who ended the relationship?"

"Yes."

"Why was that?"

"I don't see what my relationship with Jade has to do with anything," Luce said.

"Maybe it doesn't, but could you tell me what happened, why you ended the relationship?"

"I was no longer interested in what we had together," Luce said. "I changed, Judith didn't . . . Jade, I mean. She used to call herself Judith, her so-called *pen name*."

"Did Dr. Bradshaw help you change?"

There was a short pause. "She helped me get okay with what I'd been before. It's weird that you ask that. That's what Judith thought for a while — Jade, that is — that Dr. Bradshaw had changed me. But that wasn't true at all. I changed on my own. I realized how stuck I'd been in old, twisted ways — patriarchal ways. I was able to pull myself out of it, but Judith was still stuck."

"S and M, you mean?" Carel said.

"Acting out our oppression, yes. Power games. Reproducing the victim-oppressor dynamic."

"And Dr. Bradshaw helped you pull yourself out of it?"

"She helped me understand my involvement in it, what it meant, and then to move on."

"But Jade thought Dr. Bradshaw was responsible for your changing?"

"For a while she did. She thought Dr. Bradshaw *brainwashed* me — that was Jade's word. But later, she decided Dr. Bradshaw was into S and M herself and that she and I were having a sexual relationship."

"I see. Was there any truth to that?"

"Of course not. Jade's mind was twisted when it had to do with me. No, Dr. Bradshaw and I had a therapist-client relationship, nothing more. Jade's the one who became lovers with her, not me."

"When did you find out about that?" Carel asked.

"Oh, right away. Judith...Jade...couldn't wait to tell me about her conquest. She wrote to me in San Francisco. 'Your ex-therapist's not a bad fuck,' she said. 'She likes it rough just like you used to.' I probably wouldn't have believed it if she hadn't sent the photo — a picture of Dr. Bradshaw wearing Jade's red and black scarf. Jade used that scarf during some of our...scenes."

"Do you think she got involved with Dr. Bradshaw *because* Bradshaw had been your therapist?"

"Obviously."

"To get back at you?"

"Yes. I told you she wasn't thinking straight. After our breakup, she totally cracked."

"How do you mean?"

"She was an emotional wreck. She talked about suicide, she even threatened..."

"Threatened what?"

There was a pause. "They were just words."

"What words?" Carel said.

"Just empty threats. Not really threats, just wishes. She said she'd like to kill them both — my instructor at Northeastern and Lyla Bradshaw. She blamed both of them. It was just talk, though, the violence part."

"What exactly did she say?"

"She said all kinds of things." Luce took an audible breath. "The worst was after I moved to San Francisco. She showed up one day out of the blue. There was a terrible scene. That's when she accused me of having had an SM thing with Dr. Bradshaw. I finally had to call the police to get her out of my apartment. Before she left, she said she was going to *get* both of us, Dr. Bradshaw and me. It was freaky. She was really out of control then. Her eyes looked wild, almost...demented."

"When was this?" Carel asked.

"A year ago; it was last June. About a month after

that, I got the note about her and Dr. Bradshaw being lovers. That really did disturb me, the thought of the two of them together."

"So you figured Jade's affair with Dr. Bradshaw was her way of *getting* both of you?"

"Yes. That was her revenge. I feel sorry for her. Her attachment to me was . . . it wasn't healthy. It was too intense, not right. It drove her to . . . well, I suppose she could have done something worse than she did, worse than seducing my therapist."

"Maybe she did do something worse," Carel said.

"What do you mean? You're not implying that Jade could be the one who assaulted those rapists? Not a chance. She may be messed up emotionally, but she's no killer."

"You said yourself she wanted Lyla Bradshaw dead."

"Lots of people say things like that when they're angry and hurt. Instead of getting Dr. Bradshaw by any kind of violence, she got her in bed. That's definitely more Jade's style. But I think her plan backfired, in a way. She's apparently still seeing Dr. Bradshaw after all this time. Obviously she got over her anger and got into something else."

"What about the possibility that she assaulted those men in order to frame Dr. Bradshaw?"

"Do you think that?"

"I think it's a possibility."

"A man was murdered. Jade McGrath would do a lot of things, but not that. No, she's not your killer, Detective. And the idea of Dr. Bradshaw killing anyone is totally absurd. She's a gentle, sensitive person. Violence would be unthinkable to her. There's no way she'd ever harm anyone, not even a rapist."

"You still think so highly of her despite her involvement with Jade?"

"Yes. Although, that did tarnish my image of her somewhat. I know Dr. Bradshaw has a partner. I suppose Jade's goal was to destroy that relationship. Did that happen?"

"I don't know," Carel said.

118

"Jade's such a pro at it."

"At what?"

"Seducing people. Getting them to do what she wants, to see things her way. But Dr. Bradshaw being seducible is a big leap from thinking she could commit those crimes. You people couldn't be more wrong about that, Detective."

"I know you believe that," Carel said. "I hope you're right."

CHAPTER 16

The next day, Carel was in her office when the intercom buzzed. "Someone here to see you," the desk sergeant said. "Says it's about the tattoo case. Should I bring her in?"

"Yes." Carel closed the file she'd been reading and looked through the open door. The woman being escorted by the officer was Caucasian, had curly brown hair, and wore a gray blazer with the sleeves rolled up.

"Have a seat." Carel noticed the thick silver bracelet on the woman's left wrist.

"I'm the one who did the tattooings," the woman said.

"Just a second." Carel picked up her phone and pushed two buttons. "Jake, get in here, will you? Now."

"What's your name?" Carel asked the woman.

"Connie Knight. The one who died...that was unintentional. I just wanted to wipe out some brain cells."

Jake entered the office.

"Would you repeat what you just said?" Carel asked the woman.

"I tattooed and drugged those rapists, all three of them. I don't regret it."

"Do you mind if I tape record this?" Carel asked.

"Go ahead," Connie said flatly.

Carel took her recorder from her desk drawer and turned it on. She recited the Miranda rights to Connie Knight.

"Yes, yes, I understand," Connie said. "I've come here to tell you what I did. I don't want an attorney present at this time."

"Your name is...." Carel said.

"Constance Knight."

"All right, Connie, tell me about it."

"I knew where the rapists lived," Connie began. She handed Carel a sheet of paper containing a list of names and addresses, including those of the three tattooed men.

"I lured them to come to me by telling them they'd won VCRs. I held a gun on them and forced them to put handcuffs on. Then I gave them an injection of Seconal to make them sleep. I taped a tube of airplane glue to one of their nostrils. While they slept and breathed the glue, I tattooed *Rapist* on their foreheads."

"Mm-hmm," Carel said. "And then?"

"That's it. And then I left."

"How were you dressed?" Carel asked.

"Same as I am now. I wore a mask until after they were asleep, a rubber Frankenstein mask."

"Where's the mask now?"

"I cut it in pieces and threw it in the garbage."

"And the gun?"

"In the Chicago River. I tossed it after I heard Lyla Bradshaw was arrested." Connie Knight took off her wig and laid it on Carel's desk. Her own hair was straight and lighter in color. Next to the wig she placed a key. "That's the key to Lyla Bradshaw's car."

* * * * *

Two hours later, after Connie Knight had signed a confession and was booked, Carel left the station and drove to Lyla's house. Lyla's Honda was parked out front. Carel tried the key Connie had given her; it opened the door. She tried the ignition; the car started. She went up the porch stairs and rang the bell.

"Hello," Lyla said glumly, ushering her in. "I suppose you heard about the indictment."

"Looks like it was a waste of time," Carel said. She smiled warmly at Lyla.

Lyla led her to the living room. "Oh? Why is that?"

"Because the real killer has confessed."

Lyla's jaw dropped; her eyes became round as Susan B. Anthony coins. "You've got the killer?" Her voice was raspy.

"I just left her at the police station. I wanted you to be the first to know."

Lyla sighed audibly and collapsed on the sofa. There were tears in her eyes. She sat dumbfounded for awhile, then looked at Carel admiringly. "How did you find her?"

"She turned herself in."

"Well, who is she and why —"

"Her name is Connie Knight. Thirty years old, a secretary at a downtown insurance company. No criminal record. She says she knew of you, and that she'd met you once socially, but that you probably wouldn't remember her. She called you an elitist."

"The name isn't familiar," Lyla said. "So, did she explain why she did it? And why she blamed it on me?"

"She hated rapists, had been raped herself two years ago. The perpetrator was never caught. She thought you were a snobby, liberal do-nothing who was getting credit for helping with the rape problem without doing what really needed to be done."

"Tattooing and killing rapists, you mean?"

"That's what she meant. Except she claims Lester's death was an accident. She just wanted to kill some of his brain cells. She decided she'd arrange it so you could

122

make a real contribution, not just, quote, *patch up the survivors with bandaids after the evil had already been done.*"

Lyla shook her head. "Poor woman. So, why did she confess?"

"Guilt," Carel said. "Feeling it was wrong to let someone else take the blame. That you didn't deserve that."

"Thank God for consciences."

Carel chuckled. "I thought you'd thank Freud for superegos."

"That too. Did she follow me? Did she use my car?"

"Yes and yes. She found the car key you lost at that Halloween party. Apparently that's where she met you, and felt snubbed by you. She decided to keep your key, and then she decided to do what she did."

Lyla was leaning back heavily on the sofa. "I don't know whether to cry, or shout, or just pass out."

"Don't pass out," Carel said. "Let me get you some water."

"I'm going to call Candace." Lyla went to the phone and pushed buttons with shaky fingers. It seemed to take hours before someone finally answered.

When Candace heard the news, she declared she was coming home immediately.

Lyla went back to the sofa. Then she jumped up again. She called Kate Ralla and left a message with her secretary, Rhonda. She left a message on Patrice's answering machine. She tried to call Jade, but there was no answer. "I wish I knew where Leslie was," she mumbled to herself.

Again she returned to the sofa. Carel continued watching her. "Are you all right?"

Lyla's eyes were glazed. She was staring across the room. "I've been born again," she said.

"I'm very glad it turned out this way," Carel said.

Lyla knew she meant it.

"This has been a painful case for me," Carel continued. "One of my worst. And for you it's been a trip to hell, I know. Welcome back."

Lyla smiled weakly. The phone rang. As Lyla went to get it, Carel said she'd let herself out. "I'll be in touch," she added.

It was Kate Ralla calling. She seemed as happy as Lyla about the news. After they hung up, Lyla called her mother. Then Candace got home. They embraced and held each other so warmly and tightly, it seemed neither could stop. Both were crying.

The phone in Jade's apartment rang again. "Should I get it this time?" she asked.

"Go ahead," Leslie said. "We could use a three minute break." She chuckled and pinched Jade's bare nipple.

"Mm-m, I could just let it ring."

"Go on, answer it," Leslie said. She got up and left the room.

Jade took the phone from the bed table and laid it on her pillow. She picked up the receiver. "Hello."

"Jade!" Lyla said excitedly. "It's over. The killer has confessed."

Jade sat up straight on the bed. "Someone confessed?" She took several deep breaths. "Fantastic! Who is it?"

"Some woman named Connie Knight." Lyla told Jade what she had learned from Carel.

Jade kept shaking her head. "I . . . I'm flabbergasted," she said.

Leslie was standing in the doorway. "What is it?"

Jade put her hand over the mouthpiece. "I'll tell you in a minute," she whispered.

"You're with someone," Lyla said. "I should have known. Return of the libido, huh?"

"Do I detect a note of jealousy?"

"The only emotion I'm capable of at the moment," Lyla said, "is pure joy. I'm still stunned. I . . . I've got my life back, Jade. And you do, too. Candace and I are going to Hawaii to celebrate."

"Great." Jade watched as Leslie left the bedroom

again. "When you get back, I suppose your Wednesday nights will be taken. Dance lessons or whatever."

"Jade!"

"Just kidding."

"I'm not so sure you are."

"I've got other wrists to bind," Jade said, chuckling.

"You sleaze."

"You're right about that, girl. I might take a trip to celebrate, too."

"I feel like dancing in the streets. You haven't seen Leslie, have you? She hasn't heard the news yet."

"If I see her, I'll tell her to call home. And Lyla, when you get back from Hawaii, give me a call, will you?"

"Sure," Lyla said, a note of uncertainty in her voice.

When Jade hung up, she called to Leslie. "Get back here where you belong, pussy cat."

Leslie slinked sexily into the room, sidled over to the bed, and stood seductively in front of Jade. "So what's all the excitement?" she asked, gliding her blond crotch hair over Jade's bare leg.

"Oh, nothing much. The tattoo killer confessed, that's all."

"What!" Leslie jumped a good foot. All the muscles of her lithe body were tensed.

Jade told her what she had learned from Lyla.

Leslie flopped on the bed, lying stretched out on her back, arms raised. "Kwo-am be praised," she said. "Glory be."

"Cut that religious crap, my little flower." Jade pushed a finger into Leslie's slippery vagina. "What's in here? There's something in here and I'm going to find it. I think it's a come. I think it's a big bang glorious come to top all comes."

Leslie's hips gyrated.

"Come to me, come to me."

"Oh-h, I'm on my way."

125

CHAPTER 17

When Carel got back to her office, Jake told her someone was waiting. "She says she'll only talk to you," he said. "Says she's got something on the tattoo case."

Carel looked at him. "What's the matter?"

"You're not going to like it," Jake answered. He gestured toward a young woman sitting in the hall. She had curly hair and wore a gray tweed blazer with the sleeves pushed up above her elbows.

"Oh no."

"She's wearing a nice silver bracelet."

"Shit."

Jake sent the woman to Carel.

"I drugged and tattooed the rapists," the woman said. She laid a key on Carel's desk. "This is the key to Lyla Bradshaw's car."

Over the next three hours, seven more women came and confessed. At one point, Carel met with several of them at a time. They all told the same story. They hated rapists. They saw the key fall out of Lyla's pocket at a Halloween party. They thought Lyla wasn't doing anything significant about the rape menace. They followed Lyla and learned how she spent her Wednesday nights. They lured the three men to offices in buildings on Irving Park Road, Montrose Avenue, and Fullerton Avenue. They wore Frankenstein masks. They set it up to look like Lyla Bradshaw was the killer. They threw the gun into the Chicago River.

Carel had a pile of wigs on her desk and a pile of car keys. There were three more curly-headed women waiting to see her. "This isn't funny," Carel said to the woman sitting across from her. "You're each going to be charged with obstructing justice. I'd advise you to call your friends off."

"I have no idea why they're all lying," the woman said. "I'm the real tattooer. I did it alone."

"Get out of here," Carel said, waving her away. The woman removed her curly-haired wig, laid it on Carel's desk and left.

Jake came in laughing. "Are you having fun yet?"

Carel threw a wig at him.

"The press is out front interviewing the flock of killers," Jake said. "Channel Seven News is there. Who are these kooks? Lyla Bradshaw's fan club?"

"They aren't telling yet," Carel said. "What I want to know is how they know so much about the case? They know details that were never in the newspapers."

"Maybe Bradshaw put them up to this. Or her P.I."

Carel's phone rang. "Yeah," she spat into the receiver.

"Is this Detective Carel Lopez?"

"That's right."

"My name is Sarah Greenspan. I'm calling from Minneapolis. I want to confess to the tattooing and drugging of those three rapists. I have a key to Lyla Bradshaw's car. I disguised myself to look like her and I . . ."

Carel held the phone limply in her hand. She said nothing.

"Well?" the caller said.

Carel still did not reply.

"I've called the Minneapolis *Star Tribune.* A reporter is here with me now."

Carel handed the phone to Jake. "Handle this," she said. "I'm going home. And take care of the release of Connie Knight, will you?"

By the time Carel got to bed that night, four more women had confessed. One was from a suburb of Chicago, another from Minneapolis, one from San Francisco.

CHAPTER 18

The Hawaii pamphlets were spread out on the table. Lyla's mouth was set in a perpetual smile. She was thinking again of her mother's reaction to the good news. She'd had that lilt of delight in her voice that Lyla remembered from her childhood.

"So, the big island, and then Maui," Candace said. "We'll do some snorkeling."

"For sure. I can't stop smiling."

"I know. I love your smile." Candace took her partner's hand and squeezed it.

"I never knew being alive could feel this good," Lyla said.

The doorbell rang. Lyla kept smiling. Another friend, she thought, coming to tell me how happy and relieved she is. Candace let in the visitor. It was Carel Lopez.

Carel's news about the rash of identical confessions stunned Lyla into numbness and immobilization.

"How could they do this to her?" Candace kept saying. "What kind of sick game are they playing?"

"They probably think it will help her," Carel said. "That with so many people confessing, nobody can be convicted."

Lyla stared dully into space. Candace rubbed her back soothingly. "Well, what about that?" Candace said to Carel.

"Obviously the confessions are bogus."

"Don't be so sure," Candace said. "Of course all of them didn't do the actual drugging and tattooing, but maybe they were all in on it together."

"Remotely possible," Carel said. She reached into her pocket and pulled out a handful of car keys, each with a cardboard tag tied to it. "These seem to match the key from Connie Knight, but I'd like to try them in Lyla's car to make sure. I didn't see your car on the street," she said to Lyla. "Is it in the garage?"

"My mom won't be able to handle this," Lyla said, shaking her head. Her eyes were glazed.

"Lyla, try to be optimistic, honey," Candace said. "The only thing all these confessions mean is that Connie Knight didn't do it alone."

Tears slid down Lyla's cheeks. Candace went to her and held her. "There's a garage key in the kitchen," Candace said to Carel, "on a hook near the door." Candace was crying also.

When Carel returned from the garage, Lyla and Candace were sitting silently on the sofa, their eyes red.

"All the keys fit," Carel said.

"Who are these women?" Candace asked. "Are they

LUSAR members, by any chance? Obviously they know each other."

"We're looking into it," Carel said. "We'll find out, but I doubt —"

"Are they under arrest?"

"No."

"They did the assaults," Candace said firmly. "One of them found Lyla's key at that party and they all got together and planned the whole thing. Including the confessions. You may never find out which of them actually drugged those men, but you'll have to let Lyla go. Honey," she said to Lyla, "don't you see? It's the perfect crime. They never planned to let you take the blame. They'll stick with their stories. If there's a trial, Kate will have each of them tell her story in court and, of course, you couldn't possibly be convicted."

Lyla nodded dully. "Right. I'll tell my mom that."

"One of them, or maybe three, did the actual assaults," Candace continued. "How many did you say confessed?"

"Sixteen," Carel said, "including two from Minneapolis and one from San Francisco."

Candace rubbed Lyla's neck. "If they stick to their stories," she said, "and if the cops can't find anyone to contradict them, then you'll have to be freed, Lyla."

"Yes," Lyla said, actually beginning to believe it. She felt a little life coming back into her. "You could be right, Candace. Maybe the confessions aren't just a farce, or a publicity thing . . . maybe those women actually did do the crimes."

"Right," Candace said. "But even if they didn't, if they stick to their stories, then it doesn't really matter anyway."

"It matters," Carel contradicted. "We're going to get to the bottom of this."

"If they did plan it together with one or several of them doing the actual assaults, could they all be convicted?" Candace asked.

"Possibly," Carel said.

"I bet *they* don't think so."

Carel looked at Lyla. "The indictment against you has been reinstated," she said. "At this point, you remain the only one we have any substantial evidence against."

Lyla said nothing.

Carel glanced at the Hawaii pamphlets. "Don't leave town," she said.

"It's really rather clever," Lyla said. "Someone found my key. Reggie, maybe, or her girlfriend, or Sid, the one who gave the Halloween party. They knew about my Wednesday nights. Reggie admitted that. It has to be LUSAR. They took my car each of those nights — one of them did. She dressed like me. She drugged and tattooed the first one, Thomas. Then she returned my car. Then the same thing happened the next time, and the next. If that anonymous phone call hadn't come, they might have continued. It could still be going on. The next and the next and the next."

She rose and began to pace. "But why did they blame it on me? That wasn't necessary. I bet that was Reggie's idea. To make me suffer. It was her revenge." Lyla paced some more. "I wonder if they'd have confessed if I hadn't been indicted. Probably not. The confessions were probably their backup plan. Maybe none of the sixteen did the drugging and tattooing. Maybe it was someone else, one of their friends." Lyla looked at Carel. "Someone you'll never find. Maybe she lives in San Francisco, or Minneapolis, or New York, or L.A., or Des Moines, Iowa. You'll never find her. No one will ever be convicted."

"I'm sorry about this, Lyla. I really am," Carel said.

Lyla nodded. "Thanks," she said, "I know you mean it."

"For what it's worth, there is one other thing," Carel said. "The women who confessed knew about the airplane glue, the Frankenstein mask, how each of the victims was handcuffed —"

"How could they have?" Candace interrupted. "The only way is if they actually did it," she exclaimed. "You see, I'm right."

132

"Or if there was a leak," Carel said. "I'm sure your lawyer cautioned you about talking too freely."

"Oh, you think I leaked it," Lyla said. "No way. Sure, I've talked to friends about what's going on, but I didn't tell a soul about the details, not even my mother. I know better than that."

"I didn't tell anyone either," Candace said. "I'm sure Jade didn't. Kate warned her the same way she did us. Those women know because they did the crimes," Candace asserted.

"Well," Carel said, standing and walking toward the door, "obviously I've got work to do. I'll be in touch."

CHAPTER 19

The morning paper had several stories about the mass confessions; one of them included the women's names. Patrice checked her back copies of the LUSAR newsletter and found references to several of the women, including Connie Knight. "I bet they're *all* LUSAR members," she said aloud, tapping her pen on the table.

She phoned Connie Knight. By telling her she was a journalist, Patrice got Connie to agree to talk with her. They met in front of Rickies, on the corner of Belmont and Broadway.

"You're one of the new LUSAR members," Connie said when she saw Patrice. "Did you join so you could write about us?"

"Partly," Patrice replied.

They went inside the restaurant and sat at a window booth. "Are the rest of the women who confessed connected with LUSAR also?" Patrice asked.

"I agreed to talk about myself," Connie said, "about why I had to resort to drugging and tattooing those rapists. If you want to know about other people, ask them."

The two women ordered their drinks.

"I never saw violence as the answer," Connie said, "but it had come to the point where I felt I had no choice. Rapists have made all women prisoners of fear. I'm sure you feel it yourself. The criminal justice system is totally inadequate. It was time for somebody to act."

"I know, I know," Patrice said. "I read all that in the paper. Are the confessions just to give you a chance to make those points or did your group really commit the assaults and killing?"

"You aren't a cop, by any chance, are you, Patrice? Could it be that you joined LUSAR to find out if we did the crimes?"

"Yes, that *is* why I joined," Patrice acknowledged. "But I'm not a police officer. I'm a private investigator, working for Lyla Bradshaw."

"I see." Connie grinned. "Well, your cover's blown now."

"Whose idea was it?" Patrice asked. "To do the mass confessions? Yours?"

"I don't know why the others are lying," Connie said. "I stand by my own confession. I did what I had to do. And what *I* did in Chicago was just the beginning. More women will rise up and do the same thing all over the country."

"And that's the purpose of the confessions? To stimulate other women to form vigilante groups and go mutilate and murder men who they think are rapists?"

Connie smiled. "The number of rapes has been decreasing since all this started," she said.

"How long do you and the others plan to stick with your stories?"

"I can only speak for myself. What I've already said to the police is what I'll keep saying until ..."

"Until when? Until the trials begin?"

"You have to admit, if they bring this to trial it will be quite a circus."

"Do you realize how much time and energy this is going to take away from finding the real perpetrator?"

"*I'm* the real perpetrator," Connie said. She smiled smugly at Patrice.

"You just might end up convicted."

"Right," Connie replied sarcastically. "Me and a dozen others."

"There's talk that LUSAR really is behind the assaults."

"We're definitely *behind* them. Maybe we even wish there had been more of them."

"It was Reggie Hirtz's idea, wasn't it?"

Connie was clearly caught off guard. "Uh ... what do you ...," she stammered. "I have no idea what you're talking about."

"Your emotions betray you, Connie. So Reggie put you all up to this. Why?"

"I didn't say that. I think I've talked enough to you."

"A woman is fighting for her life," Patrice said angrily. "I'm spending valuable time talking to you. Lyla Bradshaw is innocent and LUSAR is just making it worse for her."

"Quite the opposite," Connie retorted. "We're saving her."

"You're wrong. If that's the motivation for the confessions, you people are way off base. You're hurting her."

The waiter brought their drinks.

"Anything I tell you now, I'll deny to the police," Connie said.

Patrice nodded, holding Connie's eyes.

Connie took a deep breath. "Don't you see how clever

this plan is? With sixteen confessions, no one will be convicted."

"Reggie convinced you of that?"

"She didn't have to convince us. It's obvious."

"So how did it all start?" Patrice asked.

"I truly have nothing against Lyla Bradshaw," Connie said. "I know it's been hard on her, but she'll be glad in the end. The end will justify our means."

"Maybe so," Patrice said. "So tell me about it."

Connie took a sip of her Sprite. "It started last fall, just after Halloween. Sid Mazer had given a Halloween party. Lyla Bradshaw was there. The day after the party, Lyla called Sid and said she'd lost her car key at the party. A couple days later, Sid found the key in a sofa. Before she got around to letting Lyla know, she mentioned it to Reggie. Reggie told her *she'd* give the key to Lyla. That's when the plan started. It was at a LUSAR meeting last November. We were talking as usual about how many men obviously guilty of rape have been set free because of technicalities or other flaws in the criminal justice system. Reggie said maybe we could do something about it, something a bit different from what we'd been doing so far. She said she knew a way we could get even with freed rapists and get away with it. She said if anybody was interested, to meet with her later. Ten of us did."

Patrice felt excitement as she listened, thinking of the tape recorder she had running in her purse, and that now she might be hearing a real confession. She also felt amazement and disgust that this group of women would actually resort to violence, including homicide. Blind radicalism, she thought.

"Our plan is to drag this on as long as we can. For the publicity. That's why we framed Lyla Bradshaw. Most of us thought it was a pretty rotten thing to do to her, but finally we all were convinced that it was the best way to go."

"Reggie saw to that, huh?"

"She had good arguments. No one's going to get convicted."

"So, who did the actual drugging and tattooing?" Patrice asked casually.

Connie shrugged. "No one knows except the persons themselves. Six of our members said they would be willing to do it. Don't ask me which ones because I won't tell you."

"Were you one of them?"

"Yes. And that's what all ten of us will say."

"I see. So what happened with the six?"

"We took care of three rapists," Connie answered proudly. "All ten of us worked on the preliminary part — getting the names of acquitted rapists, coming up with the Ames Enterprises plan, getting the wigs and drugs and things, and finding the offices. One of our members ran off the Ames letter on her computer at work, then we made copies of it and sent it to the rapists on our list. We knew about Lyla Bradshaw's Wednesday nights. Each Wednesday we'd have a LUSAR Strike Force meeting. The women at those meetings had all agreed to participate in the plan. None of the other LUSAR members knew about it. One of the Strike Force women got the gun — I don't know who or how. Someone else got the drugs and syringe. All six of us who agreed to do the action — the Savage Six, we called ourselves — knew where the gun and drugs and the tattoo equipment were, and we all had access to them."

"Where was that?"

"Hidden in the john at the church where we meet. On the tattoo nights, at about seven-thirty, the Savage Six would each draw a slip of folded paper from a bowl. There were six slips in the bowl; one had an X on it, the others were blank. The six of us would leave the meeting, one by one. We'd go to the john. The one with the X'd paper would take the package — the gun, the syringe and drugs, and the tattooing kit. We'd go our separate ways; five would go alone to movies at different movie theaters. All six of us have cars. In our trunks, we each had a curly wig, a Frankenstein mask, a blazer, a silver bracelet, and handcuffs. The one with the package would go to Vicky Kranz's neighborhood to find Lyla's car. We each had a key to it."

"So no one but that night's tattooer knew who did the tattooing each time."

"That's right," Connie said. "Clever, isn't it? We'd hoped to get more of the rapists than just three. That was a bit disappointing."

"Yes," Patrice said, concealing her repulsion.

Connie continued detailing how the *Savage Six* pulled off the crimes. Patrice listened with continued fascination.

"And you don't intend to tell all this to the police?" Patrice said.

"I just did. Indirectly."

Patrice nodded. "But you'll deny that you told me."

"For a while. You know the truth now, and you can tell Lyla Bradshaw and give her some peace of mind. Eventually, we'll tell all this to the police. As I said, we want to drag it on as long as possible. They've dropped the charges against Lyla, I assume."

"No."

"It doesn't matter. She won't be tried. We'll see to it."

"But the ten of you will be?"

"I don't know if they'll actually bring us to trial." She looked at Patrice. "What do you think?"

"I think you'll all be charged with homicide. Your three out-of-state friends, too."

"Those three will recant as soon as we come out with the real story. I think it was a clever touch to have them confess, too, don't you?"

"Brilliant," Patrice said.

"Do you really think they'll try all ten of us for murder? Without ever knowing who actually gave the injections and used the glue?"

"Yes. You're all equally guilty." Patrice watched her closely for a response. She didn't appear surprised or frightened.

"That's true, we are," Connie said.

"You're going to spend some time in jail."

"We've disabled two evil creatures and eliminated a third."

Patrice shook her head. "I think your values are a bit twisted, sister," she said, "and that you and your friends are in big trouble."

CHAPTER 20

"So it was Reggie," Lyla said. She and Candace were on the back porch with Patrice.

"I thought so all along," Candace said, gloating.

"She's much more disturbed than I ever knew." Lyla stared out at the garden, feeling pity for her former lover. "And you played the tape for the police?"

"Yes, Carel Lopez has it," Patrice said. "The cops are rounding up the women now."

Lyla smiled at Candace. "Shall we call the travel agent, hon?"

Candace looked worried. "Nothing will go wrong this time, will it, Patrice? That tape of Connie Knight's confession is all the prosecutor will need, isn't it?"

"I'm sure the tape won't be admissable in court,"

Patrice said, "but that's okay. The LUSAR women will eventually tell the truth. But even if they never admit who did the actual tattooing and drugging, it shouldn't make much difference. I think they'll all end up being prosecuted."

"You did a great job," Lyla said.

"To tell the truth, I'm surprised it was LUSAR," Patrice said. "Usually my hunches are more accurate. Before the confessions started, I had narrowed it down to either Jamie Tremaine — the son of the woman raped by Henry Lester, or Aldo Pranza — the one whose girlfriend was raped."

"Really? Why Jamie Tremaine?" Lyla asked. "I thought he had alibis."

"I don't know," Patrice said. "There was something about that guy." She shook her head, frowning. "And as far as Pranza goes, the evidence was piling up. But obviously I was wrong about both of them."

"Well, no matter," Candace said. "All's well that ends well. Pardon the cliché."

"I won't feel really free until those women are indicted," Lyla said. "When do you think the charges against me will be dropped?"

"Soon, I'm sure," Patrice said, giving Lyla a broad, pleased smile.

A short time after Patrice left, Reggie Hirtz telephoned. "Well, you're off the hook now, Bradshaw."

"Aren't you in jail?" Lyla said.

"Not yet. I'll turn myself in when I'm ready. I thought you'd want a chance to express your appreciation. We're saving your life, girl."

"Oh, right. First you go on a violent rampage and frame me and make my life unbearable, and then you *save* me by admitting what you did. Thanks, pal."

"Such an ingrate."

Lyla laughed sardonically. "You're lost, Reggie. Your

mind is so twisted I don't think you know up from down.
You've turned into a monster."

Reggie laughed. "Sticks and stones," she said. "And I
thought our arguing days were over."

"They are," Lyla said.

Reggie laughed some more. "You're doing this very
well, Lyla. But it's not necessary. I'm sure no one's
tapping your phone."

"What are you talking about?"

"Pretending you believe I'm the killer."

"Pretending! Jesus, Reggie, it's over. Connie Knight
has confessed. The police know about you. Connie's in jail.
And your other friends. So will you be soon."

"See what we're willing to go through to save you."

"You're nuts."

"Lyla, really, the police aren't bugging your phone.
They think you're innocent. You can talk straight to me."

"I hate your fucking mind games," Lyla said. "I hate
this conversation." She slammed down the phone.

The next afternoon, Leslie and Jade were sitting on
webbed lawn chairs on the roof of Jade's apartment
house. "Lyla's almost her old self again," Leslie said.

"I know the feeling," Jade responded. "Last night, I
slept well for the first time in three weeks. I'd like to
wring the necks of those LUSAR morons." She scanned
the bird's-eye view of nearby buildings. "What about the
money your Kwo-femazonians put up for Lyla? Will she
have to pay it back?"

Leslie shook her head. "That was a gift, not a loan.
But since that Defense Fund group and the other donors
came up with more than enough for Lyla to pay her
lawyer and Patrice Fedor, Lyla said she's going to give
the leftover to the Kwo-femazonians. If I know her, she'll
eventually want to pay the rest of it back. I tried to
convince her that's not necessary. New Page is a wealthy
community."

"I suppose you'll be returning there now that Lyla's been cleared."

"I suppose. Want to come along? It's a great place to visit."

"But I wouldn't want to live there, right?" Jade said.

"You might. There are other kinky people in New Page."

"Hey, I resemble that remark," Jade said, chuckling. "If you think I'm *kinky* now, you should have known me a couple years ago. On second thought, maybe it's a good thing you didn't."

"That bad?"

Jade tilted her head. "I don't think *bad* is the correct word. *Intense,* maybe. Anyway, I've definitely toned it down since then."

"Since Luce, you mean. You said you'd tell me more about her some day."

"Luce Reagan — the woman who pushed buttons in me I never knew I had." Jade was quiet for a while. "Before I met her, I played around a little with power games — light stuff, like now." She grinned at Leslie.

Leslie nodded knowingly.

"With Luce, my whole life became centered around it — the domination-submission thing. What a time that was. I swear I lived in a constant state of erotic excitement." She sighed loudly. "We took it right to the edge, Luce and I. I don't think my crotch was ever dry the whole time we were together." Jade chuckled nostalgically. "I was trying to write a novel at first, but that quickly faded into nothing. All I cared about was my time with Luce. Day after day, living with that tingling edge of excitement. I loved it. We had some very wild scenes, Leslie. I experienced moments of true ecstasy. I never stopped craving more the whole time we were together." Jade stopped talking and stared out over the city.

"So what happened?" Leslie asked. "You finally had enough?"

"Not me," Jade responded sharply. "Luce did." She

took a sip of her iced tea. "She started to lose interest. I'd persist and she'd get back into it for a while, but then she'd back off again."

"Do you know why?" Leslie asked.

"I know the changes started when she was taking that course in Lesbian Politics at Northeastern. Luce would come home from class with these critiques of SM. Head stuff. I argued back, but that prof had really gotten to her. The point came when she refused to play at all anymore. I told her it was her fear of being politically incorrect that was driving her, not her real feelings. We had some terrible arguments. And then she moved to San Francisco."

"When was that?"

"A year and a half ago." Jade shook her head. "I have to admit I was a mess for a while." She smiled at Leslie. "But, as you can see, I pulled myself together. Getting involved with Benny helped."

"And with Lyla?"

"By the time I met Lyla, I was doing fine."

"I see. How did you two meet anyway?"

"She never told you? At a karate demonstration. I'd just gotten my brown belt and was showing off. I think your sister liked how I moved."

"You mean *she* came on to *you*?"

Jade laughed. "Well, no. Actually, I made the first move. And the second and third. She resisted for a while."

"Did she tell you about Candace?"

"Yes. And I told her not to be so uptight, that I had a girlfriend, too." Jade smiled seductively at Leslie. "But I don't now. I'm *available*, as they say." She laughed playfully and Leslie laughed with her.

By the following day, all the LUSAR Ten were in police custody. Carel Lopez questioned the women individually and in groups. They admitted conspiring to commit the crimes, but had not yet acknowledged who did

145

what. Carel was in Interrogation Room Three when there was a knock on the door.

"A woman to see you," the uniformed officer said. "Says she's got something important about the case."

"Did she say what?" Carel asked.

"Photographs."

"Hmm, all right. I'll see her in my office."

The woman was short and plump with nearly white hair. "My name is Marge Savage," she said. "I'm a photographer for *Windy City News*."

One of the city's gay and lesbian newspapers, Carel knew. "Have a seat."

Marge took a photograph from a manila envelope and laid it on Carel's desk. It was a group shot of about thirty women. "This was published in *Windy City News* on May twenty-second," she said. "It was for a story we did on LUSAR. I took the photo on May nineteenth."

Carel eyed the picture. Reggie Hirtz was straddling a chair, Connie Knight was in front of her. Jess Brown was there, and Sylvia Schneider, and Tessa Rodriguez.

"They're all there, all ten of the women you have under arrest."

Carel spotted two more of the LUSAR Ten. "So?"

"May nineteenth, I said. That's when I took this picture. That was the night one of the tattooings took place, right? I have a bunch of other photos I took that night." She spread them on the desk.

"What time on the nineteenth?" Carel asked.

"I was at the church between eight and ten. So was Marian Alexander. She's the one who wrote the story."

"Are you a LUSAR member?" Carel asked.

"No way."

"Friends with any of them?"

"Nope."

"That can be checked."

"I never met any of them before May nineteenth. Check all you want. Maybe they did the other tattooings, but those ten women sure as hell weren't out drugging and branding anyone on May nineteenth. Not between

146

eight and ten, at least, which is when the tattooing took place if the newspapers have it right."

"You're sure you were with them during those times?"

"Absolutely," Marge said. "Marian and I got to the church a little before eight. I took a few stills and then Marian got them talking and I started videotaping."

"You have them on video?" Carel asked.

"An hour and a half worth. Marian talked with the whole group first, and then interviewed some of them individually. I taped it all. It's for a documentary we're making."

Carel looked over the other photos, recognizing face after face. She counted the women she recognized. Ten. All ten were there. "What the fuck is going on?" she spat.

"A scam," Marge said. "These women will do just about anything to *Stop All Rape*, but they're not your tattooing killers."

Carel ran her fingers through her hair. She looked at Marge. "The other one from your paper — Marian — she'll verify the date and times?"

"Yes, of course. So will my lover, Deanna Black. She picked us up at ten."

"And none of the LUSAR women left during that time, between eight and ten?"

"They were all there the whole time. I did more group shots at the end. And you can see the tape if you want."

Carel nodded. "Yes, I'll want to see it."

"This whole business is so crazy," Marge said. "I believed they did the tattooings at first, when the story first came out. But then yesterday I was reading one of the *Tribune* articles, the one that listed all their names and had the dates of the assaults. May nineteenth, I thought. Wasn't that the day we filmed the LUSAR group? I checked my files." She looked at Carel. "They're lying to you, Detective. The false confessions is one of their *actions*."

Carel slammed a fist on the desk. "Fuck a duck," she mumbled.

"Should I leave now?" Marge said warily.

"Stay!" Carel said. She picked up the phone. "Get Regina Hirtz from the lockup," she said. "Bring her to my office."

The next day, Carel Lopez arrived at Lyla's house. "I hate to be the one to tell you this," she said.

Lyla got a sinking feeling in her stomach.

Carel told her about Marge Savage's photographs, and that the LUSAR women had finally told the truth. "Reggie Hirtz believes you're guilty," she said. "She thought the phony confessions would stop the prosecution against you."

Lyla was speechless. She stared at the floor.

"The whole thing was Reggie's idea. She presented it to the others after your arrest. Of course they knew that the photographs and videotape would prove their innocence. They'd hoped not to use them until later, if it became necessary. Then Marge Savage jumped the gun. I'm sorry, Lyla. We're back to where we were before the false confessions started."

"I can't deal with this," Lyla said. She rubbed her temples.

"We'll pick up where we left off. I've got some leads I'm following up."

"I feel like a yo-yo."

"I know. You realize that you're still under indictment and —"

"Yes, yes," Lyla interrupted. "I know the drill by now."

"I really am sorry."

"Those fuckers."

"Apparently they truly did believe they were helping you."

"Assholes."

"The prosecutor may go forward with obstructing justice charges. The LUSAR Ten may even get some jail time, if that's any consolation to you."

"I believed it was them. I kept thinking of Reggie being responsible for brain damaging those men and killing Henry Lester. How her mind must have been working to justify it. How deep her hatred of me must have been to frame me, keeping the key, plotting her revenge." She looked at Carel. "Why did she keep my car key then? That doesn't fit."

"She got it from Sid Mazer last November. She forgot she had it until you and she had that conversation two weeks ago, when she mentioned her lover losing her wallet at that party."

"Maybe the photographer is lying. Maybe she's part of their plan."

Carel shook her head. "We checked out her story, looked at the tape. They were all there at the church on May nineteenth. Most of them can account for their whereabouts on the nights of the other tattooings, too. Regina Hirtz included."

"How did they know so many details about how the crimes were committed then?"

"Your attorney's secretary told them."

"What? Rhonda?"

"Rhonda Folletti's lover is a LUSAR member."

"Great. Does Kate know?"

"Yes. She already fired Rhonda. There's no doubt that LUSAR did not commit the crimes, Lyla."

Lyla buried her face in her hands. "I can't stand any more of this."

"I know," Carel said. "Where's Candace? You need to be with her now."

"She's at work," Lyla said bitterly. "She thought our lives were returning to normal. I called my boss. I was making plans to go back to my job after our trip to Hawaii. And now . . ." She started sobbing.

Carel put her hand on Lyla's back. "Call Candace," she said. "I'll wait with you until she gets here."

CHAPTER 21

The evening shift was in full swing at the Colton Manufacturing Company. Patrice Fedor followed Dutch into the deserted locker room. Dutch started working the combination at one of the battered lockers while Patrice watched for intruders. When the locker was open, Dutch did the watching and Patrice searched the locker. She saw green work pants, a couple of T-shirts, a bowling ball, a stack of envelopes and papers, but no gun or syringe. She pulled the pile of papers out from beneath the bowling ball bag. Mostly junk mail. She saw an old phone bill among the ads, a detective magazine, a letter from Ames —

"Hey, someone's coming," Dutch said.

Patrice shoved the letter into her pocket, closed the

locker, and slipped around a corner. A man in a denim shirt entered the room and went right to the john without seeing Patrice. Dutch occupied himself at his own locker.

When the man was gone, Patrice pulled the letter from her pocket and read it. *Dear Winner,* it began.

Aldo Pranza sounded hoarse on the phone. Patrice wondered if he had a hangover.

"I'm an insurance investigator with State Farm," she told him. "Your name has come up in connection with a hit-and-run accident, Mr. Pranza, and I'd like to ask you some questions."

"What are you talking about? I didn't have no accidents."

"That's what I'm trying to determine, sir. The accident in question took place on the evening of May nineteenth, at nine p.m. A witness got a license plate number but wasn't sure of the last digit. All the other numbers match your plate."

"It wasn't me," Aldo said. "What kind of car was it?"

"A red Subaru, nineteen-ninety."

"That's what I drive."

"I know that, sir. Do you know where you were on May nineteenth?"

"How could I remember that? That was more than a month ago."

"Well, it would help if you'd try. It was a Wednesday night, the day of the big fire at the Convention Hall."

"Oh yeah, I remember that all right. Second time the place went up in flames, and they said it could never happen again. All those boats burnt to a crisp. I think it was arson."

"So do a lot of other people. Do you remember what you were doing that day?"

"I wasn't at work, I remember that. I heard the news on my car radio late in the afternoon. I was tempted to take a ride over there and watch the barbecue. Yeah, I remember where I was that night. I was with my sister at her place, until ten or ten-thirty. We watched clips of the fire on TV. *Sprawling inferno,* she called it."

"Did you have your car at your sister's?"

"Sure did. It was parked in front of her house. It wasn't me that got in no accident. Ask my sister, she'll tell you."

Patrice wrote down the sister's name and phone number.

"Anna will verify what I told you," Aldo said. "Remind her it was the night of the big fire."

"I'm sure this will be cleared up with no trouble," Patrice said.

She hung up and dialed Aldo's sister's number. Busy signal. When she tried again, there was no answer. She tried several more times over the next few hours, but still got no response.

Candace had rented *Steel Magnolias,* in an effort to distract Lyla from her misery. They were in the middle of watching it when Patrice Fedor showed up. The three women gathered around the dining room table to talk. Candace brought coffee and cookies.

"I've got some news," Patrice said, "but don't get too excited about it. It may turn to nothing."

"What, another confession?" Lyla said.

"It's about Aldo Pranza. I searched his locker."

"You found the syringe?" Candace said hopefully. "And the gun?"

"No, a letter," Patrice said. "From Ames Enterprises."

Candace almost jumped out of her chair. "*The* letter?" she shouted.

"Right," Patrice said. "The one about the VCR raffle."

"That's fantastic!" Candace exclaimed. "So Pranza must be the killer!"

Lyla sat quietly, staring into space.

"Calm down, Candace," Patrice cautioned. "Yes, it

looks very likely that he is, but don't get your hopes up too high."

"Maybe he put the letter there to *save* me," Lyla said bitterly.

Patrice scrutinized her, then turned to Candace. "I thought she was doing better."

"Oh, I'm fine," Lyla said. "Aldo is obviously the killer. But then, after he's cleared, that's okay. Soon we'll be sure it's someone else, then someone else, and on and on and on until they electrocute me."

"I shouldn't be telling you about my findings," Patrice said.

"No," Lyla said. "I meant what I said before, I want to know. It's a kick. Maybe Reggie put the letter there to *save* me."

"She'll be okay," Candace said to Patrice. "This is her defense, that's all."

"That's all," Lyla said. "I explained it to Candace. I'm defending myself against more roller coaster riding. So tell us more about Aldo Pranza. You found this incriminating piece of evidence in his locker, but..."

"But... well..."

"Go on," Lyla said.

"He claims he was with his sister the evening of May nineteenth. I haven't been able to get hold of her yet, but she'll probably back him up."

"So? Jade backs me up," Lyla shot.

"I know, but eyewitnesses identified you, Lyla. The only thing concrete we have so far on Aldo Pranza is the Ames letter. I want you to be hopeful, but don't go to extremes. As you said, you don't need any more roller coaster rides."

"Don't worry," Lyla said. "You could find videotapes of Aldo Pranza doing the actual tattooing of each of the rapists and I still wouldn't be *too* hopeful."

"Just try to keep a balance," Patrice said.

"You want to know what I really think?" Lyla said. "I'm not letting myself feel it yet, but I'll tell you what I think. I think we've got the real killer now. It makes perfect sense." Her voice grew more excited. "We know Aldo was enraged at rapists because of Angela being raped. He'd seemed preoccupied in the last six months or so, according to Angela. We know he had a gun and a syringe if that guy, Dutch, is telling the truth, and that he was seen at the court building where he could have been gathering information about men acquitted of rape. We know he was seen driving a car like mine. And now the letter, that's the clincher. He has to be the one." She looked at Candace. "Don't you think so, hon?"

"Yes, absolutely," Candace asserted.

"Now all we have to do is prove it," Lyla said. "Have you told the police about the letter?"

"Not yet," Patrice said.

"Do you have the letter?" Candace asked.

"No, of course not. I left it in his locker."

"He might get rid of it," Candace said worriedly.

"I don't think he knows it's there. I wish I'd found a wig in his locker, too."

"Yeah, and a Frankenstein mask," Candace said.

"This obviously is a hopeful development," Patrice said to Lyla. "But you have to realize that we have nothing definite yet. I wanted to let you know. I probably should have waited until —"

"No, you did the right thing," Lyla said. "We agreed you'd keep me updated."

"Yeah, but if it doesn't pan out . . ."

"I'll handle it," Lyla said. She felt as if she could, but maybe that was because she believed Aldo Pranza was guilty and her nightmare would soon end. "Will the police get a warrant and have his locker searched?"

"I'll talk to Carel about it," Patrice said. "I have a couple more things to check out first."

After leaving Lyla and Candace, Patrice returned to her office. She tried once more to reach Aldo's sister by phone. This time, she succeeded. She told Anna the hit-and-run story and asked if she knew where Aldo had been on May nineteenth.

"With me," Anna said immediately.

"That was a long time ago," Patrice replied. "Are you sure?"

"Positive. He was at my place."

"Did you talk with Aldo today?" Patrice asked.

"No."

"You're sure."

"I'm sure."

"And you're also sure that Aldo was with you on the nineteenth of May."

"Yes, I told you that."

"Would you swear to it under oath?"

"Yes, of course. It's true."

"What did you do that night?"

"What did we do? Well, we ... uh, I don't know. We talked. Maybe we watched some TV."

"Maybe, huh? Could you have the dates mixed up, Anna?"

"No. I know it was the nineteenth because the next day ..."

"Go on."

"He came over that night because I had some trouble. I needed his help. On May twentieth, there was something I had to do and Aldo was helping me."

"What was it you had to do?"

"I'd rather not say. It's really not ... you know, it's not your business."

"You'll be asked in court."

"Why don't you just look at Al's car?" Anna said. "If he supposedly hit someone, his car would be damaged, right?"

"He could have gotten it fixed," Patrice said. "It sounds to me like Aldo told you to say he was with you on May nineteenth, but that he really wasn't. Do you know the penalty for perjury?"

"He *was* with me," Anna insisted. "He never told me to say anything." There was a moment of silence. "I'd gotten into some trouble with the police," Anna said. "I had a court date on May twentieth. Aldo was with me because I needed him. There, so now you know."

Two days later, on Wednesday, Lyla came to Patrice's office. Patrice offered coffee but Lyla refused it. "So what happened with Pranza?" she asked. "I haven't heard from you."

"How've you been, Lyla? Are you sleeping any better?"

"He's not the killer, is he?" Lyla braced herself.

"No," Patrice said softly. She avoided Lyla's eyes.

Lyla fought her tears. "But the Ames Enterprises letter," she protested.

Patrice sighed. "It was sent to him. He received it in the mail like all the others."

Lyla felt the crashing disappointment. "You mean —"

"Yes. He'd been acquitted of rape charges three years ago."

"Shit," Lyla said. "Damn, damn, damn," she said. "Are you sure?"

Patrice nodded.

"But what about all the other stuff?" Lyla persisted. "The gun, what about that? And the syringe? And his being seen in the white car and at the Criminal Court Building?"

"He was at the court building because of his sister. It seems that she was charged with selling heroin and Aldo's been pretty shaken up about it. The white car he was driving was hers. He's been spending a lot of time with her. His sister wants to keep it quiet and so Aldo never told Angela. I don't know about the gun and the syringe. Maybe he *is* a junkie. Or maybe he was hiding his sister's works, or maybe he's a diabetic. It doesn't really matter, he's not the one we're after, Lyla."

Lyla felt absolutely miserable. "Angela obviously doesn't know he was accused of rape," she said.

"I'm sure he doesn't broadcast it."

"I was so sure it was him."

156

Patrice didn't reply.

"All right, so one more down," Lyla said, trying not to let herself completely crash. "I'm getting used to it." She managed to keep the tears back. "Anything else? What about Jamie Tremaine? You said before you thought he might be the one."

"I'm trying to arrange a meeting with him," Patrice said. "He's not eager to talk with me."

"Well, that sounds suspicious."

"Maybe."

Lyla shifted nervously in her chair. "How about Larry Hunt?" she tried. "He's still a possibility, isn't he? Anything new on him?"

Patrice said nothing.

"Tell me," Lyla said. "I want to hear."

"Actually, I've known for a while that he's not the one. Before all the phony confessions started, Carel Lopez thought Hunt was our boy and she was hot to nail him. She'd gotten hold of a couple of his drinking buddies in Silver Lake, Michigan. It didn't go as Carel had expected. His buddies told her Larry had gotten to the bar at nine o'clock on May nineteenth. Carel's convinced they were telling the truth."

"I see," Lyla said flatly. "So that finishes Larry Hunt. Any other news you've been holding back?"

"I hit a dead end with your ex-patient, Eric Hefner," Patrice said. "We can rule him out. He's in some kind of structured workshop program which includes a lot of group therapy meetings. They meet on Monday and Wednesday nights. He was at group meetings on the three tattooing nights."

Lyla nodded. "I'm glad it wasn't him," she said matter-of-factly. "Our suspects are certainly dropping like flies."

"We still have some left," Patrice responded. "Besides Jamie Tremaine, there's your neighbor, Jim Julian. I've been having trouble getting hold of him, but I finally did. I'm going to meet with him tomorrow, supposedly to get his advice on designing a flyer for my pet grooming business. I hadn't been able to contact him at home so finally I called the real estate office where he works. I told them I liked their flyers and needed some advice. They put Jim on the line."

"It'll be another dead end," Lyla said bitterly.

"There's still Jade's people," Patrice said. "Benny, and that Leon, the homophobic vandal who Jade and her friends sprayed with stink juice." She looked pointedly at Lyla. "And there's Jade herself."

"What do you mean?"

"Carel Lopez talked to one of Vicky Kranz's neighbors, a woman named Elizabeth Graham, and —"

"So Carel Lopez is back to trying to pin it on us," Lyla said angrily.

"Not you, just Jade," Patrice corrected. "The neighbor told Carel that she regularly saw you and Jade on Wednesday nights."

"Well, that's good. Then she can verify that Jade and I were in Vicky's building those nights."

"Yes, but not every Wednesday, unfortunately. She's fuzzy about which nights she saw you."

"So how did this make Lopez suspect Jade?"

"Ms. Graham said that a number of times she saw Jade leave the building for a while during the evening, and then return. She wasn't sure of the times or dates when that happened. She said Jade would be gone for an hour or more."

"That happened only once," Lyla said, "that time Jade went to the drug store."

"Maybe," Patrice said. "You don't know for sure, though, since you always fell asleep after making love, right?"

"Oh, come on, Patrice. Are you suggesting Jade could have gone out and committed the crimes while I was asleep. That's ridiculous."

"Carel's been checking her background," Patrice said.

Lyla shook her head disgustedly.

"Should I stop?"

"No, go ahead. Obviously there's more."

"It involves a woman named Luce Reagan."

"Luce Reagan?" Lyla exclaimed.

"An ex-client of yours, right?"

Lyla was feeling extremely uneasy. "How is Luce involved?"

"She and Jade were lovers," Patrice said.

"That's not true." Lyla's uneasiness escalated.

"They broke up before you and Jade met."

"Not so," Lyla said adamantly. "I knew Luce's history. There was no Jade in her life."

"How about a Judith?"

Lyla frowned. "Yes. So?"

"Jade used to go by the name Judith."

Lyla's heart was pounding. "No, that's impossible." Her mind raced. "Judith was obsessed with Luce. That was a major theme in our therapy. It couldn't have been Jade. No, you're mistaken."

"There's no mistake. It wasn't by accident that Jade and you got together."

Lyla shook her head vigorously. "Are you suggesting that —"

"Jade became lovers with you out of revenge."

Lyla's head flopped back against the easy chair. "Oh, God. Jade is Judith? She's Luce's Judith? I can't believe it."

"You had no way of knowing."

Lyla closed her eyes and took several deep breaths. "Things like this don't happen in real life." She was on the edge of hysteria. "It's like a house of mirrors. What seems to be isn't."

"Hard to know who to trust," Patrice said.

Lyla's jaw tightened. "She was using me."

"Apparently so," Patrice said. "In the beginning, at least."

"And, of course, she told Luce about our affair."

"As soon as it started."

"That bitch." Lyla blinked rapidly. "And Carel Lopez thinks Jade slipped out when I was asleep and got the rapists. But why? To frame me in order to get back at Luce?"

"Partly," Patrice said. "And to get back at you for having a sexual relationship with Luce."

"What?" Lyla was aghast. "Good Lord, now I'm being accused of that, too? That's crazy."

There was a knock at the office door. Patrice went to get it.

"Ah, two birds with one stone," Carel Lopez said as she walked in. She took the chair Patrice had been using. Patrice pulled the rolling chair out from behind the desk for herself.

"I've got some good news and some bad news," Carel said. "The good news is that we might know who the killer is."

"And the bad news is you think it's Jade McGrath," Lyla said.

Carel's eyebrows lifted. "Tell me more." She looked fixedly at Lyla.

"I just told her you suspect Jade," Patrice said. "And why."

"It's ridiculous," Lyla said. "Even if Jade became lovers with me because I was Luce's therapist, that doesn't mean she'd mutilate and kill people. She might have fooled me, but not that much. She's not a sociopath. You're dead wrong about her."

"If we're so wrong, then why has she disappeared?" Carel looked from one woman to the other. "She's packed up and gone. This morning we searched the garage where Jade keeps her painting equipment. Guess what we found?"

Lyla just stared at her.

"An Ames Enterprises letter. It was under an old chest of drawers."

Lyla's mouth was agape. "Impossible!"

"Her painting partner was there during the search. She saw what we found and, I suspect, tipped Jade off. When I went to Jade's apartment, she was gone. Her roommate said she'd packed a suitcase and left."

"It's absurd. Impossible," Lyla said. "No, wait. The killer put that letter there. Of course. It's part of the frame."

"Let's explore the more likely possibility," Carel said. "After you made love with Jade you always fell asleep, right? For at least an hour, you said."

"And so did Jade," Lyla said defensively. "Usually, at least."

"She could have drugged the wine," Carel said.

Lyla shook her head vehemently.

"An hour would have given her enough time." Carel leaned forward. "Here's the way I see it." She kept her eyes fixed on Lyla. "After you fell asleep from the drugged wine, Jade would take your car key and leave the apartment. She'd go to her own car where she had a wig, a mask, a revolver, et cetera."

Lyla stared at the floor, her muscles tight.

"She'd drive her car to where yours was parked."

Not Jade, Lyla was thinking. *It can't be. Jade is Judith? No! She thought I was having sex with Luce? Jade, a killer. No, none of this is true.*

"She'd transfer her supplies to your car, then take your car, leaving hers in your parking place," said Carel. "She'd put on the blazer and the wig."

Lyla forced herself to keep listening.

"In the dark, from a distance, she could pass for you, Lyla."

I never really knew her very well, Lyla thought.

"She'd drive to an office building where she already knew she'd be able to get inside and use an office. From the office, she'd start calling potential victims from her list. When she'd find one of them at home, she'd give the Ames Enterprises VCR story. She'd tell him he had to come that night."

Lyla was shaking her head.

"And then, when the victim arrived —"

"No!" Lyla said. "It can't be."

"It's plausible," Patrice said.

"After she was done with him, she'd leave him handcuffed in the office. She'd drive your car back to hers, removing the wig and blazer as she drove. She'd park your car back where you'd left it, and transfer her supplies back to her own car. Then she'd return to Vicky's apartment. You would still be asleep."

"Farfetched," Lyla said.

"Each of the office buildings was within a ten-minute drive of Vicky's apartment," Carel said. "And each of the victims lived nearby."

"All the men who reported receiving the Ames letter lived in the area," Patrice added.

Lyla was shaking her head. "The real killer planted that letter in Jade's garage. If Jade has run, it's because she knows how you people work."

"She's your only witness," Carel said.

Lyla did not respond.

"She hated your guts, Lyla." Carel looked at her sympathetically. "She assaulted those men and framed you as revenge against you and Luce Reagan."

"It can't be," Lyla repeated. "I know Jade. She's not like that."

"Maybe you only knew the Jade she wanted you to know," Patrice said gently, "not the real one."

"She convinced you she was what you wanted her to be," Carel said. "A couple hours of fun each week. No attachment. No strings. But that wasn't true. There were strings, all right. You should be happy, Lyla. If I'm correct, your troubles really are over this time. We'll find her, you know. She won't be able to hide for long."

"It just couldn't be," Lyla said once more. Her eyes brimmed with tears.

Patrice reached over and touched her shoulder.

CHAPTER 22

The moment Lyla got home, she phoned Jade's apartment. Jade's roommate, Helen, told her Jade was away on a trip. "I don't know where or with who or anything else about it," Helen said.

Lyla persuaded Helen to give her the phone number of Lori, Jade's partner in their decorating business. There was no answer that night or the next morning when Lyla tried reaching Lori. She'd just hung up from another attempt when Leslie stumbled into the kitchen. "Is it morning yet?" she said, rubbing her eyes.

"You must have had quite a night," Lyla said. "What time did you get home?"

Leslie poured some coffee. "Late."

"That I know. You didn't see Jade last night by any chance?"

Leslie plopped into a chair. "Why do you ask that?"

Lyla told her sister about the police finding an Ames Enterprises letter in Jade's garage. "They went to arrest her, but apparently, she's left town. Carel Lopez thinks Jade's the killer."

"Lopez is a fool," Leslie said.

Lyla spelled out Carel's speculation about how Jade could have drugged and tattooed the three men while Lyla slept. "She thinks Jade's motive was to get revenge against me and an ex-lover of hers."

"What! Oh, come on."

"Jade's ex-lover was a client of mine," Lyla said. "I had no idea about that until yesterday. Carel Lopez found out. Jade apparently thought I was responsible for her lover splitting with her."

"Are you talking about Luce Reagan?" Leslie said, looking stunned.

"How do *you* know about her?" Lyla demanded.

"Jade told me. You were Luce's therapist?"

Lyla nodded. "It's pretty obvious that Jade and I meeting and becoming lovers was no accident. Jade thought Luce and I had been sexually involved."

"What!"

"That's what Luce told Carel Lopez."

"This is crazy."

"It sure raises some ugly questions about Jade."

Leslie was silent for a long time. "Even if Jade did think you were making it with Luce, Lyla, that doesn't mean she'd . . . that sure as hell doesn't make the rest of Lopez's theory true. You don't believe it, do you?"

"I don't know," Lyla said. "I don't want to."

"Maybe Luce got it wrong. I don't think Jade even knows you were Luce's therapist."

"Don't be naive, Leslie. She sent a letter to Luce Reagan the moment she got me in bed."

Leslie's eyes widened.

"That's what Luce told Carel. What reason would she have to lie?"

Leslie shook her head. "There has to be some other explanation." She chewed nervously on her lower lip.

"Even if Jade did get involved with you because of Luce, that doesn't mean she's the one who did the crimes. Someone's framing her, Lyla, like they did you. I bet the real killer planted that letter in Jade's garage."

"I hope you're right," Lyla said. "I think Jade's friend, Lori, warned her about the Ames letter, and that's why she ran."

"That's right," Leslie said. "She didn't want what happened to you to happen to her."

"What do you mean?"

"Being arrested for crimes she had nothing to do with."

"She told you this?"

Leslie nodded. "I was with her last night. When Lori told her the cops had found one of those letters in her garage, she figured they'd come for her so she decided to split."

"I see," Lyla said.

"What did you want her to do, let them put her in jail?"

"Running makes her look guilty," Lyla replied.

"Which helps you," Leslie retorted. "If the cops believe Jade did the killing while you slept off the drugged wine, then you're home free, Lyla. You should be happy if she looks guilty."

"I'm not happy at all." Lyla glared at her sister. "*Is* she guilty?"

"Lyla!"

"She deceived me," Lyla said defensively. "She got involved with me because she thought I'd been Luce Reagan's lover. She manipulated and used me, Leslie. If she could do that, who knows what else she might have done?"

"Don't be disgusting."

"She ran away."

"She's hoping they'll find the tattooer while she's gone," Leslie said.

"Did you encourage her to leave?"

"I didn't *discourage* her."

"Where did she go?"

"I can't tell you that. I mean, even if I knew, I couldn't."

"You do know, don't you?"

"I know neither you nor Jade attacked those men and I'm doing what I can to protect both of you." Leslie's voice cracked as she spoke.

"I can't stand any more of this," Lyla said, pulling at her hair. "People I thought I knew well, I don't know at all." She got up and paced. "Maybe Carel Lopez is right about Jade. I just don't know. And you? Maybe Jade has you under her spell? Would you throw me to the wolves to protect her, Leslie?"

"You're cracking up," Leslie spat.

"Am I? Or am I finally seeing things clearly? Maybe Jade really did blame me for Luce dumping her. Maybe she did think Luce and I had a sexual relationship. So, to Jade, I would represent the destruction of her world. Maybe she hated me all along. So she pretends to be attracted to me. She sets it up so I'll be blamed for crimes she commits. Maybe that is what happened. Maybe hot-in-the-sack, barrel-of-laughs Jade McGrath is a sociopathic killer."

"I can't believe you could even have such thoughts," Leslie hissed. "You're flipping out."

"And now she's using you," Lyla said. She sat heavily in a chair and stared into space.

"You're jealous because I have her now and you don't!"

Lyla glared hatefully at her sister. "You won't have her for long. They'll find her, Leslie. She'll be convicted of murder."

"You don't know what you're saying."

"It all fits when you really think about it. How blind of me not to see it sooner. She charmed me, manipulated me in typical sociopathic fashion. She'd fuck me, then drug me, then go out and destroy brains and kill, using my car, dressing herself to look like me. And now she's charming you, sister. Using you to help her get away." Lyla looked pointedly at Leslie. "And I think I know where she is. Where you'd tell her to go. Where she'd be safe. Where she could hide for a long, long time, the rest of her life if necessary."

Leslie turned her head away.

"It's true, isn't it? Where else would you send her but your paradise in the mountains, your retreat from the real world, your community of fanatics. Circle Edge. New Page, Colorado." Lyla stood up angrily, almost knocking the chair over.

"Where are you going?" Leslie demanded.

"To phone Carel Lopez and tell her where the killer is hiding."

Leslie went after her. "No, Lyla, don't!"

"Did you think we wouldn't figure it out?"

"You're so wrong about her, Lyla. Don't turn on Jade like this. She's no more guilty than you are. Leave her alone. Please! Patrice will find the killer. Or the police will. Jade would never hurt you or anyone."

"Wake up, little girl. Don't you see she's pulled you in, too? She's disturbed, Leslie. Pathologically. And now she's using you. Perfect. *My* sister. Another jab at the person who Jade's sick mind believes is her enemy. She's worse than sick, she's evil."

"I can't believe I'm hearing this from you."

"Don't you understand?" Lyla said frantically. "If the police don't find Jade, I'm going to be tried for those crimes, including murder!"

"No, no, Lyla, that won't happen. They'll find the real killer."

"Jade *is* the real killer. Face it, Leslie."

"You just want that to be true so you'll be free."

Suddenly, Lyla's shoulders sagged. She felt totally drained. Neither woman spoke for a while. "Maybe so," Lyla said at last.

"You know Jade," Leslie said. "You know she'd never do anything like that. She really cared about you, Lyla. She still does. It's your own pain and fear that make you think twisted things like that."

Lyla wondered if that could be true. "And you and Jade?" she asked. "What's going on between you two?"

"I don't know," Leslie said softly. "We're attracted to each other. Maybe it's more than a fling. I don't know, Lyla."

"Do you think she can hide at Circle Edge indefinitely?"

"If a woman needed to disappear, an innocent woman who was being accused of horrendous crimes, that would be the place to do it."

"You don't think the police could find her there?"

"Not if the community didn't want them to."

"Someone will tell. Eventually."

Leslie shook her head. "No they won't."

Lyla was quiet, thinking. "And what if the real killer isn't found? What if the prosecutor decides to go ahead and try me? Jade is my only witness. Will she show up then?"

"That won't happen," Leslie said. "You won't be tried."

"The case against me is much stronger than the one against Jade — my car being seen, eyewitnesses identifying me. The prosecutor could decide Carel Lopez's theory about Jade is all wet. I suppose he could even argue that *I* planted that letter in Jade's garage."

"We have to find the real killer, Lyla. That's the only hope for both of you."

"Right now, Carel Lopez thinks Jade is the real killer. And Patrice thinks she might be right. They're going to put all their resources into finding Jade, not looking for anyone else."

"Even Patrice?"

"She's out right now trying to make contacts with people who know Jade."

"Shit."

"Tell Jade to come back, Leslie."

Leslie shook her head. "Maybe you really *don't* know her very well. You think she'd do what I tell her?"

"If you explain it to her. If she understands that hiding only makes things worse for both her and me. As long as the cops think it's her, they won't be looking for the real killer. Explain it to her, Leslie. She might listen. Or I could talk to her if you tell me how to reach her."

Leslie narrowed her eyes. "She freaked when Lori told her about the cops finding that letter. She was in jail once, Lyla. Only overnight, but it was complete torture for her. I think she's claustrophobic or something."

"Yes," Lyla said. "A cage *would* make Jade nuts."

"I might be in love with her."

"I thought so."

"She's . . . fascinating . . . exciting, and —"

"I don't want to hear about that, Leslie," Lyla snapped.

Both sisters were silent, then Lyla said, "I don't think she'd take well to living the rest of her life in hiding."

"She's supposed to contact me," Leslie said. "I could tell her what you said. See what she thinks."

Lyla nodded.

"I'll talk to her," Leslie promised.

CHAPTER 23

The next day, Lyla had just finished giving Gal a bath and was sitting on the kitchen floor drying her when Leslie came in the back door.

"I talked to Jade."

Lyla turned off the hair dryer.

"She said she'll come back if they take you to trial."

"That's nice," Lyla said flatly.

Candace entered the kitchen. "What's nice?"

Lyla began brushing the dog.

"I didn't know you were here," Leslie said. "Aren't you going to get in trouble, missing so many days of work?"

"That's the least of my worries right now," Candace replied. "Besides, I have a lot of sick days coming."

Lyla got to her feet and grabbed the dog's leash. She started toward the door.

"Oh, hon," Candace said, "if you're going to walk Gal, why don't you take that cookie plate back to Jenny? I keep forgetting." As she handed the plate to Lyla, she looked into Lyla's sad eyes and gave her a hug.

"I think I'll drive to the grocery store after I walk Gal," Lyla said. "We need milk."

"Get some potatoes, too," Candace said.

Lyla took her pack from the kitchen chair, hung it on her shoulder, and she and the dog went out the back door.

Five hours later, Lyla still had not returned. Candace was frantic. She'd been calling everyone she could think of who Lyla might have gone to visit.

"No luck, huh?" Leslie said.

"I'm going to start calling hospitals."

"I still think she probably just drove down to the lake and lost track of time."

"Lyla wouldn't do that. Besides, if she were going to the lake, she'd have taken Gal along instead of leaving her in the yard."

"She's under a lot of strain, Candace. She's bound to do some things that aren't normal for her."

"She'd know I'd worry. She'd call." Candace chewed her lip. "It must have been a car accident."

Candace called Ravenswood, Lake Shore, Illinois Masonic, and three other hospitals. No Lyla Bradshaw. She called the police. There had been no reports of traffic accidents involving a Lyla Bradshaw.

"What exactly did that neighbor say?" Leslie asked. "The one Lyla was taking the cookie plate to?"

Candace was staring out the window. "I already told you. She said Lyla brought back the plate, they talked for five or ten minutes, and then Lyla left. That's all."

"Well, I'll take a bike ride down to the lake and see if she's there," Leslie said. "Don't worry," she told Candace reassuringly. "She'll show up."

But she didn't. The next morning, Candace called Patrice. Patrice tried to calm her but was clearly worried herself. She called Carel Lopez.

"This is the goddamnedest case I've ever had," Carel hissed.

An hour later, Carel arrived at Candace and Lyla's house, catching Leslie as she was about to leave. "I need to talk to you."

"All right. Come on in."

"I think Lyla might be with Jade," Carel said when they were seated in the living room.

"Oh?"

"Jade might have kidnapped her," Carel said somberly. "Or worse."

Leslie rolled her eyes. "That's ridiculous."

"You and Jade are lovers, aren't you?"

Leslie glared at the detective. "What would that have to do with anything? If it were true."

"You might be blinded by your infatuation with her. Jade's a dangerous woman, Leslie. She messed up the brains of two people and killed a third. She may well be planning to do something to Lyla, if she hasn't already."

Leslie shook her head. "You've lived too long on the seamy side. Or are you out to get Jade because you have the hots for Lyla? Don't deny it, I've seen how you look at her."

Carel glared at her. "Your sister disappeared nearly twenty-four hours ago," she said. "Aren't you worried?"

"Of course I'm worried," Leslie snapped, "but Jade has nothing to do with Lyla being gone."

"I think you're wrong."

"I *know* you're wrong."

"Oh? Because Jade's convinced you she's a wonderful person? Or do you have something more concrete?"

172

"I can tell you this," Leslie said, "when Lyla disappeared, Jade was miles away from Chicago."

"How do you know that?"

Leslie said nothing.

"Talk to me, Leslie. We're dealing with homicide here. If you know something, I need to hear it."

"I know that Jade is far away from here, in another state. She left the night before last."

"How do you know that?"

"I know."

"Did you see her get on a plane?"

Leslie didn't respond.

"Maybe she lied to you about leaving."

"I talked to her by phone Thursday night," Leslie said. "After she got there."

"Who called who?"

"She called me."

"How do you know she didn't call from around the corner?"

"Because . . . I just know. Because she said things that proved she was there, things she couldn't have known if she wasn't really there."

"I see. She's in Colorado, isn't she? At that commune or whatever, where you were staying."

"I didn't say that."

"New Page, Colorado."

"I didn't say anything about Colorado."

"Did you talk to her again, since Thursday night?"

"Yes, yesterday morning."

"And I bet *she* called *you* again, right? You didn't call her."

"That's right, that's the way we agreed to do it."

"Figures," Carel said. "You don't really have any proof that she left Chicago at all."

"I know she did."

"You're sweating, Leslie. You're not sure, are you? Maybe she didn't leave. Maybe she was still here yesterday at noon when your sister mysteriously disappeared. Maybe she was waiting near the house until she saw Lyla coming out to walk the dog."

"That's crazy," Leslie said. "Leave me alone! Leave Jade alone! It's Lyla you should be searching for. Something's happened to Lyla and Jade had nothing to do with it."

"Jade has a gun," Carel said. "We know that from the survivors she tattooed. She could have forced Lyla to go with her."

"No! Jade was far away when Lyla disappeared. I don't want to tell you where she is because you'll arrest her. She's innocent and I can't let that happen. Don't waste your time looking for Jade. Find Lyla. And find the killer. That's what you should be doing." Leslie voice was high-pitched and frantic.

"That's exactly what I'm trying to do and you're not helping," Carel said coolly. "Leslie, Jade is a sick woman. She might already have killed Lyla, or crippled her mind. It might be too late, but maybe it's not."

Leslie began to cry. "You even have Lyla thinking Jade might be the killer."

"Look at the facts, Leslie. Jade believed your sister stole from her the woman she was totally obsessed with. She'd go to any lengths to get revenge. She already has."

"She couldn't have done that to those men."

"She's disturbed, Leslie, insane maybe. She brain-damaged two people and killed another in order to frame Lyla. And then, when it looked like the truth was emerging and Lyla was going to go free, she decided —"

"No!"

"Come on, Leslie, open your eyes. The stakes are too high to keep kidding yourself. If we move fast, there still might be a chance. Every minute we waste might be bringing Lyla closer to ending up with a damaged brain . . . or dead."

"You're trying to scare me."

"You should be scared."

"No woman would maim a bunch of people because a lover left her."

"No sane woman."

"Not Jade."

"Yes, Jade. Is she at New Page?"

Leslie began to sob.

"I want you to go there with me, Leslie. Help me get her and bring her back."

"I can't."

"You must," Carel said. "For Lyla's sake."

Leslie wiped her eyes on her sleeves. "I know what I *could* do. I could call and ask when Jade arrived. If they tell me Thursday night like Jade says, then that will be the proof that Jade didn't do anything to Lyla."

Carel crossed the room in three strides and brought the phone back to Leslie. Leslie sat with it in her lap for several seconds, just staring at it, then she shielded it from Carel's view and began pushing buttons.

"I'm going to listen on the extension," Carel said. She got to the kitchen phone in time to hear, "Riley, here. Who's there?"

"Hi, Riley. This is Leslie."

"Hi, darlin'. We miss you. Are you still in Chicago?"

"Yes."

"Everything cool?"

"You tell me."

"A few developments here. Your friend took off. Thanked us and said she wouldn't be staying after all."

"She left? Why?"

"I don't know."

"When did she go?"

"This morning. Nicole gave her a ride to Denver — Jade and another woman, Beth Wrightwood. Beth's a friend of Nicole's who was visiting from San Francisco."

"When did Jade get there?" Leslie asked.

"To New Page? Late Thursday night, like you said she would. Is something wrong?"

"No, I just . . . no, everything's fine. So she was there between Thursday night and this morning? She was there the whole time?"

"That's right. I don't think it was smart of her to leave. Maybe she figured the Chicago police might guess she'd come here, since she knows you. So, any progress in finding the real villain?"

"Not yet," Leslie said.

175

"Too bad. I'm sure Jade will call you soon, Leslie. And we'll keep mum about her, count on it. Maybe she went to San Francisco with Beth Wrightwood. Do you want me to give you Beth's phone number?"

"No, that's all right. Jade will call me. Thanks, Riley."

"Kwo-am be with you," Riley said.

"And us all," Leslie responded.

Carel returned to the living room.

"So that's that," Leslie said. "You heard it. Jade got there Thursday night. Now will you try to find out what really happened to Lyla?"

Carel stared pensively out the window. "San Francisco," she mumbled. She turned and faced Leslie. "Well, that's a relief. It looks like Jade may *not* be involved with Lyla's disappearance."

"You actually believed she was?"

"Yes," Carel said. "Now I'm worried about the other one — Luce Reagan."

"Oh, come on."

"Lyla must have freaked and run," Carel said, mostly to herself. "The pressure finally got to be too much for her."

"But you still think Jade —"

"At best, Jade is just intent on saving her own skin right now," Carel said. "At worst, she plans to do at least one more brain destruction — or murder. Luce Reagan. I wish you'd gotten Beth Wrightwood's phone number. I'd like you to call Riley back. Get the address, too."

"Fat chance," Leslie hissed.

"It would save me some time," Carel said. "Cooperate, Leslie. I don't want to have to lock you up for obstructing justice."

"You're wrong about Jade and I'm not going to help you find her. Threats won't change my mind."

"We can hold you for forty-eight hours without bail."

"I'm not saying another word to you."

Carel stood in front of her. "You have two options, Leslie — call Riley and get me the information I want . . ."

Carel pulled out her handcuffs. "Or we can go down to the station."

"Don't be a pig, Lopez."

"Don't obstruct justice," the detective shot back. "We'll find Jade anyway. You do what I'm asking and that will just make it a little faster. And it will save you from the unpleasantness of being locked up. Jade McGrath is a loose cannon, Leslie. A very dangerous person. Everything points to it. You and your sister got mixed up with a bad apple. I'm trying to clean out the barrel."

Leslie stared silently at the floor. "You can't be right about her."

"I know it's hard to accept."

"If you are right... damn, well, how could I be so wrong about her? And Lyla? Lyla's a psychologist, for Gods sake, she ought to be able to spot a psychopath."

Carel shook her head. "They can fool the most astute observers," she said. "Jade is a sick, dangerous women, Leslie. Make the call."

Leslie looked at the phone, then at Carel. "What about Lyla? I still think something's happened to her."

"She'll surface as soon as Jade is in custody," Carel said. "Lyla is running scared, too. Look what she's been through. She's probably a bit unbalanced herself at this point. I bet she's holed up in some motel somewhere."

Leslie picked up the phone. "I hope you're right about that." When Riley answered, Leslie told her she'd like to call Jade after all, and maybe go visit her. She wrote down Beth Wrightwood's address and phone number on a note pad.

"You did the right thing," Carel said, slipping the piece of paper into her notebook. "Now you're not going to like this next part."

Leslie looked at her.

"I have to lock you up anyway."

"What?" Leslie's mouth was agape.

"A precaution. You could have a change of heart. You could decide to call Jade and warn her. I don't mind going to San Francisco, but I don't want to have to run around the whole country looking for her."

"I'm not going to warn her," Leslie protested. "I've got enough doubt about her to ... I got you the damn address, doesn't that convince you?"

"Like I said, you might change your mind. I'll make sure you have your own cell. It'll be boring. Bring some books along. Sorry, Leslie, but there's really no other way. And you won't be able to make any phone calls until I give the okay. I'll let Candace know you're safe."

"I'll sue you for false arrest," Leslie spat.

Carel laughed. "Get your toothbrush, change of underwear, books, whatever."

"Let me go with you to San Francisco," Leslie blurted.

Carel looked askance at her.

"Maybe I can help."

Carel shook her head. "Too risky. Too much trouble. I'd have to watch you every minute."

"Come on," Leslie pleaded. "I don't want to sit in any jail cell. My going with you is a compromise."

Carel shook her head. "Nope. You'd be a hindrance. It's out of the question. The stakes are too high to play games with this."

"Then just leave me here," Leslie tried. "I swear I won't warn Jade."

Carel scrutinized her. She was quiet for a few moments. "All right," she said.

Leslie looked much relieved.

"You can come with me. Maybe you will end up being helpful. When I'm not right there to watch you, I'll handcuff you, so be prepared for that. You better not give me any trouble."

"I won't."

"Tell Candace that you're going back to Colorado. In fact, tell her you think Lyla might be hiding out there."

CHAPTER 24

Before catching the Saturday night red-eye to San Francisco, Carel had Leslie make one more phone call.

"No," Beth Wrightwood told Leslie, "Jade didn't come with me to San Francisco. Nicole dropped her off in Denver."

"Did Jade tell you her plans?" Leslie asked.

"Just that she's going to continue traveling around the country. I don't think she had any specific plans."

"Well, if you hear from her, will you tell her I'm worried and ask her to call me?"

"I don't expect to hear from her, but sure, if I do, I'll tell her."

Leslie thanked Beth and hung up. Carel hung up the other phone.

"So," Leslie said, "do we go to Denver instead?"

Carel shook her head. "Beth was lying. Jade's in San Francisco."

They spent the night at the Diva Hotel in downtown San Francisco, Leslie handcuffed to the bed. In the morning, Carel drove them in their rented Ford to the Mission District. She parked near Beth Wrightwood's apartment building on Sixteenth Street. "Wait here, will you?" she said, cuffing Leslie to the steering wheel.

Carel went to the building next door to Beth's. She rang doorbells and spoke to one person after another. It was Sunday morning, the fourth of July, and most of the people were home, but none of them was helpful. Carel next went to the building on the other side of Beth's. The third person gave her what she wanted.

"Police," Carel said, flashing her badge. "I'm trying to locate this woman," she said in Spanish, showing Beth's neighbor a photograph of Jade. "Have you seen her around here in the past couple days?"

The woman scrutinized the photo. "I don't think so."

"Do you know Beth Wrightwood?" Carel asked.

"Oh, yes. She lives next door. She isn't in trouble, is she?" the woman asked worriedly.

"No, not at all," Carel said. "Did you know she was out of town recently?"

"She was on vacation. To Colorado. But she's back now."

"You've seen her since she returned?"

"Not to talk to, but I did see her. She came back yesterday. I saw her arrive with her suitcase and —"

"And?"

"And a friend, a woman. The woman had a suitcase, too."

"What did the other woman look like?" Carel asked.

"I didn't see her too well."

Carel held up the photograph of Jade again. "Could this be the woman you saw?"

"Well, I couldn't say for sure, but maybe so. She had dark hair like that."

"Have you seen either of them since they arrived yesterday?"

"No, I haven't," the woman said. "Is the other one in trouble, the one in the picture?"

"I need to ask her some questions," Carel said. "If you do see Beth or the other woman, don't tell them I was asking about them, all right?"

"All right, but... well, Beth is a good person. She wouldn't be involved in anything... illegal or anything."

"It's not Beth I'm looking for," Carel reassured her.

Carel went next door and rang Beth Wrightwood's bell. She waited, then rang it again. Finally she heard footsteps. Through the door window she saw a young black woman in a terry cloth robe coming down the stairs.

"What is it?" the woman asked irritably through the closed door.

Carel showed her badge. "Police," she said. "Are you Beth Wrightwood?"

The woman nodded. "What's the problem?"

"I need to talk with you. Can I come in?"

Beth opened the door. "You woke me up," she said. "What do you want?"

"Can I come upstairs with you?"

"What for? What's this about?"

"Let's talk in your apartment."

"No," Beth said, "let's not. If you have something to say, say it here."

"I want to talk to Jade McGrath."

Beth gave her a steely stare. "I don't know anybody by that name."

Carel moved past her and started up the stairs.

"Hey, what are you doing?" Beth protested. "You have no right to do that." She followed after Carel.

No one was in Beth's living room. Carel went to the bedroom, then the john and the kitchen. No Jade. She went back to the bedroom. Beth followed her. "Whose suitcase is that?"

181

"It's mine," Beth said. "What's this all about?"

"Why's your suitcase out?"

"I just got back from a trip. Why are you asking?"

Carel pulled a pair of jeans from the suitcase. She held them up. "These look kind of short for you."

"Quit touching my stuff." Beth grabbed the jeans from her.

Carel glanced at the unmade double bed. "She slept with you last night, didn't she? Don't lie, Beth. I know that you not only know Jade McGrath, but that she came here with you from Colorado. Don't get yourself in trouble, just tell me where she is."

"I have nothing to tell you," Beth said firmly. "And I want you out of my home."

"You're protecting a murderer," Carel said. "Jade McGrath has already maimed two people and killed a third. She came here to kill another. You better have something to tell me."

"Yeah, I do. You're full of shit. And you're trespassing, too. Let me see that badge again," Beth demanded.

Carel showed it to her.

"You aren't even a San Francisco cop. You have no right to be here messing with me like this. You get out or I'm calling the real cops."

"How are you going to feel if Jade pulls off this next murder?" Carel said. "Knowing you could have helped me stop her? The next one is no rapist, Beth. It's her ex-lover. A woman. I need you to help me prevent it."

"I need you out of my face," Beth spat.

They stared angrily at each other for several seconds, then Carel turned and left the apartment.

She got into the car and uncuffed Leslie. "That was a mistake," she said.

"Jade was never there, right?"

"Oh, she was there, all right. But she's not now. Her stuff is still there. The mistake was not coming earlier. We should have skipped the nap."

Carel drove to a phone booth and dialed Luce's

number. It rang twenty times before someone finally picked it up.

"Hello," a groggy voice said.

"Luce Reagan?"

"Yes."

"This is Detective Lopez, from Chicago."

"Yes?"

"Have you heard from Jade?"

"No. Why would I? What's going on?"

"Quite a bit. I want to talk to you about it in person. I'll come to your place."

"Come here? You're in San Francisco?"

"Yes."

"Well, all right, but . . . I was sleeping."

"Sorry, it can't wait. I'll be there in ten minutes."

Luce lived in the Richmond District just above Golden Gate Park. Carel parked a block from her apartment and, again, left Leslie cuffed in the car.

Luce had coffee ready. They sat at the kitchen table.

"Jade is in San Francisco," Carel said. "I think she intends to do you some harm."

"Oh, great," Luce said nervously. "What makes you think that?"

"Many things," Carel replied. "And I mean serious harm. I think she'll show up soon, probably today. She's over the edge, Luce. I think she thinks she has nothing left to lose."

"What are you talking about?" Luce demanded.

"Murder."

"No," Luce said, shaking her head vigorously. "No way."

"I know you want to believe she's not as disturbed as she is. But the evidence against her is piled nose high, and it stinks."

"You think Jade's the one who got those rapists?"

"There's nothing else I can think."

"And that now she wants to get me?"

"She's moving fast. I think she'll show up here soon."

"God!" Luce's hands shook as she tried to drink from her cup.

"I'll stay here and wait for her. You should make yourself scarce. Go visit a museum or something."

"What evidence are you talking about?" Luce asked. Her voice quivered.

"Take my word," Carel said. "The sooner you're out of here, the better."

Luce pushed her coffee mug aside. "All right." She stood. "Can I make a phone call first?"

Carel listened as Luce told someone named Tina that she was coming over, that she'd be there right away. "No, no, I'm all right. I'll tell you about it when I get there."

"Leave me a phone number where I can reach you," Carel said, "and a key to your apartment."

As soon as Luce was gone, Carel went to the car and retrieved Leslie.

"I really don't think you'd do anything stupid," Carel said when they were inside Luce's apartment. "But on the other hand, how can I know that for sure? So, here's the plan. You have to be somewhere out of sight when she comes, so I'm going to handcuff you to the bed. You're getting used to that, right? And when the doorbell rings, I'm going to gag you. Just so you know. You got it?"

"It's totally unnecessary," Leslie protested. "For one thing, we don't know for sure Jade is even in San Francisco. That suitcase could have been Beth's. Maybe she likes her jeans short, or maybe they were a gift for somebody. But even if Jade is in the city, I think you're dead wrong about her planning to hurt Luce. We could wait here for weeks and she'll never show."

"She'll show."

"If she did do those rapists, I bet she's on her way to Brazil or someplace by now."

"Into the bedroom," Carel said. She told Leslie to get onto the bed, then cuffed her to the bed post.

"This is uncomfortable," Leslie complained.

"It was your choice," Carel responded. "You could have chosen a comfy jail cell."

Leslie pushed a pillow behind her back. "I want to call Candace to find out if there's any word from Lyla."

Carel thought a moment. "All right," she said, "but make it short." She brought the phone to Leslie and dialed, then gave Leslie the receiver.

Candace answered on the first ring. "Leslie!" she exclaimed, as soon as she heard her voice. "Are you at Circle Edge? Is Lyla there?"

"No," Leslie said. "Unfortunately, she's not."

"Damn."

"Anything new on your end?"

"No," Candace said dejectedly. "The police have an all-points bulletin out for Lyla's car, but nothing so far. You'd tell me if she were there, wouldn't you?"

"Of course I would."

"Your mother called last night. I lied to her. I told her Lyla had to get away for a while, that she and some friends rented a cottage in Michigan."

"Good. Mom doesn't need anything else to worry about. How're *you* doing?"

"Not great. Paula's here with me. She's playing mother hen."

"I'm glad. You shouldn't be alone. I'm sorry I left, but I had to."

"It's all right, Leslie." Candace paused. "Another bad thing happened."

"Oh, great. What now?"

"You remember our neighbor down the alley, Jenny Wocjak?"

"The one who baked the cookies? Yeah?"

"She committed suicide."

"You're kidding."

"Carbon monoxide in her garage."

"Jeez. That's a shame. Did you know her well?"

"Not really. I chatted with her sometimes. She always seemed to be in good spirits. I guess you never know about people."

"I guess not," Leslie said.

185

"It seems like everything's falling apart." Candace's voice caught. "What's your phone number there, so I can call you if anything develops."

"I'm staying in a cabin in the mountains," Leslie said. "There's no phone. I'm calling from a restaurant in town, but I'll keep in touch with you, Candace. Hang in, huh? You'll hear from Lyla. I'm sure she's just hiding somewhere and is afraid to call because she probably thinks your phone is tapped."

"That's what I'm hoping."

"Is the phone tapped?"

"I don't know. But, you know, Leslie, even if that is why she hasn't called, she could call someone else and get a message to me."

"Well, maybe she's afraid to, afraid the cops will find out somehow."

"Yeah, maybe."

After they hung up, Leslie said, "I hope I'm not kidding both of us about Lyla being safe."

"She'll turn up," Carel said. She switched on the small black and white TV on Beth's dresser, then sat on the wooden chair next to the bed to watch it and to wait.

The wait continued. An hour passed. Then another. "I'm hungry," Leslie said, tossing her magazine aside. "Order a pizza."

"No," Carel said. She took a candy bar from her jacket pocket and handed it to Leslie. Just then, the doorbell rang.

"Do you think it's her?" Leslie said nervously.

Carel had her spare handcuffs ready. The bell rang again. "Can I trust you to keep your mouth shut?" she asked, "or do I have to cuff your other hand and gag you?"

"I won't make a sound," Leslie assured her.

The bell rang again. "All right," Carel said, stuffing the handcuffs into her back pocket. She went to the living room, closing the bedroom door behind her. She pushed the buzzer to unlock the downstairs door, then opened the apartment entry door part way. She stood behind it flush against the wall, her revolver in her hand.

The footsteps on the stairs got closer and closer.

186

"Luce?" a female voice called.

Carel remained quiet.

The door moved inward. The moment the person crossed the portal, Carel slammed the door shut with her foot and crouched spread-legged, holding the gun with both hands.

Jade turned. Her eyes widened at the sight of Carel Lopez. Then, like lightening, her foot flew out in a sharp karate kick that sent Carel's gun flying. The next blow doubled Carel over. Jade tore out of the apartment.

By the time Carel recovered enough to pursue her, Jade had reached the bottom of the stairs and was sprinting across Fulton Street. Carel saw her bounding toward the bushes and trees of Golden Gate Park. She ran after her into the woods, catching glimpses of Jade's red jacket from time to time. She ran as fast as she could, but the distance between them was growing. She got to the peak of a small hill and could see Jade ahead. Then Jade stumbled. Carel sprinted, gaining on her prey. She was getting closer and closer, was within forty feet, then twenty, then ten. She leaped and tackled Jade. The two women wrestled among the twigs and undergrowth. Carel nearly had her subdued when Jade's elbow swung in a swift arc and caught Carel in the throat.

Carel lay groaning on the ground, gasping for air. She could feel Jade pulling her gun from her holster, but was powerless to stop her. When she recovered enough to breathe almost normally, Jade was standing over her, pointing the pistol at her.

Carel pulled herself to a sitting position.

"Move slowly," Jade said. She was panting heavily. "Don't get up. Scoot over to that tree."

Carel pushed herself along the ground and leaned against the tree. She pushed strands of hair from her face.

Jade leaned against another tree, about eight feet away, still pointing the gun at Carel. They were far from any paths or roads, too far to be visible to anybody in the park, Carel realized. She took a deep breath and rubbed her throat.

"Sorry about your neck," Jade said.

"You're quite a fighter," Carel responded. Her voice was hoarse.

"I'm not the killer," Jade said.

"Running away makes it look like you are."

"Well, I'm not. But apparently you even got Lyla thinking I am."

"You'll be treated fairly, Jade. If you're not guilty, you'll be freed."

"I can't count on that, Detective." Jade shifted her grip on the pistol. "How did you know about Luce?"

"I'm a cop," Carel said. "It's my business to know."

"And you know I killed Henry Lester, huh? And brain damaged the others?"

Carel shrugged. "I think you might have."

Jade didn't respond.

"You can't keep running. That's no way to live."

Jade stared at the gun. "Maybe I'll just execute myself, save you guys the trouble. That's one solution, right?"

"A stupid one," Carel said. "Too final."

"Prison is final, too."

"Not necessarily. Give yourself a chance, Jade."

"That's what I was trying to do. I was thinking of heading for Mexico."

"And also thinking about Luce?"

Jade laughed hollowly. "That's right. I just spent two hours down by the ocean thinking about Luce. Trying to decide."

"Decide what?"

"Whether or not to see her one more time. I guess I made the wrong decision."

"Maybe not. You now have a chance to come back with me instead of continuing to run."

"Chance of a lifetime." She moved a foot closer to Carel. "Give me your handcuffs." Carel didn't move. Jade waved the gun at her. "Come on, I'm not kidding."

Carel pulled the cuffs from her pocket and started to get up.

"Stop!" Jade said. "Throw them."

Carel did. They landed in the grass in front of Jade.

"And the key," Jade said.

Carel tossed the key.

"What I could do is handcuff you to a tree," Jade said. "Then I could take off for Mexico, or Hawaii maybe, or Tahiti. Somewhere far away."

"You won't like living as a fugitive," Carel said. "If you're guilty, then stand up and acknowledge what you did. If you're innocent, come back and fight to clear yourself."

"I've been thinking about that," Jade said.

"Good."

"You freaked me out there in Luce's apartment."

"I noticed," Carel said. She looked pointedly at Jade. "I want you to give me back my gun now."

Jade smiled. "I probably should." She ran her palm pensively along the pistol's handle. "But, the problem is, Carel, that I just hate the idea of being locked up, even for one day, for one hour. It's weird, but I can handle just about anything better than that. Even if I can convince you people that I'm innocent, it'll take some time, and during that time, I just know you're going to want to lock me up. You see my dilemma?"

"Maybe Lyla can help you get over your claustrophobia," Carel said.

Jade smiled. She slid down along the trunk of the tree and sat in the grass. "Lyla's mad at me. She's ready to sacrifice me to save her own neck."

"You hated her from the beginning, didn't you?"

Jade cocked her head. "Yes," she said, "I did. I blamed her for what Luce did to me. I suppose you know about that."

Carel didn't answer.

"I thought she and Luce were fucking each other. But later I decided I was wrong about that. Wrong about a lot of things. I stopped hating Lyla. In fact . . ."

Carel waited. "In fact, what?" she prompted.

"Mm-m, let's say I grew rather fond of her. Tell me this, Detective Lopez, if I keep running and you guys never find me, what will happen to Lyla?"

"It could go either way," Carel said. "The charges could be dropped, or she could be prosecuted for homicide and the other crimes."

"That suggests you people aren't completely convinced that I'm the killer?"

"You're a suspect, that's all," Carel said. "And so is Lyla."

"But there's a chance they'll let Lyla go if they think I'm the murderer."

"A chance."

"So maybe I could save Lyla by staying away."

Carel looked askance at her. "That's your interest — saving Lyla?"

"Oh, I forgot, you think I hate her guts and framed her for the tattoo business. How's she doing, anyway?"

"I don't know," Carel said. "She disappeared."

"Disappeared? What do you mean?"

"Lyla's been gone since Friday. No one knows where she is, including Candace."

Jade looked flustered. "I don't get it. Why? She's the one who thinks it's stupid to run. Did something happen to her?"

"I don't know. Jade, let's stop this now. Put the gun down, will you?"

"You don't seem to understand, Detective. I'm not going to jail. Period." She picked up the handcuffs and tossed them to Carel. "Fasten one side onto your wrist, the other on your ankle, then I'm going to tell you about this wonderful memory I had today. Go on, do it."

Carel picked up the handcuffs. She opened one side, bent over as if to lock it onto her ankle, then suddenly flung the handcuffs through the air. They hit Jade's face, just below her eye. Carel bolted up and was on top of Jade in a split second. She pummeled her with staccato blows, then twisted her wrist until the gun dropped to the ground.

Carel groped for the weapon and managed to get hold of it while still sitting on top of Jade. She shifted, rolling Jade over, then pressed her knee into Jade's back, holding

190

the gun tip to the back of Jade's neck. Stretching her arm, she retrieved the handcuffs from the grass, pulled Jade's hands behind her back, and locked on the cuffs.

Then she got to her feet.

Jade turned over and looked at her. "You are so butch," she said.

"Get up."

Carel walked her to a path and then out of the park and across Fulton Street. Inside Luce's apartment, she opened the bedroom door and told Jade to go in.

Jade's jaw dropped when she saw Leslie.

"You're bleeding!" Leslie said.

Jade stared at the shackle attaching Leslie to the bed post. "Does she think you're a murderer, too?"

"Sit over there," Carel ordered, pointing to the wooden chair.

"What happened?" Leslie asked.

"You tell me," Jade said, sitting on the chair. "What are you doing here?"

Leslie looked chagrined. "I helped Carel find you. Jade, it wasn't you, was it? You didn't do the killing, did you?"

Jade's eyes suddenly filled with tears. "*Et tu,* Leslie?"

Leslie shook her head. "No," she said. "I never believed it, not really."

"Well, before mad dog Lopez went into her violent rage in the woods," Jade said, "I was about to tell her what I remembered while I was sitting at Land's End. It's a way to prove that I'm not the killer."

Carel was leaning against the wall still holding the pistol. "Go ahead, tell me," she said.

Jade shifted on the chair. "Could you take these handcuffs off first?" she asked.

"Just tell your story," Carel said.

Jade shifted some more, then began to speak. "I was there by the ocean. I was thinking about Luce, wondering how it would feel to see her again, and I was also thinking about how it feels to be locked up in a cell. I remembered that time I was busted for possession. They locked me up overnight. It was bad. And as I remembered that, I remembered something else — buying dope one night last February." Jade smiled at Carel. "It was a Wednesday. I'd forgotten all about it. Wednesday, February tenth, two days before Benny's birthday. I was getting her some marijuana as a gift."

"The night of the Anastopoulos tattooing," Carel said.

"That's right. Lyla was asleep. Most of the time, I would sleep, too, but on that night, February tenth, I went to visit this straight couple I know. They live not far from Vicky's place. I bought a bag for Benny."

"Oh, that's great, Jade!" Leslie said excitedly.

"But proving it presents a slight problem," Jade said. "How could I do that without incriminating my friends? That would be a lousy thing to do, don't you think?"

"What choice do you have? You're facing a homicide charge," Leslie said.

"If you're telling the truth," Carel interjected, "it could be arranged so no charges are brought against your friends."

"The guy's the dealer," Jade said, "not his wife." She lifted up her shoulder and wiped her cheek. She looked at the blood on her shirt. "You got a washcloth or something?"

"In a minute," Carel said. "Keep talking. Were they both there that night?"

Jade nodded. "And the woman's brother, too. I forget his name. He was helping her with her income tax forms. I gave her a tip that saved her some money. She'd remember that, don't you think? That I was there that night."

"Yes," Leslie said. "I'm sure she would. She has to."

"If this story is bogus," Carel said, "it'll get you nowhere, Jade."

"It's the truth."

"What are their names?" Carel said.

Jade didn't answer.

192

"We'll give them immunity from prosecution," Carel said.

"Shouldn't I have a lawyer for this?" Jade said to Leslie.

"Fine," Carel said. "We'll talk about it some more in Chicago, then."

"I can't believe you forgot about that Wednesday night," Leslie said.

"Me neither," Jade replied. "I was on that cliff looking at the ocean and thinking life was shit and I had no choice but to run and hide, and then I remembered."

"I'm sure glad you did," Leslie said.

"Leslie, why are you handcuffed to the bed? Is there something you two want to tell me?" She grinned. "Or is it Luce? Is she back to her old tricks?"

"Carel was afraid I'd warn you," Leslie said. "Can you take this off me now?"

"Not yet," Carel said.

"So where's Luce?" Jade asked. "She didn't want to see me, huh?"

"Carel thought you were coming here to kill her," Leslie said.

Jade looked at Carel disgustedly. "You have a sick mind, you know that?" She looked at a photograph on the dresser, Luce and a butch-looking Asian woman. "So did Luce believe it?"

Carel put her gun in her holster and walked over to Jade. "Stand up and turn around," she said.

Jade did as she was told. Carel unlocked one of her wrists then attached the free end of the handcuff to the unoccupied bedpost.

Jade sat on the bed and moved close to Leslie. "Hi, cutie. I missed you."

Carel went into the bathroom and washed the dirt from her hands and arms. There were grass stains on her pants. She combed her hair, then brought a wet wash-cloth and a tin of bandaids back to Jade. She unlocked Leslie's handcuff.

193

"Thanks," Leslie said, rubbing her wrist.

Carel went into the living room to make a phone call.

With the blood wiped off, Jade's wound was smaller than it had appeared. Leslie took the washcloth from Jade and finished the cleanup. Then she put a bandaid over the cut. "You look sexy," she said.

Jade shrugged. "Yeah, I know."

"Why'd you come here?" Leslie asked. "To Luce's?"

"That's what I kept asking myself," Jade said. "Maybe just as the final step . . . in getting over her."

"It could have backfired. You might have gotten all stirred up again."

"I know."

"And why did you leave Circle Edge? I told you it was a safe place to stay."

"I decided that between Lyla and Carel, they'd figure out where I was. I didn't want to cause trouble for those women. I was planning to go hide out in Mexico."

"So you just came to San Francisco to see Luce?"

Jade shook her head. "I didn't think I would see her. No, I came here with a woman I met at Circle Edge."

"Beth Wrightwood. That's how we knew you were in San Francisco. Riley told me you left with Beth."

"And you told the cops."

"I'm sorry. Carel got me all confused."

"Yeah, well, aren't we all?"

"So, did you and Beth . . .?"

"Did we what?" Jade said testily.

Leslie shrugged. "Never mind."

Carel returned to the bedroom. "We're booked on a five-thirty flight to Chicago," she said. "And I talked to Luce. She gave me the okay for us to stay here until it's time to go to the airport."

"She didn't want to see me, right?" Jade said.

Carel just looked at her.

"I knew she wouldn't."

"I need you to go to our hotel and get our stuff," Carel said to Leslie. "The bill's taken care of. Then come back here and pick us up." She handed Leslie the car key.

"What about *my* stuff?" Jade said. "I have a suitcase at Beth's."

"She can send it to you," Carel said.

"I could pick it up," Leslie offered.

"I'll call Beth and tell her it's okay," Jade said. "Otherwise she won't let you near my things. That woman is one tough cookie."

"A cream puff," Carel said.

On the flight back to Chicago, the women sat three abreast, Jade in the middle.

"Did you know Lyla was Luce's therapist?" Leslie asked Jade. "Yes," Jade said.

"And you thought they were sexually involved?"

Jade nodded. "For a while I did. I wasn't thinking real clearly when Luce cut me off, Leslie. I needed someone to blame."

"Do you still believe it?"

"No, of course not. In fact, I don't think I ever really did."

"But you seduced Lyla to get back at her and Luce?"

"Not to get Lyla, just Luce. But that was only part of my reason. When I first met Lyla I was very attracted to her. That was before I found out she was *the* Dr. Bradshaw. After that, I got even more interested."

"Because you blamed her for Luce ending it with you?"

"No," Jade said. "By that time I knew that wasn't true. I'd calmed down quite a bit by then, but I was still angry at Luce. I got involved with Lyla because I was interested in Lyla. Getting some revenge against Luce was a bonus."

"According to Carel, you sent Luce a letter telling her you were having an affair with Lyla." Leslie glanced at Carel who was pointedly listening to the conversation.

"I told her her ex-therapist was a good fuck. I also sent a photo."

"You're nasty, Jade."

"I know." Jade gestured to the handcuffs on her wrists. "But look at me now. I guess I'm paying for it."

CHAPTER 25

On Monday afternoon, Kate Ralla met with Jade at the State Street lockup. "How're you doing, kiddo? You look terrible."

"Just get me out of here," Jade said.

"We're working on it. Lopez and the assistant State's attorney met with your witnesses. They were given immunity. Unfortunately, they're not talking yet."

"Shit."

"Their lawyer's negotiating some guarantees," Kate said. "I think they'll work out a deal. Once your witnesses do agree to talk, let's hope they have good memories. I'll be there for the questioning." Kate put her notes into her briefcase.

"Make sure you mention the income tax stuff."

Kate smiled condescendingly. "Thanks, Jade," she said.

"Keep your spirits up, kiddo. If all goes well, we'll have you out of here by tomorrow morning."

That evening Patrice went to Lyla and Candace's house. Leslie was making coffee and Candace was sitting stiffly at the kitchen table. Candace was pale and expressionless, and she looked exhausted. "Well, at least it looks like Jade will be cleared," she said flatly.

Leslie poured Patrice coffee and offered her a sweet roll. "What's the matter?" she said to Patrice. "You look like you have bad news."

"Is it about Lyla?" Candace said in a panicky voice. "Have you heard something?"

"No, there's no word on Lyla," Patrice said without looking at either of them. "It's not that." She sipped her coffee.

"Well, come on," Leslie prodded. "Out with it."

"Another Ames Enterprises letter turned up." Patrice stared at the table. "At the WICCA office. A woman who works there — Joyce Tilton — called the police yesterday. Said she'd found the letter in the bottom of one of the desk drawers."

"Impossible," Leslie said.

"It was in a folder where Lyla kept notes for some article she and Joyce were writing. The folder had Lyla's name on it. Joyce says she found the letter yesterday, but the cops think she might have found it earlier, that she warned Lyla . . . told her about the letter and that she was going to report it. And that's why Lyla fled."

Candace's whole body started to shake. Then she was crying, great rasping sobs. Leslie and Patrice did what they could to comfort her, finally giving her a sleeping pill and getting her into bed. Leslie stayed with her, talking softly, holding her hand, until she slid into a restless sleep.

When Leslie returned downstairs, she said, "The letter is part of the frame. The killer planted it there."

Patrice nodded. "Maybe."

"You do still believe Lyla is innocent, don't you?"

Patrice said nothing.

"Oh, come on, Patrice. You're not giving up, are you? You're going to keep looking for the real killer, aren't you?"

"Yes," Patrice said flatly. "I'll keep looking. I'm feeling discouraged, though, Leslie. I'm running out of other possibilities."

"What do you mean *other?* You mean besides Lyla?"

"I didn't say that."

Leslie sat at the table. "Jade's roommate told me you questioned Benny."

"She has alibis for two of the tattoo nights. I'm checking them out."

"Did you ask her about her crack to Jade about enjoying her Wednesday nights while she could?"

Patrice nodded. "She claims she was referring to her intent to tell Candace about Jade's affair with Lyla. Apparently Benny knew about the affair for some time. She said it annoyed her, but didn't rile her too much because she's very hot for a new lover and was thinking of dumping Jade anyway."

"I see. Is she believable?"

"I don't think she's the killer, Leslie."

"Well, somebody is, goddamn it!"

Patrice was silent.

"What about that guy, Leon?" Leslie said. "Have you checked him out yet?"

"He was in the hospital on May nineteenth," Patrice replied. "Allergic reaction to a bee sting."

"Great."

"There's still the fellow who lives up the alley, Jim Julian. He was supposed to meet with me last week, but he didn't show. And he doesn't answer his phone or his doorbell. I'll keep trying. And there's Ruth Tremaine's son, Jamie. Him I definitely would like to talk with, but his mother tells me he's away on a vacation now. He has alibis for two of the tattoo nights, but I'm not totally convinced. There's also that ex-patient of Lyla's — Ivan Dorley. He apparently fell in love with her like the other one, Hefner. Dorley's not crazy, but very weird, according to Lyla. He's still a possibility. I'm going to meet with his brother tomorrow."

"You don't sound optimistic."

"I'm still working," Patrice said.

"That letter found at WICCA does make things look worse for Lyla, but so did the letter in Jade's garage, and she turned out to be innocent."

"Mm-hm," Patrice said.

"The killer planted both those letters. I hope the police figure that out."

Neither woman spoke for a while, then Leslie said, "Maybe that woman from WICCA did warn Lyla, and then Lyla figured they'd rescind her bail and put her back in jail, so that's why she split. Maybe Joyce had agreed to wait a while before reporting it." Leslie ran her fingers through her hair. "But if that's it, I just know Lyla would have let us know somehow that she's all right. I try to convince myself that she's run away and is safe, but . . ." She shook her head. "I really don't think she's safe at all. No word in three days. I think something awful has happened to her."

"Such as?" Patrice said.

"Such as the killer kidnapping her." She looked intently at Patrice. "You've thought of that, haven't you?"

"For what purpose?" Patrice said. "Why would the killer kidnap Lyla?"

"I don't know," Leslie said. "Why did the last person who talked with Lyla kill herself that same night? Maybe Jenny Wocjak didn't kill herself. Maybe there's some connection."

CHAPTER 26

Candace awoke from her drugged sleep and made her way sluggishly down the stairs. Leslie was in the kitchen. "Sorry I freaked last night," Candace said.

"I'm freaking myself," Leslie responded. "You want some breakfast?"

Candace dropped onto a kitchen chair. "I thought you're not supposed to dream when you take sleeping pills. I had nightmares. Ames Enterprises letters were turning up everywhere — in the dishwasher, under the covers on the bed, overflowing in the bathtub. Does Patrice believe Lyla's guilty?"

"I don't think so," Leslie said. She poured some cereal in a bowl and set it in front of Candace. "She's still investigating other suspects." She poured on the milk.

"Kate Ralla called. Jade's witnesses talked. They backed up Jade's story."

Candace nodded. "Good," she said tonelessly.

"The cops still have to check a few things, but Kate's sure Jade will be released today. Her roommate and I are going to pick her up as soon as we get the word, so I want to go over to their apartment and wait for the call. I didn't want to leave until you woke up."

Candace didn't reply.

"Will you be okay?" Leslie asked. "You don't mind if I'm gone for a while?"

"I'm okay," Candace mumbled. "My head feels heavy, that's all."

Leslie watched Candace mechanically lift the spoon to her mouth. "Do you wish Jade *was* the killer?" she asked.

Candace didn't answer, just looked at Leslie then looked away. She continued chewing. "You're right about the letter at WICCA," she said. "I heard you saying it last night, but I just couldn't think straight. Of course the killer planted the letter."

"There's no other explanation," Leslie said.

"I got so scared. So much evidence pointing at Lyla."

"So much *contrived* evidence."

"But where is she, Leslie?"

"Hiding somewhere. We have to hold onto that hope."

"Afraid to call."

"Yes."

"That must be it," Candace said.

Leslie put on her jacket. She looked guiltily at Candace. "I'm going to go now, okay?"

"I'll be fine," Candace said.

"I'm taking Lyla's bicycle. I'll call you later."

Candace nodded and continued eating. She finished the cereal, then made her way sluggishly into the living room and collapsed on the sofa. Through glassy eyes, she watched from the window as the mail carrier climbed the porch steps. She remained motionless on the sofa until Gal jumped on her lap. Her tears dripped on the dog's soft fur as she petted and stroked her. She thought about the Ames letter, feeling afraid the police would believe it was the final proof of Lyla's guilt.

Suddenly she was on her feet and dialing the phone. She asked for Carel Lopez.

"Did you people go to the WICCA office?" she said angrily to Carel.

"What's the matter, Candace?"

"Bright thing for Lyla to do, huh? Mutilate and kill people and then stash some major incriminating evidence in a folder with her name on it. I suppose you're convinced, though."

"Hey, come on, calm down."

"The WICCA office is in the basement of a church," Candace said. "Anyone could get into it. If you'd go check, you'd see that the real killer would have had no trouble putting the letter there."

"We checked," Carel said.

"And?"

"It's possible that someone put the letter there. We haven't ruled that out. We're doing what we can, Candace."

"You're still investigating?"

"Yes. I know how hard this is on you. If anything new develops, I'll let you know."

Candace sat with the dead phone in her lap for several minutes, staring into space. Finally she mobilized herself. She went to the kitchen, put the milk away, and placed her bowl and spoon in the dishwasher. She wiped some crumbs off the counter, then wandered into the hallway and stood at the front door looking out the window. She recalled that first night when the police had come and arrested Lyla for unpaid parking tickets. She laughed hollowly.

"Get the mail," she told herself.

She opened the front door and reached into the mailbox. There were four solicitation letters to Lyla from various ecology and political groups, and three for her. She put Lyla's on the growing pile on the hall table. There was a department store ad, a gas bill, a letter . . .

Candace's heart crashed against her chest. She felt dizzy and had to brace herself against the wall. A letter to her, in Lyla's handwriting!

She took it into the living room and sat on the edge of the sofa staring at it — a plain white business envelope, addressed to her. She opened it with shaky fingers.

Dear Candace, it said, *All those rapists, freed to rape again and again. I know it was wrong but I feel no regret for what I did to them. I did what I felt I had to do. I'm finished now, with everything. I don't expect you to understand. I am sorry for the pain I've caused. Lyla.*

"No!!!" Candace screamed. She fell heavily to the floor, the letter crumpled in her hand.

When the doorbell rang an hour later, Candace still lay where she had fallen, conscious, but numbed to immobility. The ringing continued and there were loud pounding sounds. Slowly, Candace sat up. She looked toward the sounds. Someone was on the porch, looking at her through the living room window, rapping on the glass.

"Candace, open the door!"

Candace blinked her swollen eyes until they focused. She struggled to her feet, and to the hallway. She unlocked the door.

Patrice Fedor walked Candace back to the living room and got her onto the couch. She got a glass of water and a wet cloth. She laid the cloth over Candace's forehead, then felt her pulse. "What happened?"

Candace turned her head and stared at the crumpled letter on the floor.

Patrice picked it up and read it. "Oh, shit!" she said. She read it again. "Is this Lyla's handwriting?"

Candace nodded.

Patrice checked the postmark on the envelope. Chicago. "Shit," she said again.

"She's dead," Candace said dully.

Patrice handed her the water. "Here, drink this. We don't know that, Candace."

"He killed her."

"Who?"

"Whoever made her write the note."

Patrice didn't reply.

Candace pulled herself to a sitting position. Her head felt very light. She drank some water. "You don't believe it, do you? The confession? The allusion to suicide?"

Patrice slowly shook her head. "Did you tell Carel about this? No, of course you didn't. I'm going to call her now."

CHAPTER 27

At noontime on the previous Friday, Jenny Wocjak had been sitting in her yard on a plastic lawn chair when Lyla Bradshaw had arrived at her back gate.

"I've got your plate," Lyla called.

"Come in, come in," Jenny had said. "I'm sitting here *catching some rays,* as my nephew would say."

Lyla sat in a matching plastic chair next to her neighbor. "Good day for it," she said, trying to sound cheerful. She hoped some light conversation might distract her from her anger and disappointment about Jade running away. "The cookies were delicious. Thanks again."

Gal lay on her back in front of Jenny. Jenny reached down and rubbed her belly. "I wish I had a doggie biscuit for you, little Gal. Such a cute name you have."

Lyla decided not to tell her that the name stood for *gay and lesbian.*

"How are things going, Lyla? Is your detective any closer to finding out who did it?"

"Not yet," Lyla said. Her eyes wandered to the six-foot, solid cedar fence separating Jenny's yard from Jim Julian's. She wondered idly how Jim's garden was doing.

"I wish there was some way I could help," Jenny said. She shook her head. "Such a terrible mistake the police are making. Is that other young woman your sister? The one I see walking Gal sometimes."

"Yes, that's Leslie. She came in from Colorado when the trouble started."

"It's good to have family around at such times."

Lyla nodded. "Your petunias are doing well," she said. She thought of Jim again and wondered why he hadn't shown up for the meeting with Patrice yesterday. "Have you seen Jim around lately?"

"Jim next door? Oh, I see him coming and going every once in a while. I haven't talked to him for a time, though." Jenny suddenly looked very pensive. "Lyla, you're a psychologist. What do you call it when a man dresses up like a woman? Is that what they call a transsexual?"

"Transvestite," Lyla said, looking questioningly at Jenny. "Why do you ask?"

"Oh, I don't know." Jenny glanced up at Jim's back porch window. "It could have just been for a costume party, I suppose. You know, Jim has been acting strange ever since that terrible thing happened to his mother." Again Jenny's eyes flicked to Jim Julian's window.

"What happened to his mother?" Lyla asked.

"You never heard? Why, a man broke into her house and raped her."

"What? Jim Julian's mother was raped?"

"Raped and beaten. She doesn't live very far from here, you know. I don't know what's happening to our neighborhoods. It was a year or more ago. Poor woman. They caught the man and there was a trial. And then they let him go free. I don't know why. According to Jim, his mother was absolutely sure the man was the one who raped her."

Lyla leaned forward anxiously. "And afterwards Jim started wearing women's clothes?"

Jenny nodded. "Could a thing like that, you know, your mother being raped and you being so close to her — could that drive a man to become . . . not normal? Oh, I suppose it's none of my business, but I just thought . . . you being a psychologist. Well, I feel sorry for him."

Lyla could barely breathe. "What did he have on when you saw him?" she asked. "A dress, or . . .?"

"No, slacks and a blazer. And he was wearing a wig. I just happened to notice . . . from my bedroom window upstairs, you see. It's right over his living room. The movement caught my eye, I guess, and I just happened to notice. His drapery was caught on a chair and I could see in. I saw it quite clearly — Jim wearing that wig and the blazer. He really did look like a woman, I swear. Then he straightened the drape and I couldn't see any more."

"He saw you looking?"

"I hope not. I wouldn't want to embarrass the poor boy." Jenny looked sincerely sympathetic. "Why do they do it, the transvestites? Do they wish they were women?"

"When was it you saw him like that?" Lyla asked.

"Oh, months ago. Last winter. Before Christmas, I think. Or maybe it was just after Christmas."

"And since then?"

"I just saw him that one time. I suppose it could have been for a costume party."

"Jenny!" a voice called. Jenny's husband stood in his undershirt at their back door. "Phone call!"

Jenny looked at Lyla. "I could have them call back," she said.

"No, you go ahead," Lyla said, trying to sound calm. She felt close to passing out.

Jenny took the cookie plate and dashed inside.

On shaky legs, Lyla went out into the alley with Gal.

* * * * *

208

Jim Julian had entered the alley at the same moment. In his right hand was the paring knife he'd intended to use on the orange that was to have been his dessert. He'd brought his lunch out to the garden and had been on the lounge chair near the fence when he'd heard *her* next door. The sound of her voice first brought the warm chill. And then the rage.

He overheard Jenny Wocjak accusing him of being a transvestite. That would have been laughable if the ramifications weren't so frightening. And the old gossip didn't stop there. She told the dyke bitch about mother, and that the rapist scum had been acquitted. The dyke bitch would put it all together, Jim knew.

He showed Lyla the knife. "It would give me great pleasure to use this on you," he said through clenched teeth. "But I won't, if you do what I say and don't make any noise."

There was fear in her eyes this time, not pity like before. Jim liked that. He held the knife to her ribs and walked her down the alley. He had her put her dog in her yard and then he closed the gate. He made her open her garage and get into her car. He got in next to her, holding the knife to her ribs. "Drive to Irving Park Road," he told her, "and then go west."

He's the killer, Lyla thought, pulling out of the garage. *And he knows I know.* She could feel the sweat on her brow. When they neared the highway, he told her to take the entrance going north.

"Where are we going?" Lyla asked, trying not to reveal her terror.

Jim took in deep lungsful of air. "I used to love the sound of your voice." He leaned back into the seat. "I thought you were so special," he said sadly, "that you weren't like the rest of them. But you turned out to be even worse." His voice was angry then. "My mother warned me. I should have listened."

"Jim, I never meant to —"

"Shut up! Don't talk." His grip tightened on the knife. They drove silently for a while.

Jim sighed deeply. "I thought about you constantly

after that time in your yard, when we first met. At night, before I'd go to sleep, I'd always have the same fantasy — you and me together, loving each other, being together forever. I thought you were the one I'd marry."

Lyla's mind was racing. She considered intentionally crashing the car.

"There'd never been any woman I felt that way about," he said dreamily. "Then finally I got up the nerve to ask you out." His breathing was audible. "Even after you rejected me, I couldn't get you out of my mind. I'd think about you all day, and at night you were in my dreams. I'll be patient, I thought. Someday she'll be mine." He chuckled hollowly. "I never thought it would be like this. Going for a drive in the country, me holding a knife on you. It didn't have to be this way," he said angrily.

"Jim, believe me, I —"

"Shut up!"

Several minutes passed before he spoke again. "It had never crossed my mind that you were a queer. You were just not ready, I thought, but someday you would be. I would wait. But then . . ." He sucked air through clenched teeth. "That night . . . my cat was out . . . I was looking for her . . . she ran into your yard and I went in after her."

From the corner of her eye, Lyla could see his clenched fist, holding the knife.

"When I saw you and the other pervert through the window that night, it was like someone had kicked me in the gut with lead boots." He shuddered. "The other one was naked from the waist up. The two of you were all over each other, hugging and kissing. Disgusting! First I was just shocked, then totally revolted. I actually threw up in the alley on my way back home. An abomination!"

He slammed his fist down on the car seat. "How could you?" he screamed. "How could you do that to me?"

"It isn't about you, Jim," Lyla said softly.

"Shut up, bitch!" He brought the knife tip to her throat. "I told you not to talk. You're going to do what I say. I'm in charge of you now."

Lyla chilled with fear. She was afraid she'd lose control of the car. She gripped the wheel, trying to concentrate on the road. He took the knife away.

They drove silently for several miles, Lyla's mind working frantically. Finally, she said, "Can I say something, Jim?"

"Go ahead."

"Candace forced me to be with her."

"Bull."

"She's the one who wouldn't let me go out with you."

"Lies."

Lyla said nothing more.

Finally Jim said, "You're just saying that because you're scared of me. You think I did those things to those rapists."

They drove another mile or two, neither speaking. "His name was Henry Lester," Jim said at last. "Pure scum. What he did to my mother couldn't go unpunished."

Lyla nodded. "I agree."

"He violated her." Jim shuddered. "He hurt her, hurt her terribly."

"Evil," Lyla said.

"Straight from hell." Jim's voice caught.

"And now he's back there," Lyla said, "in hell where he belongs."

"Yes, exactly."

They went another five minutes, then Lyla asked, "Where are we going, Jim?"

"To my cabin."

Lyla remembered once when they had been playing backgammon he'd mentioned that he owned a cabin in Wisconsin. He usually went there by himself, he'd told her. *Maybe we could go together sometime,* he'd added. *Maybe,* she'd said, then had changed the subject.

"Will you tell me why?" Lyla asked.

"You'll find out," he said testily. "Just shut up and drive."

They crossed the border into Wisconsin. After another thirty miles, Jim told her to take the next exit. Lyla drove for several miles on a county road, then he had her take a dirt road for another mile or so. The area was wooded and seemed deserted.

"There's a road on the right after that next clump of trees," he said. "Take it."

Lyla reviewed the moves she'd learned in her self-defense class, foot to the knee, heel of the hand to the nose. Jim was only slightly taller than she, though quite a bit stronger, she suspected.

The road ended in front of a small wooden cottage. Jim reached over and took the keys from the ignition, holding the knife on Lyla with his other hand. "Out," he said.

The cabin had four small rooms. It reminded Lyla of cottages her family had rented for summer vacations in Virginia. Jim told her to sit at the kitchen table.

"Jim, you and I really do have to talk now. I have a lot to tell you that you've had no idea about."

"Sit!" he ordered, brandishing the knife.

Lyla sat on the padded aluminum chair. "I was never free to tell you what was really going on," she said.

"Shut up!" he barked. "It's too late for talk. I don't want to hear your lies, anyway." He opened a drawer and took out a hunting knife, keeping his eyes on her. From another drawer he got a box of business envelopes and a pad of plain white writing paper. He put them on the Formica table along with a pen, then he stood several feet behind Lyla. She started to turn.

"Don't move!" he said.

From the corner of her eye, Lyla could see the hunting knife in his hand.

"Address the envelope to the other pervert," he said.

Lyla started to turn toward him, then stopped. "To who?" she asked.

"Candace Dunn, your lover. Write her name and address on the envelope."

Lyla wrote.

"All right, push the envelope to the side. Now take a sheet of paper and write what I say. *Dear Candace*..."

Lyla wrote it.

"*All those rapists, freed to rape again and again.*"

Lyla didn't move.

"Write!"

"Why, Jim? Tell me what this is for?"

"Just write, dyke bitch!" he hissed. He moved closer to her.

Lyla wrote the sentence.

"Now write this: *I know it was wrong, but I feel no regret . . .*"

Lyla put the pen down. "I won't do it, Jim."

He lurched at her and Lyla felt a sharp sting just above her elbow, then saw a circle of blood growing on her shirt. She felt woozy. "My God, you —"

"Do what I tell you or I'll cut you much, much worse."

Lyla pulled up her sleeve and looked at the wound. It wasn't deep, but it was bloody and it hurt.

"Write!"

She didn't move.

"I'll tell you what I'm going to do if you don't write. I mean it." He moved to the drawer and got out a meat cleaver. "I'll tie your hand down, your left one. I'll cut your fingers off, one at a time until you do what I say. I mean it. You write or I'll hack you to pieces."

"All right!" Lyla said, looking at his crazed eyes. "Just calm down, Jim. I'll write the letter."

He put the cleaver away and, still holding the hunting knife, stood behind her again.

When the letter was finished, he had Lyla seal it and put a stamp on the envelope. "Good, you're doing well," he said. He took a coil of rope from the cupboard. "Now into the living room."

As Lyla rose she was hoping for an opportunity to kick him, then get the knife. But he stayed too far behind her.

"Sit on the sofa," he said.

The sofa was heavy, wooden-framed, with removable cushions. Seating himself on an upright chair about eight feet from Lyla, Jim began cutting the rope into segments, each about five feet long. He made loops at the ends of three of them. "Put this around your wrist," he said, tossing a piece of rope onto Lyla's lap.

Lyla slipped her hand through the loop. She glanced at the door. Could she make a run for it? She had a horrifying flash of his hunting knife plunging into her back.

"Tighten it," he said.

Lyla pulled the end of the rope until the loop grew smaller.

"Now this one on your other wrist." He tossed another rope segment.

Lyla did as he said, her mind jumping from one possible means of escape to another.

"Sit in the middle of the sofa."

Lyla shifted to her left. He was going to tie her up, but why, she thought. What was going on in his crazed mind?

"OK, now don't move." He walked around the sofa and stood behind her. Lyla turned her head to see what he was doing and immediately felt a sharp crack on her skull. "Don't move," I told you. "Look straight ahead."

She felt rough rope slip over her head. It settled loosely around her neck. Panic rising, she grabbed at it. The cold knife blade was instantly at her throat.

"Hands down," he said.

She put her hands at her sides.

"Don't worry, I'm not going to strangle you. I just don't want you going anywhere. Now, sit still, all right?"

"All right," Lyla whispered. She wondered if the blade had punctured the skin on her neck. Her heart was pounding so loudly it seemed like drums.

He took the knife away. He was still behind her but she couldn't tell what he was doing. She felt the rope grow slightly tighter on her neck, forcing her to sit far back on the sofa.

He came around to the side and pulled at the rope on her left wrist forcing her to extend her arm. He tied the loose end to the wooden arm of the sofa. Then he tied her right arm the same way to the other side of the sofa. "The harder you pull, the tighter they'll get," he said.

He wrapped another length of rope around her ankles and tied her feet together. Then he stood back and looked at her. "I used to dream about you being here with me," he said with a sneer.

Lyla swallowed. "So did I," she said.

He slammed his palms over his ears. "Stop your goddamn lies!"

"Candace was blackmailing me. If she reported my father he would have gone to jail, so I had no choice."

Jim shook his head rapidly back and forth. "I'm not listening," he yelled. He began pacing in front of her. "My mother told me about this, how they lie. Lies, lies, lies! I'm not listening."

He turned and left the room. Lyla could hear the bathroom door close. She stretched her fingers trying to reach the knots. Impossible. She held onto one of the ropes and pulled, checking if the sofa arm had any give. It didn't.

When Jim returned, he seemed calmer. "Goodbye, Lyla," he said. "You can yell all you want. No one will hear you." He smiled malevolently. "Have a nice day."

She heard the front door lock, then her car starting and moving away until there was no sound at all except for the tick-tick of the clock on the wall. It was two-thirty. Lyla wondered how much time she had left to live.

CHAPTER 28

Jim parked Lyla's car in the crowded DePaul area, then took a bus home. He phoned his mother. "You're right, Ma, I do need a vacation. I'm going to go to Florida."

"Well, this is sudden."

"I just decided."

"Do you want me to go with you?"

"Not this time, Ma. I'm going to drive. It'll be a long trip. I'm leaving in the morning."

"So soon? Well, that's probably best. If you sit around thinking about it you'll end up not going. You come for dinner tonight and we'll say goodbye."

"All right, Ma."

He drove to the flea market on Lincoln Avenue where he'd gotten the other handcuffs. He bought three more pairs. On the way home, he stopped at the hardware store and bought some chain. Then he went to his mother's house.

She had prepared his favorite meal — chicken and spaghetti. They talked about his trip, Ruth commenting on how strained he seemed and what a good idea it was that he would have a chance to relax. "Stay in Holiday Inns," she said. "They're the best."

At nine o'clock, Ruth Tremaine walked her son to the door.

"You sure you'll be okay without me?" he asked.

"I'll be fine, Jamie. The alarm system gives me great peace of mind, and I'm sure Reverend Pearson will look in on me. You have a wonderful time," she told him. "Don't forget your swimsuit."

"I won't, Ma."

"Be sure to call me."

"I will."

At his house, he packed the things he would need, then sat in front of his TV to wait. He thought about *her* — tied up, frightened, miserable. Good, he thought. She *should* suffer.

When it was nearly one a.m., he walked next door and rang Jenny Wocjak's front doorbell. He knew her husband worked the night shift and that she would be alone. He waited a long time on her front porch until he finally saw the curtain on the door window move.

"Jim!" Jenny said. She opened the door. "What's wrong?"

"My mother," he said in an alarmed voice. "She's very sick. I just talked to her on the phone. She won't let me call an ambulance."

"Oh, dear."

"I need to get her to the hospital but my car won't start. I'm too nervous to drive anyway. Do you think you could drive me to her house? I know it's a lot to ask. And then maybe to the hospital?"

"Well . . . yes, of course. Come in, I'll just be a minute."

Jim waited nervously in the front room until Jenny

217

reappeared, dressed in slacks and a loose jacket. She had her purse over her shoulder. He followed her through the house to the back door and out into the garage. As they walked, he slipped on a pair of gloves.

Inside the garage, Jenny was about to get into her car when he grabbed her. She struggled but he easily overpowered her. He tied her hands behind her back with the thick length of cloth he had in his jacket pocket. He stuffed a handkerchief into her mouth, then tied another piece of cloth around her face. Whimpering and moaning, her eyes darted in terror as he pushed her into the front seat of her car. He retrieved the car keys from where they'd fallen on the floor.

Jenny was struggling to get out. When he came near her, she kicked at him. Jim raised his fist as if to smash her in the face. "Sit still," he ordered through clenched teeth. She quieted. He tied her ankles together with more cloth, then checked the bonds on her wrists. Assured that she would not be able to get loose, he pulled at one side of her unbuttoned jacket until it hung out over the passenger door's threshold. He closed the door on the jacket.

Next he went around to the driver's side. He took her house key off her key chain, then started the car. Jenny made moaning hums beneath her gag. When the engine was idling smoothly, he got out of the car leaving the driver's door open.

He took Jenny's purse into her house and left it on the kitchen table. Then he went to his own house to wait. Sitting on his back porch, he stared at Jenny Wocjak's garage, thinking about Lyla Bradshaw waiting for him at the cabin, and thinking about death.

When he figured enough time had passed, Jim Julian returned to the garage. He freed Jenny Wocjak's jacket from the door and let her flop across the seat. She was dead, or if not, close enough for there to be no risk of her escaping. Nosy, gossipy spy, he thought as he untied her ankles, wrists, and mouth. As he'd hoped, the soft cloth had left no marks. He took the handkerchief from her mouth and stuffed it in his pocket. He put the house key back on her key chain and left the engine running.

Jim felt jittery excitement as he drove the quiet, late night streets to where he'd left Lyla's car. He transferred his things from his trunk to hers, including the bag with the wig and blazer. Then he drove Lyla's car to the highway and north toward Wisconsin.

Lyla's wrists were sore and her neck stiff. She'd dozed off a couple of times in the hours since he had left her, but mostly she thought — about Jim, wondering how crazy he was, about how she might get out of this, trying to believe there was some hope that she would. The cabin was pitch dark. The only sounds were the ticking of the clock, and the occasional soft scrape of a tree branch against the living room window.

When she heard a car approaching, she felt both hope and dread. A car door slammed, then another. She heard footsteps, a key in the lock. The cabin door opened. The room filled with light.

"Ah, you waited for me." Jim Julian put two small suitcases down on the floor and set a satchel on the coffee table. "Have you been having happy thoughts?" he asked.

"I have to go to the bathroom," Lyla said.

"I imagine you do." He went behind the sofa, untied the rope and lifted it up over Lyla's head. From the satchel, he took handcuffs and a long, thick chain, and carried them to the kitchen. When he returned, he was pulling the chain behind him. A pair of handcuffs was attached to the last link. Jim took a pistol from the satchel and shoved it into his belt.

He stood before Lyla, dangling the handcuff and chain. "What do you prefer, ankle or wrist?"

Lyla looked at him. "That's up to you, Jim. You're calling the shots."

He looked pleased. "True," he said. He fastened the cuff to her left wrist, then he untied her ankles and her right hand. He immediately backed away, pointing the gun at her. "Don't try to get up yet," he said. He went

219

around and untied her other hand. "All right, you can go to the john."

Lyla removed the segments of rope from her wrists. She stood up. Her muscles ached. Jim had backed away, holding the gun on her. She went toward the bathroom, dragging the chain. Through the kitchen door, she could see that the other end of the chain was locked by another pair of handcuffs to the leg of the old-fashioned sink.

What's he plan to do, she thought worriedly, terrified by every possible answer that came to her mind.

When she returned to the living room, Jim was leaning against the far wall. "You hungry?" he asked.

Lyla nodded.

"There're some cans of soup in the cupboard. Help yourself."

Lyla went to the kitchen and heated barley soup in a battered pan atop the old gas stove. Jim stood in the doorway, holding the gun, watching her. When she went to get the spoon, she stared at the knives in the drawer, wondering if she'd be able to use one on him if she got the chance.

"You want some?" she asked.

"Sure," he said.

He sat at one end of the table and told Lyla to sit at the other. He laid the gun next to his bowl as they ate. Lyla was surprised she had any appetite, but she nearly emptied her bowl.

"The busybody is dead," he said.

She stared at him.

"Jenny Wocjak. She committed suicide in her car with carbon monoxide."

Lyla felt her stomach roll. Her hands began to tremble. She put them on her lap.

"You're going to do the same thing."

Her mind raced. She took slow, deep breaths. "If only I had been free to talk with you, Jim."

"There's a deserted place I know about fifty miles from here. I brought some tubing. I'll attach it to your exhaust pipe." He smiled at her across the table. "I'd thought about killing you sooner — last winter, after I saw you with the other pervert."

"She forced me," Lyla said. "When I told her I wanted to go out with you, she hit me."

Jim raised his eyebrows.

"*Never!* she told me. *You can only be with me or I will ruin your father. Stay away from Jim Julian.* That's what she said. I was afraid if I had told you about it, you would have done something desperate and then she would have made good on her threat and my father would be jailed."

"You told her you wanted to go out with me?"

"The only thing keeping me going was those backgammon games you and I had, Jim, and the other little snatches of time we had together. At least she allowed me that."

Jim's jaw was tight. "You had sex with her."

Lyla lowered her eyes. "I had no choice."

"You defiled yourself. The only woman I ever really wanted and you did filthy, perverted things."

"But only because —"

"Shut up!" He glared at her. "I don't want to hear about it. I know you're lying, anyway, trying to trick me." Spittle accumulated on the sides of his mouth as he spoke. "Get up, it's time to sleep."

Pistol in hand, he made Lyla go into one of the bedrooms and lie on the bed. After attaching another handcuff from a link of chain to the grate of the metal headboard, he left the room without another word.

CHAPTER 29

Carel Lopez arrived at Candace and Lyla's house a little after noon. She read the letter from Lyla that Candace had received that morning.

"Patrice believes Lyla's the killer," Candace said, glaring at Patrice. "Do you, too?" she asked Carel.

"I didn't say that," Patrice protested.

"Neither of you knows Lyla," Candace said. "If you did, you couldn't believe it for a second. The real killer forced her to write that letter. He's going to kill her and make it look like suicide. Maybe he already did."

"We're doing everything possible to find him," Carel said.

"Find who?" Patrice asked.

"Jim Julian." Carel put the letter in her pocket. "I know you've been trying to get hold of him, Patrice. So have we." She looked at Candace. "The woman Hank Lester was accused of raping was Ruth Tremaine."

"Yes, I know," Candace said. "I know all their names. So?"

"Ruth Tremaine is Jim Julian's mother."

Candace looked aghast.

"I found out this morning. Julian's boss at the real estate office gave me his mother's name — Ruth Tremaine."

Patrice's eyes were wide. "Jamie," she said. "I met him. I had no idea he was Jim Julian."

"No one made the connection earlier because of the names," Carel said. "Ruth Tremaine remarried after her first husband — Jonathan Julian — died."

"He's the killer!" Candace croaked.

"When his mother remarried, she gave Jim the house he now lives in."

"It's Jim Julian," Candace gasped, "and he's got Lyla!"

"His mother says he's on vacation in Florida," Carel said. "That he left Saturday morning."

"Why would he grab Lyla when his frame was working so well?" Patrice said.

"He's going to hurt her!" Candace wailed.

"And why did Jenny Wocjak kill herself?" Carel said. "If Julian did kidnap Lyla, maybe there's some connection with Jenny's death."

"The why's don't matter," Candace cried. "He has Lyla! He's had her for four days. Find him, please find him before . . ." Her flow of words turned into pitiful moans.

CHAPTER 30

Lyla had awakened after her first night in the cabin long before she'd heard the knock on the door.

"I'm coming in," he had said.

The door was not fully closed because of the chain. Lyla could see him through the crack. She didn't respond.

"All right?" he shouted angrily.

"Yes, come on in," she said.

Jim's eyes met hers momentarily. She thought she saw pain beneath his anger. He unlocked the cuff that was attached to the bed.

"I dreamed about you," Lyla said.

"I bet you did," he replied nastily. "Nightmares, huh?"

"No. We were in my backyard."

"Get up," he said sharply, gesturing with the gun. He left the room, pulling the door as far closed as it could go.

Lyla put on her slacks and shoes, went to the bathroom, then found Jim in the kitchen. Coffee was brewing.

"Your last meal," he said. "It won't be fancy. Take your pick — soup, beef stew, or ravioli."

Lyla sat at the table. "Just coffee," she said.

He poured a cup and set it before her. "There's no cream."

"That's okay."

Jim sat across from her. He laid the pistol on the table. "Jenny Wocjak was a fool," he said. "It was bad enough that she spied on me, but then she had to blab to you, too."

Lyla sipped her coffee. It was bitter.

"She got what she had coming. Just like you're going to. You'll be better off dead, anyway," he said scornfully. "All your kind."

"I understand why you hate me," Lyla said softly. "If I'd seen you with a man, I'd have felt the same way."

Jim stared stonily at the table.

"I used to think about suicide," Lyla said. "Wishing I could bring myself to do it."

He looked at her.

"But I knew it wasn't up to me to choose the time."

Jim took deep breaths. "You really messed up my life, you know."

"I know," Lyla said.

"You led me on. You were nice to me. I thought that meant you felt something for me"

"I did," Lyla said.

"And all along you were . . . with that woman, doing filthy, sick things."

"How awful it must have been for you."

"I wanted to die. I hated everything and everyone. The world collapsed for me. You did it, you ruined my

life!" His lip curled. "And now you're going to die for it."
He tightened his jaw. "I'm glad. I need it. Maybe I'll get
some peace then. I need you to be dead."

"I only wish it could have been different," Lyla said.

"You thought you were too good for me," Jim hissed.
"You just felt sorry for me. That's what Ma said. You
pitied me, but you don't now. You're scared now. You
deserve to die, dyke bitch!"

"I guess I do," Lyla said. "It does scare me, though. I
don't know if God will want me."

"You'll go to hell," Jim said matter-of-factly. He took
the gun and stood up. "Come on, enough of this stupid
talk. Let's get it over with."

Lyla's heart began to pound. She took a couple of
deep breaths. "I'd like to write a goodbye letter to my
mother," she said.

Jim was silent a moment. Thinking of his own mom,
Lyla hoped.

"All right," he said. He took the writing tablet and an
envelope from the kitchen drawer and laid them in front
of her.

Dear Mom, Lyla wrote. *Whenever I want, I can close
my eyes and feel your arms around me and hear your
loving words and your soft laughter. You're always with
me. I know that most of what is good about me came
from you and Dad. You taught me to be kind and
charitable, to love righteousness and despise evil. I tried to
live by those values. Partings are always sad, but we have
so many good memories. We will always be part of each
other. I love you so, you and Dad. I thank you both and
know some day we will be together again.* She signed it,
Your loving daughter, Lyla.

Lyla pushed the letter aside. She sat with her head
hanging, looking miserably sad. She hoped Jim would take
the letter. He did. She watched him read. Tears came to
his eyes.

"They must be good people," he said.

"Yes. I was lucky to have them. I always knew that.
They were always there for me, especially Mom." She

wiped her eyes. "We almost lost her a few years back." She said no more.

"What happened?" Jim asked.

"She was so ill and . . . the thought of her . . . dying . . . it was the most terrible, dreadful feeling."

"But she's okay now?" Jim said.

"Yes." Lyla wiped her eyes some more. "Almost fully recovered."

"My mother got sick once, real sick, I mean." He bit on his lip. "If she had died . . . I . . . I don't think I could have gone on."

"That's how I felt," Lyla said. "My father nearly destroyed himself getting the money for Mom's treatment. It was worth it, though, no matter the price we had to pay."

"She's the foundation of your world."

"Yes."

Jim was quiet for a while. "My father scared me, though," he said. "I was sad when he died, but partly relieved too."

"Was he strict with you?" Lyla asked.

"That's putting it mildly. He wanted me to be as steadfast and pure as he." Jim laughed bitterly. "One time, when I was thirteen, he caught me in my bed . . . uh . . . you know, uh . . ."

"Playing with yourself?"

"Yes. He stuck my hand into scalding water."

"Oh, no," Lyla said.

"I never did it again."

Lyla nodded. Jim pushed the envelope over to her. "I was luckier," Lyla said. "My dad was always gentle." She began addressing the envelope. "And he taught me how to do things — repair lamps, work with wood, plumbing, things like that."

"That's neat," Jim said. "I never did learn much about stuff like that. Father said I was clumsy." Jim looked deeply sad. "If you and I had gotten together," he said softly, "you could have kept our sinks draining."

Lyla smiled. "Yeah."

"And maybe taught me how to do things like that."
Lyla nodded.

"You could have fixed things — like the cabin stairs. Some of the wood is rotten, I think. I try not to step on the second stair. It probably won't hold much longer."

"I could fix it," Lyla said.

Jim didn't respond.

"Are we in a hurry?" she asked.

Jim shrugged. "I don't know. My mother thinks I'm in Florida."

"How bad are the steps?" Lyla asked.

He fingered the pistol. "Want to take a look at them?"

"Sure," Lyla said.

Taking the pistol with him, Jim went to the sink and unlocked the handcuff. "Stay there," he said.

Lyla watched as he carried the chain to the living room and locked it to the sofa arm.

"Okay, come on," he told her.

The chain allowed Lyla to go down the porch stairs and about ten feet beyond them. She examined the wood, poking and pushing on it with her fingers. "Not good," she said. She checked the railings and the porch floor. "It all needs to be replaced. Look." She showed Jim how soft the wood was. "It's hazardous."

"And you really know how to do it?"

Lyla nodded. "We'll need planks of treated wood for the steps and risers, some two-by-fours for the bannisters, one-by-ones for the railings. And some galvanized nails. Do you have tools?"

"I have a hammer," Jim said, "and a small saw that I use to trim branches. If that's not enough, I could buy what you need."

"Let's make a list," Lyla said.

They went back to the kitchen and sat across from each other. Lyla drew the plans and figured out how much wood they'd need. Jim wrote down what Lyla told him, clearly excited by the project. When the list was complete, he chained her to the bed and left to buy the supplies, saying, "I'll try not to be gone too long."

As soon as the car sounds faded, Lyla checked the bed

to see if she could somehow remove the handcuff from the headboard. Not without a metal saw, she concluded. If she took the bed apart, she'd still be locked to the headboard but at least would have some mobility. The slack Jim had left in the chain was enough for her to reach the dresser. She searched the drawers, hoping for a pair of pliers or even some scissors. There were blankets, sheets, and some women's clothes — Jim's mother's, Lyla assumed — but nothing even resembling a tool. She checked the closet and underneath the bed. Nothing.

She looked out the window, straining her eyes for any sign of human movement. The woods looked still and deserted. I guess I'm going to build a porch, she thought.

Jim returned two hours later with everything on the list, plus several bags of groceries. He took Lyla outside and attached the chain to the bumper of her car. "I'm going to put the handcuff key and the car key far out of your reach," he said. "If anything happens to me, you'll be stuck here, you know, so you better not try anything."

Lyla was examining the lumber as Jim spoke, acting as if she was barely listening. He went around the back of the cabin. When he returned, he no longer had the pistol.

"First I have to brace the eave," Lyla said, "then remove the old wood, except for the stanchions."

"I'd like to help," Jim said.

"Great. Let's get started."

Lyla began measuring the posts supporting the eaves. Jim watched her closely. She laid a two-by-four over the wooden horses Jim had bought. She measured and marked the board, then with the large handsaw Jim had bought, she sawed off a half foot. Jim brought the next two-by-four. Lyla measured it and Jim began to saw on the mark she'd made. After bracing the overhang, they took turns removing boards with the crowbar and hammer.

A couple of hours later, most of the old wood lay in a heap off to the side. Jim had gone inside the cabin and returned with lunch. They sat on boulders and attacked their sandwiches hungrily.

"How's your arm?" Jim asked, gesturing toward the dried blood on her sleeve.

"It's just a scratch," she said. "I cleaned it this morning."

Jim took a bite of potato chip. "I love to watch you move," he said. "The way you lift those boards, the way your arm moves back and forth when you rip a plank of wood out. It's beautiful to see." He was blushing. Lyla smiled.

"So skilled and competent," he said. "I really admire competence." He stared into the woods. "You know what my greatest achievement was?"

"What?" Lyla asked.

His eyes became steel cold. "Killing Lester."

Lyla felt her body tighten. She said nothing.

"And making it look like you did it, you and Jade McGrath."

Lyla reached for a potato chip. "It must have taken a lot of planning."

"I had to coordinate everything perfectly. It was a full-time job for a while."

"I bet."

"After that scum was acquitted, something snapped in me. I wasn't myself. I started to crack up, I think. It was horrible . . . frightening, like I was losing my mind. There were the nightmares, and I'd have these horrible images even when I was awake — seeing Ma the way I'd found her, tied up, bleeding." Jim's fists were clenched. "And they let the monster go!"

"That never should have happened," Lyla said.

Jim seemed not to hear her. "He was out there, free, living his life. That was wrong! It shouldn't be! I'd pace back and forth in my house. I'd pound on walls." He looked at Lyla. "And I kept thinking of you." His expression softened. "I thought that you could help somehow. My thoughts got crazier and crazier. I began to believe that together you and I would take care of Lester. You would understand what was needed, and you'd help me. I figured if I told you about what he did to Ma and about his getting away with it, you'd want to help me get him. I convinced myself that you would. I was almost ready to come to you and talk about it."

"I wish you had," Lyla said.

Jim's eyes narrowed angrily. "It was then that my cat went into your yard and I saw you and the other one." He picked up the hammer. "That was more than I could take," he said through clenched teeth. "First the rejection by you, then Ma being raped, then the acquittal, and then learning you're a queer." He looked at Lyla with utter disgust. He began rhythmically banging the hammer on a rock. "It was too much for me." Bang! Bang! His eyes were glazed. "I couldn't take it."

"If only I could have told you the truth," Lyla said.

He ignored her. "I stayed in my house for days and days. I don't know how many. Just sitting there. The only person I talked to was Ma." He let the hammer fall to the ground. "I felt so powerless, so hopeless."

He said no more. Lyla watched him leerily. After a while, a slow grin formed on his face. His eyes had a faraway look.

"Then it came to me." His voice was hoarse and rasping. "I wasn't powerless. I would kill Lester." He took several deep, full breaths. He looked at Lyla. "And then I'd get you. Hurt you somehow, maybe lure you to some isolated place and do something to you."

Lyla realized she was holding her breath.

"I was in my living room, thinking about how I'd do it. The TV was on but I wasn't paying much attention to it. But then there was a guy on the screen with a big tattoo. That's it, I thought. That's what I'll do to her — tattoo *Lesbian* across her face." His smile was sinister. "And then I'll kill her." He chuckled in a way that sent shivers along Lyla's spine.

"I was going to drug you to knock you out, then tattoo you, then kill you. That was my original plan." He rubbed his hands together. "I started working on exactly how I'd do it. I needed to lure you to me. I figured out how — I'd send you a letter saying you're a finalist in a raffle and that you might win a big prize." His smile was wicked, his eyes glazed. "Then when I was ready, when I had the office and everything was set up, I'd call you and say you won a VCR. I'd talk like this." He raised the pitch of his voice. "I sound like a woman, don't I?"

Lyla nodded. Her heart was racing.

"I'd tell you to come and pick up your prize. But I had to make it so you'd come alone. I'd find an office near where you work, and I'd say you have to come by one o'clock. It would have worked, too. You'd have come on your lunch hour. And when you did, I was going to handcuff you. You'd be in my power. I'd look you in your perverted face and tell you that I knew about you being a queer. A homo! A dyke! A sick, twisted, moral degenerate!" Saliva glistened on the edges of his mouth. "You don't deserve to live!" He stood up and lurched toward Lyla, his hands open threateningly, staring at her neck through crazed eyes.

"Jim!" Lyla said. "Stop!"

He stopped in his tracks. He was breathing heavily, staring dumbly at her.

"We need to cut the step boards," she said. "Hand me the ruler, will you?"

He blinked several times. "Lunch break is over, huh?"

"That's right. Back to work. You cut the two bannisters, will you? They need to be five and a half feet long. I'll go pull the rest of the old boards."

"Yeah, okay."

Lyla moved away. She watched him out of the corner of her eye. He was busy sawing a board, seeming to be back in touch.

They worked on the porch for another three hours. "I'm bushed," Jim said. "Shall we call it a day?"

"Okay," Lyla said. "We made a good start."

After they picked up the tools, Jim retrieved the pistol and handcuff key. He unlocked the chain from the car. "You first," he said.

Lyla went around the back and into the cabin. Jim followed her, holding the chain. He attached the end of it to the kitchen sink. "I'm hungry," Lyla said. "Shall we order a pizza?"

Jim smiled. "No phone. I bought some chicken."

"That sounds good. Why don't we cook it together?"

As they worked in the kitchen, he kept his eye on her, not letting her get close to any knives. The pistol was stuck in his belt. While the chicken cooked, they took turns in the bathroom. Lyla had to slide her blouse down the chain to get it out of the way while she showered.

When the meal was ready, they sat where they had several times before, across from each other at the kitchen table. *We're just like a happily married couple, aren't we, Jim?* Lyla thought. *Is that what you're thinking?*

Jim laid the pistol next to his plate. Lyla got him talking about movies and TV shows, managing to keep light conversation flowing throughout the meal. Afterward, they watched television in the living room until both of them felt sleepy. Again, Jim used the extra pair of handcuffs to shorten the chain and keep Lyla restricted to the bedroom.

As she lay in bed, she thought about Candace, knowing how worried she must be. *Well, at least I'm not dead yet,* she thought.

The next day was the Fourth of July. Lyla and Jim spent it working on the porch. When they talked, it was about the job they were doing, or small talk about the weather, vacation spots they liked, how the Cubs were doing. At one point, Lyla said the chain was in her way, and asked Jim if he would take it off.

"So you can run away?" he said. "You must think I'm a real jerk."

"I wasn't thinking about running," Lyla said.

Jim's jaw was tight. "The chain stays on."

Lyla shrugged. She took a nail from the box and began hammering.

That evening, they again prepared supper together. For dessert, Jim served strawberry ice cream topped with fresh strawberries.

"I had strawberry ice cream on my first date," he

said, setting the dish in front of Lyla. "I was seventeen and so was she. Helen Malone." He smiled sadly. "I had a terrible crush on her for over a year before finally getting up the courage to ask her out. I thought I'd burst from happiness when she said yes."

"I bet you were nervous," Lyla said.

"God, was I. I wanted everything to go perfectly. I thought the date went okay, but then she wouldn't go out with me again."

"Really? That surprises me."

"It does?"

Lyla nodded. "You must have felt hurt," she said.

"I was crushed. I finally recovered enough to ask another girl out. That was almost a year later. Same thing happened with her. One date and that was it."

"Mm-m," Lyla said sympathetically.

"I'd been shy before, but I really was after that. Withdrawn, I guess. I didn't much like high school anyway. Felt kind of like an outsider."

"Different in some ways from the other kids?"

"Yeah. Ma told me not to worry about it. She said most of them were too wild anyway, and that they were probably jealous of me, that that's why they didn't ask me to their parties and things."

"It was lonely for you, I imagine."

"Yeah. It was even worse in college. I only lasted a year. I really felt left out there, like a total outcast." He took a bite of his ice cream. "I took some courses in graphic design after leaving college. I liked that. I really got into it. I was pretty good."

"I'd like to see some of your work," Lyla said.

"You would?"

"Sure."

"Most of it's at home, but I have a few things here," he said excitedly. "I'll get them."

He jumped up from the table and started to leave the room, then immediately turned back and grabbed the gun. He glared at her. "I suppose you'd just love to put a bullet in my head," he said angrily.

"It never crossed my mind," Lyla replied calmly.

He left the kitchen and returned a few minutes later with a large brown portfolio. "Sometimes I work here at the cabin," he said.

He laid some sheets of paper on the table. One was a poster advertising a church picnic, another was letterhead for a shoe manufacturing company; there were several logo sketches.

Lyla examined the poster. "This is excellent," she said. "You have a good eye, Jim."

"The pastor liked it. Of course, I didn't charge for it. After my father died, I worked at an agency for a while. I was doing pretty well, but the people were nasty there, so finally I quit. Soon after that, Ma remarried. Bert Tremaine. He was a member of our church and she'd known him for years. I didn't like him much. She moved into his house which was about a mile from ours. I stayed at the old house. I got that job at the real estate place. I didn't really need the money because of the inheritance from Dad, but it was something to do. Ma was afraid I was lonely so she kept trying to fix me up with girls from church. I kept saying no until one Sunday she introduced me to Shirley. I really liked that girl. I didn't feel so shy with her. She was the only woman I . . . who I actually got involved with. We dated for nearly a year. I got very attached to her, overly so, according to her. She said I was too dependent on her. I didn't know what she meant. I told her I just liked her a lot."

His lower lip was quivering.

"After she broke up with me, I was . . . well, a real mess." He blinked and wiped at his face. "For months, I hardly went out of the house. I didn't shave for days on end. Ma was worried about me. She told me to stay away from women, that that was my problem, and she made me join this Bible study group. They were nice to me there. I started to feel a little better. I took Ma's advice and stayed away from girls. I wasn't very happy, but at least I wasn't miserable anymore. About a year later, Bert died. Ma was broken up about it, but not nearly as much as when my father had died. After Bert's death, Ma wanted me to sell the house and move in with her. I didn't want to, though. I'd gotten used to living alone and I liked it. Sometimes Ma nags too much. I think we do better living separately. We see a lot of each other, though."

"You seem very close to her," Lyla said.

"She's the one woman I can trust," Jim responded. He put his drawings back into the envelope. "I've got a surprise for you."

"Oh?" Lyla said leerily.

He unlatched the back door. "Go outside, I'll be there in a minute."

Lyla felt apprehensive. She went out the door and stood on the grass. It was a clear, warm night, stars sprinkling the sky. A moment later, Jim appeared holding two lit sparklers.

"Happy July Fourth," he said. He handed a sparkler to Lyla. They twirled them in the air and watched the glow.

CHAPTER 31

"That was the best Fourth of July I ever had," Jim had said the next morning at the breakfast table. "It almost felt like we . . ." He hesitated for a long time. "Like everything was good between us."

"Maybe things could be, Jim," Lyla said softly.

He shook his head. "Maybe they could have been, but, unfortunately, that's a dream. In real life, I have to kill you."

Lyla took a sip of coffee. She got a pensive look. "I used to think about killing Candace," she said.

Jim looked at her incredulously. "Oh, you mean because she was *forcing* you to be with her. Yeah, I really believe that. You think I'm a total jerk, don't you?"

"I think you're the man I wanted but could never have," Lyla said.

Tears came to Jim's eyes, but then he frowned and glared at her. "Yeah, right."

"It's true. I remember the first time you and I ever talked. I felt . . . I don't know, kind of light-headed, like I'd had too much wine.

Jim eyed her skeptically.

"The more time we spent together, the more my feelings for you grew. I used to daydream about you all the time."

"Shirley told me stuff like that," Jim said angrily. "Lies. All lies. Ma told me not to listen. She's right. Stop saying that stuff. Shut up, will you, Lyla, just shut up!"

"All right," Lyla said calmly.

"You mean nothing but pain and misery to me. Once I found out what you are, the only good feelings I've had about you were when I was planning how I'd send your perverted soul to hell."

His voice rose as he spoke and his eyes took on that glazed look again. Lyla felt uneasy.

"I followed you, did you know that? To learn your habits so I could figure out how to kill you and get away with it. Then one day I saw you on that TV news show, talking about rape. You made it so easy for me, you and your other pervert friend, Jade McGrath. I followed her, too. Your predictable Wednesday nights and your public declaration of hatred for rapists gave me the greatest idea of my life!"

He looked joyful. Lyla's worry grew.

"I wouldn't tattoo *you*. No, I had a better idea. I'd tattoo Lester, and kill the pig, and then make you take the blame for it." He smiled gleefully. "What an idea! It was so satisfying, I can't tell you."

"The perfect way to get both of us," Lyla said.

"It was brilliant." He seemed glutted with pride. "Of course there'd have to be a couple of other killings too, to take the focus off of Lester since the police might consider me a suspect in his murder."

"So you meant for the other two to die?"

"No, just some of their brain cells. I knew what I was doing. Clever, don't you think? I made it look like something you might do — incapacitating rapists who'd never been punished for their crimes, rather than killing them. And the death of Lester would appear to be a mistake. Accidental overdose of the Seconal."

Jim chuckled. "I was so happy when I came up with the idea of framing you for Lester's death. I felt like I'd just won the Nobel Prize. It was a stroke of pure genius."

"Brilliant," Lyla said.

"I got to work on it right away. I went to the Criminal Court Building and got a list of men who'd been acquitted on rape charges. I went back five years. I found thirty of them who lived on the north side. I sent them all letters saying they were finalists in a raffle."

"To set the stage," Lyla said.

"Exactly. As an afterthought, I planted a copy of that same letter in Jade McGrath's garage and another one at that church where you work, hoping the cops would find them." He looked at Lyla expectantly. "Did they?"

"They found the one in Jade's garage," Lyla said.

"Good. They probably won't find the other one until after you're dead."

Lyla squirmed on her chair. "So, do you think we should get to work on the porch?" she said. "I'm ready if you are."

"Not yet!" Jim snapped. "I want you to listen to me."

"All right," Lyla said soothingly.

"You're the only one I'll ever be able to tell how I got those bastards and I want to tell it."

Lyla nodded.

"You just listen." He fingered the pistol.

"I'm listening," Lyla said.

Jim leaned back. "So I sent the letters and then I went around finding offices. I needed places to do the tattooings, business offices for the phony Ames Enterprises company. I checked out buildings not too far from your Wednesday night haunt, looking for places I'd be able to get into at night, old buildings with no security guards. I found the three I needed. They all had offices inside that I could get into with a credit card."

"Clever," Lyla said.

"Then I had to get the Seconal."

"How did you manage that?"

"My cousin's private pharmacy. He's an orderly at a hospital. He's also a kleptomaniac. His apartment is loaded with pills and medical instruments and syringes and injectable meds. He doesn't know I took things."

"I see," Lyla said. "And what about the car? That really puzzled me. Did you somehow make a license plate with my number on it, and get a Honda like mine?"

"I used your car," Jim said.

"Really? How did you get into it and start it?"

"I had a key," Jim said, leaning back with self-satisfaction.

"Amazing."

"Piece of cake. I bet you can't guess how I got it."

"I have no idea," Lyla said.

"I was patient," Jim said. "And crafty."

"Obviously."

"From the second-floor back bedroom of my house, I can see into your backyard. I watched. I spent a lot of time watching. One Sunday, a couple weeks before Christmas, I saw your pal, Candace, leave in her car. Then I saw you come out and start shoveling the snow from your back sidewalk. This was my chance. When you finished the back and went to shovel the front walk, I made my move. I sneaked in through your back door. I figured you wouldn't have locked it. I found your purse, or that thing, whatever you call it, a pack. Your keys were in it. I drove to the hardware store and had a copy of your car key made. It didn't take long at all. I returned the key while you were still out front shoveling."

"Amazing," Lyla said. "I had no idea."

"I learned a lot about myself through all this," Jim said. "I'm a clever person. And I'm not afraid. I always thought I was, but I'm not."

"I can see that," Lyla said.

"This adventure has given me a new slant on life. The best part was Lester."

"That must have been gratifying," Lyla said, "to give him what he had coming."

"Oh, it was. That was definitely the high point of my life. May nineteenth, nineteen ninety-three. I remember every detail of that day. I'd tried to get him two times before that, on Wednesday nights, but he wasn't home. That was disappointing, but it turned out to be a great buildup to the finale, to May nineteenth." Jim's eyes were gleaming. "I can picture every move I made that day, starting with setting my VCR. My mother doesn't know I own one; no one does. I got it so I could record *Star Trail* — my alibi for those three nights. At six o'clock on Wednesdays, I would set the VCR, then I'd disconnect my phone, which I always have done on Wednesdays at nine anyway so I wouldn't get any interruptions during the show.

"That night, after setting the recorder, I went to the neighborhood where you and your queer lover had your get-togethers. I got there at six forty-five. I parked in the alley across the street from the building you used, like I'd been doing every Wednesday night. I went into the walkway and waited. It's dark there. I could see the street, but no one could see me. I waited until I saw your friend come and then you. As soon as you arrived, I went to my car and drove around until I found your car. I transferred my supplies into your car, then parked my own car in your spot."

"Smart," Lyla said admiringly.

"I drove your car to a phone booth and called Lester. I was thrilled when the pig answered the phone. Bingo! I thought. This is it! I asked him if he wanted to buy some carpeting. The slime was real rude to me. It made me even angrier. I drove to the office building I'd picked out, the one on Fullerton. It had a window on the first floor that was never locked. I climbed in and went and unlocked the front door of the building. Then I went up to the office I'd chosen earlier, one with a credit card lock. Fischer and Harms was the name on the door. I phoned Lester and told him he'd won a VCR. I was sure

241

the pig would come. I covered the Fischer and Harms sign with one I'd made saying *Ames Enterprises.*"

"You thought of everything," Lyla said.

"Yes, I did. I put on the blazer, one like I've seen you wear, and a shirt like yours. Also a stuffed brassiere and the silver bracelet. Then I waited. The moment I'd been living for was almost here. When I heard the knock, I asked if it was Henry Lester. 'That's right,' he said, with that ugly pig voice. I told him to come on in, that I'd be there in a minute. I went into the adjoining room. When I came out, I was pointing my gun at the scumbag. It gave me great pleasure to see him cringing with fear. I made him lie on the floor and handcuff himself.

"I said a few choice words to him then, about what happens to pigs who rape good, Christian women like my mother. I wanted him to know why this was happening to him. He was sweating. It was beautiful to see him squirm. I injected him with the Seconal, a huge dose of it. When he was out, I put a plastic bag with the airplane glue over his nose, like I'd done with the other two."

"To make it seem like you were trying to cause brain damage."

Jim nodded. "It was almost nine o'clock by then. I called my aunt to make my alibi more solid. I talked a few minutes then told her I had to go watch *Star Trail.* Then I uncuffed Lester, turned him over, and tattooed *Rapist* on his forehead. He was dead by the time I finished."

"Good riddance," Lyla said vehemently.

"I cuffed the pig's body to the radiator, then put on the wig, grabbed the gray pack thing like yours, and left by the front door. I acted as if I was in a great hurry, running to your car and screeching away. I was hoping someone would see me, but since I couldn't count on that, I called the police the next day and reported seeing your car at the scene."

"The anonymous phone call," Lyla said. "*You* made it."

Jim smiled. "Of course. Anyway, after taking care of Lester, I drove to my car from the Fullerton building. I took off the blazer and wig as I drove. I transferred my supplies back to my own car and re-parked yours where it had been originally. Then I drove home."

"What a coup," Lyla said.

"I was flying that night. I liked it, Lyla! I really liked killing him."

"I can understand why."

"When I got home, I watched *Star Trail* on the tape. The next morning I called Ma and made sure we talked about the show."

"Terrific alibi," Lyla said.

"The cops bought it, including some phony *researcher* who came to Ma's house. No one suspects me. They think you did it." He grinned. "The perfect crime."

"I'm impressed," Lyla said.

"Once I decided to do it, I made sure I did it well," Jim said, smiling. "You want some more coffee?"

By Monday evening, the frame for the porch and stairs was in place and some of the floor boards nailed in. They cooked and ate their dinner, then watched TV. There had been no more talk about Jim's perfect crimes.

After breakfast the next morning, Jim told Lyla he was going shopping and he'd have to chain her in the bedroom while he was gone. "Do you want anything?" he asked.

"I could use some underwear," Lyla said.

That seemed to embarrass Jim. "Make a list," he said. "I'll get you some clothes, too, if you want. Put your sizes down."

"Why don't I just go along with you?" Lyla tried.

"Forget it," he said.

Lyla got the now familiar note pad from the kitchen drawer. She would have taken the hammer, too, and stuck it down her jeans, but Jim was watching. When she finished the list, he chained her in the bedroom and left the cabin.

Lyla lay on the bed, thinking of Candace and the

pleasant life they used to have. It all seemed very, very far away.

When Jim returned and unlocked the bed handcuff, he handed Lyla a Sears shopping bag.

"Thanks," she said. "It'll feel good to put on clean clothes."

"Come into the living room," he said shyly. "I have something else for you."

A gift-wrapped box sat on the sofa.

"How sweet," Lyla said. She opened the box and held up a green jersey dress. "This is lovely. Are we going dancing?"

"I've never seen you in a dress."

"Candace wouldn't let me wear them," Lyla said.

"Is that true? She had that kind of control over you?"

Lyla didn't answer.

"Tell me about it," Jim said.

Lyla stared at the floor. "It's not a pretty story."

"Go ahead. I want to hear."

Lyla took a deep breath. "She was my father's secretary. I met her four years ago. She approached me in a very . . . well, blatant way. I was shocked. It made me . . . I don't know, sort of sick to my stomach. Nothing like this had ever happened to me before. I didn't even know any homosexuals."

"They try to recruit," Jim said.

"Yeah, I know. I rebuffed her in no uncertain terms. But that didn't stop her. Every time our paths would cross, she'd come on to me. I was tempted to tell my father. I wish I had. Anyway, soon after she started to work for my dad, my mother got ill. The medical expenses were way more than their insurance covered — the surgeries, the repeated hospitalizations, and especially the extended care. Mom needed around-the-clock nursing care during her convalescence. Before she got sick, Dad was already in debt from some bad investments he'd made. I gave them my savings, and he borrowed from my sister and other relatives. It still wasn't enough."

Jim's expression showed sincere concern.

"So, Dad ended up embezzling money from his company." Lyla hung her head. "What else could he do?"

Jim nodded understandingly.

"When Mom recovered from the last surgery, they moved to Pittsburgh. They're doing fine now, thank God. Dad's saving as much money as he can at his new job. He hopes to pay back what he took, to do it anonymously somehow."

"And Candace?"

"She knew what Dad had done, how he juggled the books. She had some documents that proved it. She showed them to me."

"And she threatened . . ."

"Yes, to expose my father if I didn't . . ."

"What a sick, evil woman."

"She promised it would just be once, one time together. It was so repulsive, Jim, so wrong, but I felt . . ."

"Of course."

"But then she insisted on more . . . and more. I . . . I tried to numb myself to it, to pretend I wasn't there. She began taking over my life in other ways, too. She insisted we buy the house and live there together."

"You were a prisoner."

Lyla nodded.

"But . . . well, you sure seemed to be enjoying it when I saw you through the window."

Lyla shook her head, looking mournful. "I had to pretend," she said. She sighed deeply. "I had to do so many things. Candace changed my whole life, Jim. Took over. I had to stop going to church. She wouldn't let me see any men at all. Yes, I was a prisoner "

"But she let you play backgammon with me."

"Oh, she was angry about that. I insisted. You can watch from the window, I told her. Jim and I are friends. That's what I told her. She punished me for doing it, but it was . . . well, it was worth it."

"So that's why you couldn't go out with me."

Lyla nodded sadly.

"I thought I'd picked up something. Pain. That you'd

245

been hurt. That's why I never gave up. I thought you would someday be mine."

"If only I could have been."

"If only I had known." Jim's eyes glistened with tears. "And what will Candace do now? Now that you're gone, and if you never go back, will she report your father?"

Lyla shook her head. "She'll have nothing to gain by it."

"She should be punished for what she did."

"God is punishing her," she said. "She has brain cancer. It's untreatable."

"Ha!" Jim said. "Her just desserts."

"If she hadn't gotten the cancer, I might have killed her myself," Lyla said. "But now her death will be slower and more painful."

"Exactly what she deserves," Jim said. "Do your parents know about any of this?"

"No."

"No, of course not," he said. He reached out and touched her hand.

Lyla looked at him lovingly.

"Would you try the dress on?" he asked.

"Tonight," Lyla said warmly. "I was thinking we might have dinner by candlelight."

Jim sighed. "I'd like that."

CHAPTER 32

They had worked on the porch until six o'clock that night. When they went inside, Jim removed the handcuff from her ankle. She was free for the first time since he'd tied her to the sofa four days before.

"Go ahead," he said. "Get ready. I'll make dinner."

Lyla started toward the bedroom.

"Wait!"

She turned.

"I can trust you, can't I?"

"Yes, Jim, you can," Lyla said solemnly.

"Okay, go ahead."

She got the robe Jim had bought for her and went into the bathroom. Possibilities ran through her mind. The bathroom window was tiny. No escape there. She thought about sneaking out the front door and making a run for it. Not a chance, she thought. He'll be listening; he'll hear me. The best possibility is the bedroom. She turned on the shower, then opened the bathroom door and peeked out. She could hear him banging pans in the kitchen. She slipped out of the bathroom and dashed to the bedroom. Every other time she'd been there, she'd been chained to the bed and unable to reach the window. She hoped it wasn't stuck.

She undid the latch and began slowly lifting the window. It moved easily. She was so excited, her heart was pounding. She pictured herself running through the woods, running and running, getting as far away from that madman as possible.

About a foot up, the window stopped moving. She pushed at it, but it wouldn't budge. She examined the frame. A nail had been driven into each side of it, preventing the window from opening fully. *Burglar protection,* she figured. She pulled at one of the nails; it was tight. *Damn!* She needed a claw hammer or a pair of pliers. *Freedom is just the other side of this pane of glass,* she thought. She looked at the table lamp. *Smash the window and jump through. I'll probably get cut but that's all right. But he'll hear. He'll come running. He'll have the gun!*

Angry and disappointed, she tiptoed back to the bathroom and took her shower. At least it felt good to be unencumbered by the chain.

Jim Julian's eyes widened when she walked into the kitchen. "You look . . . fantastic," he said breathlessly. She was wearing the green dress. "Here, sit. The steaks are almost ready."

Lyla thought it wise not to mention that she didn't eat red meat.

When they sat at the cloth-covered kitchen table, Lyla realized the pistol was nowhere in sight. They dined by candlelight and talked about art. Jim liked the Deco period, he told her, "the straight lines and purity of it. I could always draw well," he said. "I know I could make it as a graphic artist if I really tried. You know something interesting, I feel like I can now."

"Not afraid anymore," Lyla said.

"I feel like I can do anything."

"I think maybe you can," Lyla said.

After they finished eating, Jim told her he had another surprise. He got a bag from the kitchen counter and pulled out a backgammon game.

"Oh, great!" Lyla said. "It's been so long since we played."

They played for an hour. Jim won most of the games.

"You're too good for me," Lyla said.

"You said that before. A long time ago. Do you remember?"

Lyla nodded.

"I used to feel inferior to you. Mostly because you're so much more educated than I. I guess also because you seemed so self-assured, so comfortable with yourself. But I don't feel that way anymore; that doesn't seem important to me now."

"And I felt inferior to you," Lyla said. "Not in terms of education, but morally. I felt ... dirtied, guilty, because of what went on with Candace."

"That wasn't your fault, Lyla. There's no need for you to feel that way." He was leaning toward her, the backgammon game forgotten. "You're a very special person. I knew it from the beginning. My mother wasn't dirtied because of what Lester did to her. It wasn't her fault. The same is true with you."

His expression suddenly changed. He was silent. Lyla watched him apprehensively. His eyes had grown cold. Finally, he said, "I'm letting you get to me. I'm being a jerk."

Lyla felt anxiety creeping through her stomach, speeding up her heart rate.

"Oh, God, I so much want to believe you," Jim said. He ran his fingers through his hair.

"I know how much I've hurt you." Lyla lowered her eyes.

249

"I want to believe what you told me... about Candace, about your feelings for me. Partly I do believe it."

Lyla said nothing.

"But what about Jade McGrath?" he said. "I know she's a homosexual. She is, isn't she?"

"Yes," Lyla said.

"And those Wednesday nights. I don't understand. Were you...?"

"Lovers with her?" Lyla shook her head. "No way, Jim. Jade was trying to break free from that way of life. I was helping her. That's what we did on those Wednesday nights. We read the Bible together. We talked about getting her twisted impulses behind her."

"Ah, so that's it," he said happily. "Yes, that explains it. I had no idea."

"No one did," Lyla said. "It was our secret."

"Did it work?"

"It was working. She was starting to turn, to accept Jesus, to renounce her wrongful desires."

"I'm so glad."

"Me too," she said. "At the clinic where I work, they consider it anti-therapeutic to try to help patients get over their homosexual inclinations. So I had to do that work privately. I didn't want money for it, anyway. It felt like a calling to me. I was planning to dedicate myself more and more to that goal, helping homosexuals change."

"Fantastic," Jim said. "That is truly noble work."

"I thought so."

"You *are* special, Lyla. In so many ways. I knew I was right about you."

"Thank you," Lyla said softly.

"Maybe somehow we could..." He wrung his hands fretfully. "You understand that I had to kill Lester."

"Yes," Lyla said.

"It felt like an absolute necessity to me, a duty almost."

Lyla nodded. "I do understand."

"And I had to do what I did to the other two — Thomas and Anastopoulos — to cover up the killing of

Lester. I don't feel bad about that. They were rapists. They deserved to be punished."

"They did," Lyla said.

"But Jenny Wocjak. I feel bad about her."

Lyla nodded sympathetically.

"When I heard her telling you about my mother being raped and about how she saw me dressed as a woman, I knew you'd figure everything out. I had to stop you from telling anyone. Jenny was ruining my perfect crime and I couldn't let that happen. She would have told others. I had to kill her. I didn't want to, but I had to."

"She was ruining everything."

"Yes. You do understand, don't you?"

"Of course I do."

"And I thought I had to kill you, that that was the only way."

Lyla said nothing. She was holding her breath.

"But maybe there's another way." He leaned toward her. "Lyla, what do you think of this? The whole time I was cooking tonight I was thinking about it. There were two things I had to find out first — whether you'd try to run away if I took the chain off, and why you were with Jade McGrath."

Lyla nodded. "And now you've found out."

"Yes. So, now I can ask you." He said no more.

"Ask me what, Jim?"

He took her hand with both of his and held it tightly. "Lyla . . . Lyla . . ."

"Go on, Jim."

"Lyla, will you marry me?"

She closed her eyes. She took deep, deep breaths, needing the seconds to think how to respond, and to swallow the repulsion. She opened her eyes and looked into Jim's hopeful ones. "Yes," she said warmly.

He jumped up from the table and let out an ecstatic whoop.

Lyla used the time to think. When he settled down, she said, "Can I tell you about my dream?"

"Yes, tell me," he said eagerly.

Lyla closed her eyes. "It's all whiteness and purity,"

she said. "You and me . . . on our wedding night." She looked at him. "It's such a beautiful dream. It's the way it should be, the way God wants it to be. We're together, you and I, our bodies as well as our souls, for the first time. The first kiss. The first embrace. The touches. The love. Making love. We're married and we come together, fresh and unspoiled for each other. Our wedding night, the night of nights that is the beginning of forever together."

"What a beautiful dream. Yes, that's how I want it. That's how it should be. I can wait. I've waited so long. This wait will be beautiful."

"The beginning of forever," Lyla repeated.

"We'll go far away to live. Somewhere out of the country. Australia maybe."

"I've always wanted to go there," Lyla said.

"We'll start new lives."

"A dream come true."

"Oh, Lord. This is so wonderful. And to think, when we first came here, I was sure I was going to kill you."

"But instead, we'll bring new life to each other."

"Oh, I can't believe this is happening. I'm so happy."

"Me too."

"We'll fake your suicide," Jim said. "We'll drive your car into a river. They'll assume your body was washed away."

"It would work," Lyla said.

"I have money. That's no problem. I'll miss Ma, but . . . well, I guess I can leave her if I can be with you." He moved around on his chair excitedly. "We'll have to get you a passport. That's no problem; I'll use my mother's. We'll put your picture on it. I can fix it to look authentic. And I'll put your new name on it — Lyla Julian."

"The beginning of your new graphic arts career," Lyla said.

They continued talking excitedly, making plans. The wedding would take place in Australia, they decided. "Can you wait that long for our first kiss?" Jim asked.

"It'll be hard," Lyla said.

"You'll have to stay in hiding until we're ready to go, but I can be seen. Nobody suspects me. I'll go home and get the passports."

"Good idea," Lyla said.

"And my financial records and things. I'll have to get them, too. My mother thinks I'm in Tampa right now, but that shouldn't be a problem. She won't know I've been home. I hate to leave without saying goodbye to her, though."

"We'll have her come visit us in Australia," Lyla said.

"Yes," he said excitedly. "That's what we'll do. Oh, Lyla, I think this is a good plan. I'll leave in the morning. You'll be okay here while I'm gone?"

"I'll finish the porch," Lyla said.

"I won't be gone long, my love." His eyes glistened with tears. "And then we'll have the rest of our lives."

"Oh, Jim."

"Oh, Lyla. I know you mean it. I know you do. Right? You do, don't you? You want to be with me."

"More than anything," Lyla said.

"I'm not being a jerk."

"Of course not."

"Some women don't lie. You're not lying. I know you're telling the truth."

"Of course I am."

"You don't hate me for what I did — Jenny and Lester and the others? And laying the blame on you?"

"You did what you had to."

He sat silently for a while. "I'm afraid," he said at last.

"It's a big change, but so exciting. It's scary for me too."

"But, I mean . . . please don't hate me for what I'm thinking. Please try to understand."

Lyla got a sinking feeling. "What is it, darling?"

"There's like a voice inside, a little voice but I can't ignore it. It's saying, *Lies, lies, all lies!* Please understand, Lyla. This has all happened so quickly. I need time to let it sink in."

"Yes, we both do," she said.

"There's this little part of me that's afraid . . . it thinks that if I leave you here tomorrow . . . that you'll be gone when I get back."

"Oh, Jim. That little part of you is so wrong. Listen to the other part. That special feeling you have about me. The trust, the love."

"Yes, that's what I should do. You want to get away from Candace. You love me. You want me. You want to go away with me. You're not angry about what I did. You understand. I hated you and did a terrible thing to you, but only because I didn't understand, only because I felt betrayed by you. I love you so much. You know that, don't you?"

"Yes, absolutely," Lyla said.

"But that voice inside of me," Jim said with great pain. "I wish I could ignore it, Lyla."

"Try, my love."

"I can't. Not yet. I'm sure the doubt will fade soon. Try to understand. I can't leave you alone here. This new turn — our love, our plan — it feels so . . . fragile. It's not quite strong enough for me to trust it yet." He went to the sink and got the chain. "I'm sorry, Lyla. I have to do it this way. Please be patient with me."

"But you *can* trust me, Jim. We made a commitment now. I'm yours forever. We're linked together by love. There's no need for a chain."

"Yes, I'm sure you're right, mostly I am, but it has to be this way for now." He held up the handcuff. "Please give me your sweet hand, my love."

Lyla shook her head. "No, Jim, it feels so wrong to me now. Ugly and out of place."

His eyes became cold. "Don't argue with me," he said. "Put out your hand."

She hesitated, weighing her options, then slowly stretched out her arm.

Be patient, she told herself as he chained her to the bed. *He's almost there.* Her sleep was restless. She

254

dreamed she was falling and woke with a start. It took her a long time to fall asleep again.

In the morning, Jim avoided her eyes. "I've made a decision," he said. "I didn't sleep much. I thought about it all night."

Lyla braced herself.

"I'm going to Chicago to get *her*."

No! Lyla wanted to scream.

"Candace Dunn. I'll tell her that I know she's blackmailing you. I'll tell her that if she doesn't stop, I will kill her. I'll scare her into telling the truth. If the truth is what you told me, then I'll kill her. And I'll destroy the evidence she has against your father. If what you told me turns out not to be true, then, of course, I'll have to kill you both."

"Jim, no!" Lyla said. Her voice was shrill.

"I'm mostly sure you told the truth, Lyla, but if you didn't, if you lied to me, then you will die."

Panic gripped her. She wanted to scream and smash his face.

"And Candace Dunn deserves to die in any case."

Lyla dug her fingernails into her palms. Then she spoke calmly. "No, that's wrong, Jim. No more killing."

"I've made my decision."

"It's a bad decision, Jim. If you —"

"I don't like it when you argue with me, Lyla."

"If you need proof," Lyla persisted, "there are other ways to get it without killing."

"What's the matter, Lyla? Are you in love with her? Is that it? Is that why you're protecting her? Could it be that she's not blackmailing you at all? Could it be that you'd tell me anything to save your own skin?"

"I don't want you to take the risk, Jim. It's you I'm worried about. What if something goes wrong? What if you get caught?"

He smiled. "I'm good at taking care of evil people, Lyla. I've become a pro."

"It feels so bad that you don't trust me," Lyla tried.

"I know that. I'm sorry."

"Will you do me a favor? It's not such a big one."

He waited.

"Will you think about it a little more first?" Lyla said.

"No," he responded coldly. "I've already thought it through. I'm leaving for Chicago now. I'll have to chain you in the bedroom, but I'll put food and water in there for you. And a bucket. I shouldn't be long, though. I'll put the TV in the bedroom, too, if you want."

"Wait one more day," Lyla said. "We'll work on the porch. I think we can get it finished today. And then you can go tomorrow."

Jim looked at her. "It's so important to you?"

"It's just one day," Lyla said.

He said nothing for nearly a minute. "I suppose it wouldn't make much difference. All right, my love," he said. "One day."

CHAPTER 33

Candace got the mail as soon as she heard the mail carrier on the porch. Not that she really expected there to be anything else from Lyla. There wasn't. She went back to the sofa and lay staring at the ceiling. She'd just begun drifting into a semi-doze when the telephone rang.

"Jim Julian's car's been found," Patrice told her. "It was parked near Sheffield and Webster. I think it's a good sign, Candace. I think Julian has her with him, using her car. It's been six days. If he was going to kill her, he'd have done it by now."

"Poor Lyla," Candace moaned. "What do you think he's doing to her?"

"The police will find them, Candace. They've searched his house. They found a VCR which blows his alibi to hell. Obviously he taped that TV show on Wednesday nights. He also has a computer. The type on his printer matches the type on the Ames letters."

"Yes, of course," Candace said fretfully. "We already know Julian's the killer."

"The police are looking for them. Carel's keeping me informed, and I'll let you know if anything develops. Are you going in to work today?"

"No," Candace said. "I'm useless there."

"Is anyone home with you?"

"No. It's all right. I'm okay."

"Well, you take care. I'll call you as soon as I hear anything else."

Candace returned to the sofa, hoping she might get at least a little sleep. As soon as she closed her eyes, she was haunted by terrifying images of Lyla in the clutches of her demented captor.

As Candace tossed and turned on the sofa, seventy miles away, Lyla Bradshaw was nailing a step into place and Jim Julian was sawing a board. Lyla worked slowly, buying time, hoping to come up with a plan. By the time it started to get dark, the porch was still not completed.

"We'll finish it tomorrow," Jim said. "Then I'll go to Chicago. It's better that I go in the evening anyway since she'll more likely be home then."

They piled the scraps of wood against a tree and gathered up the tools. While Jim's back was turned, Lyla slipped the claw hammer down her jeans. She tightened her belt, hoping that would hold the hammer in place. She pulled her blouse out to cover the bulge.

Jim unlocked the chain from the car bumper and the two went into the cabin, Lyla in the lead. Jim attached the chain to the kitchen sink.

"I'm going to shower," Lyla said, hoping to get out of his sight fast. The hammer was beginning to slip.

"How about spaghetti tonight?" Jim said. "We have some ground beef."

"Sounds good. I'll come help as soon as I clean up and change."

Lyla moved toward the door. She got a few feet past the doorway when she heard, "Lyla, wait." She stopped. She didn't want to turn around. "Do you like onions in the sauce?" Jim asked.

"Sure," Lyla said, trying to sound light. She realized she was perspiring. "I'll join you soon."

She went to the bedroom and closed the door as far as she could against the chain. She undid her belt, got the hammer out, and shoved it under her mattress.

"You're quiet tonight," Jim commented during their dinner.

"There's so much to think about," Lyla said, forcing down another bite.

"I know. I've heard they have wonderful beaches in Australia. Maybe we can learn to scuba dive."

"I'll find you some beautiful shells," Lyla said. Her thoughts were far from Australian coral reefs. She was picturing herself smashing Jim's skull with the hammer, and wondering anxiously whether she'd actually be able to do it.

Lyla wore her jeans and tennis shoes to bed that night. Her sleep was more restless than it had been any of the other nights of her captivity. Her nightmares were full of blood; guns were firing, knives slashing, hammers pounding bone, pounding and pounding, and her heart began pounding so hard she awoke with a start, gasping for air.

The cabin was deadly quiet. It was still dark. She felt around beneath the covers for the hammer. Found it. Looked at her watch — 4:30 a.m. She would sleep no more this night. She lay still, staring at the blackness out the window, fingering the smooth wood of the hammer's handle. She rehearsed what she would do, practiced in her mind over and over.

When the knock on her door finally came three hours later, Lyla almost screamed.

"You awake?" he called pleasantly.

This is it. This is it. Lyla took several deep breaths. "Good morning," she called. "Come on in." She sat up in the bed, the covers pulled up to her chest. Her right hand gripped the hammer. She had hoped he wouldn't have the gun with him, but he did, stuck in his belt.

"Did you sleep well?" he asked as he took the handcuff key from his pocket.

"Like a log," she said. "I dreamed about you."

He unlocked the bed handcuff. "I've got the coffee brewing. You can tell me your dream over breakfast." He was about to leave.

"Jim."

He turned. She held her left hand out to him. He came to her and took her hand softly in his, looking into her eyes. Her right arm was at the edge of the covers. His head was in perfect range.

"I feel so close to you," she said.

He squeezed her hand. "It won't be long before —"

She swung with all her might, The hard metal of the hammer head connected solidly with the back of Jim Julian's skull. The sound was an ugly thud. His eyes grew wide for a moment then closed as he slumped to the edge of the bed then onto the floor.

Lyla jumped up. She considered hitting him again. *Is he dead?* she wondered. She reached into his shirt pocket for the handcuff key. He didn't stir. She got the key and removed the handcuff from her wrist.

Get the gun, she told herself. He was lying on it. She'd have to roll him over. She started to turn him, pulling at his shoulder. Suddenly his hand shot out and grabbed her ankle in a steel grip. Lyla screamed.

* * * * *

Carel Lopez sat in Ruth Tremaine's prim living room.

"Oh, yes, he's definitely still in Florida," Ruth said. "I got a call from him yesterday."

"You remembered what I said, didn't you? Not to mention that I want to talk with him."

"Oh, I agree with you, the last thing we want to do is worry him and spoil his vacation. I didn't mention a thing about it." She looked at Carel. "Whatever he witnessed must be something important."

"Yes, it is," Carel said. "Did you get his phone number?"

"No, I asked him for it but he's staying in a condominium that has no telephone. I don't like that. It makes me nervous when I'm not able to reach him. Like when he goes to the cabin. He's there days at a time and I just have to wait for him to call. I keep trying to get him to have a phone installed."

"What cabin is that, Mrs. Tremaine?"

"Why, Jamie's cabin in Wisconsin. I don't go there much myself. It's too isolated, off in the woods like that. He likes it, though."

"Where in Wisconsin is the cabin?"

"It's near a town called Woodward. About seventy miles from here."

"Do you know the road names where the cabin is? Can you show me on a map?"

"No, I couldn't do that," Ruth said. "Jamie always drives. I don't know the way. But why do you want to know where the cabin is? That doesn't have anything to do with Jamie being a witness, does it?"

"It might," Carel said. "Who else besides your son knows where the cabin is?"

"Well, my nephew Paul knows. I gave him the directions last summer. Jamie had written them down one time for me. And I think my sister's husband knows."

"Do you still have the directions?" Carel asked.

"They're in the buffet right under my address book."

"Could you get them for me?"

"Well, if you think it would help. I must say I'm very

curious about what kind of criminal case Jamie's a witness to. But I do understand that it has to be confidential, like you said."

Ruth went to the dining room and returned with a piece of notebook paper. She gave it to Carel.

"Thank you," Carel said. "Do you have a key to the cabin?"

"No, I don't. Jim has the only one. He keeps it on his key ring."

"Do you know if he's been there lately?"

"You know, now that you mention it, he hasn't gone for months, not since last fall, I believe. This thing that he witnessed, it didn't happen in Wisconsin did it?"

"I think part of it did," Carel said. "Thank you, Mrs. Tremaine, you've been helpful."

"I have? Well, I still don't understand any of this. But if Jamie can be of help to the police in some way, then I'm all for it. I've gotten over my anger at you people for losing the evidence in my own case. I still think most of you do a good job."

"We try," Carel said. She stood. "Remember to call if you get any new information."

On her way back to the police station, Carel passed by Lyla and Candace's house and noticed Patrice Fedor's car. She decided to stop in briefly and let them know what was happening.

"I'd say it's definitely worth a trip to the cabin," Carel said. "We'll need another warrant."

"Oh God, I hope she's okay," Candace moaned.

"I want to go along," Patrice said.

Carel thought a moment. "All right. In your own car. But stay out of the way if there's any action. Here, copy this down." She handed Patrice the sheet of directions to the cabin. "I'll call you when we're ready to go. You follow behind. Don't get ahead of us."

"Fine," Patrice said. She finished writing and handed the paper back to Carel.

The moment Carel left, Candace called the number Leslie had given her. "Carel Lopez thinks Julian has Lyla at his cabin in Wisconsin," Candace said breathlessly. "Patrice and I are going there with the police. Do you want to come?"

"Hey," Patrice said. "That's not a good idea, Candace."

"I'll be right home," Leslie said.

Two hours later, Patrice, Candace, and Leslie waited anxiously for the phone to ring. It finally did. "We'll meet you at the Irving Park entrance to the expressway in about twenty minutes," Carel told Patrice. "Look for my car. Remember, stay behind me."

"Right," Patrice said.

CHAPTER 34

Patrice, Candace, and Leslie waited in Patrice's car on Irving Park Road until they spotted Carel's blue Ford. Jake was sitting next to her. A police car with two uniformed cops was behind Carel's car. The caravan entered the highway and began the trip north.

Soon after they left the highway for the county road, Carel Lopez pulled onto the shoulder and stopped. The two cars behind her did the same. Carel marched out of her car and walked to Patrice. "You shouldn't have brought them along," she said, glancing at Candace and Leslie.

Patrice nodded. "I know, but I think they needed to come."

"You can continue as far as the turnoff to the cabin,"

Carel said adamantly, "and no farther. You're all to wait there."

"Right," Patrice said.

Carel went back to her car. The three vehicles began to move again. When they reached the turnoff, Patrice pulled off the road and parked. She, Candace, and Leslie headed on foot through the woods, walking parallel to the unpaved road.

As soon as the cabin came into view, Carel and the other officers proceeded on foot, leaving their vehicles out of sight several hundred yards from the cabin.

"That's Lyla's car," Carel said to Jake.

She told the two uniformed officers to circle around the back of the cabin. Pistols drawn, she and Jake slipped from tree to tree toward the front. Carel stood flush against the front cabin wall next to a window. She listened. Nothing. As Jake kept an eye on the front door, Carel inched toward the window. Slowly she moved her head until she could see inside.

Her mouth opened. She uttered a barely audible gasp, then bit her lip.

"What?" Jake whispered.

"Lyla Bradshaw," Carel said. "On the sofa. Bleeding. She looks . . . dead." Carel took a deep breath. "We're going in. Julian's probably still there."

Carel ducked under the window and moved along the front of the cabin to the newly built porch. Jake was right behind her. Carel went up the stairs. She tried the door. It opened.

Carel went in first, crouching, turning, pointing her gun in one direction, then another. Jake moved cautiously toward one of the bedrooms. Carel made her way to the kitchen. No sign of Julian. She let the other officers in the back door. While the three men continued searching the cabin, Carel went to the bleeding figure on the sofa.

Jake returned to the living room. "Julian's not in the cabin," he said.

"Yes he is." Carel was staring at the dead face.

Jake followed her gaze. The wig on the corpse was slightly askew; the tweed blazer was spotted with blood.

Carel looked from the gun on the floor to the bleeding hole in the dead man's temple. "Looks like suicide," she said.

Jake shook his head. "Dressed for the final kill."

"So where the hell's Lyla?" Carel mumbled to herself.

"Or maybe it was set up to look like suicide," Jake said.

Carel didn't respond. She went outside to check Lyla's car while the other officers began searching the area around the cabin. Carel was about to join them when she spotted Patrice in the woods. She beckoned her to come forward.

"Julian's dead," Carel said. "Probably suicide. Lyla's not here. We're looking for signs of her. Where's the rest of your crew? We could use their help."

"Candace!" Patrice called. "Leslie. Come on."

The two women came out from behind the trees. Patrice told them the news.

"Lyla's okay," Candace said vehemently. "She got away. She has to be okay."

Leslie and Patrice took a peek through the cabin window. "It looks just like Lyla," Leslie said. "Freaky."

Carel instructed the women to look around the area but not to touch anything.

A short time later, about a hundred yards into the woods, Patrice found the claw hammer. She called Jake and showed him. "Looks like blood on the handle." Patrice said.

"Sure does."

"There's more blood here on the grass," Patrice said. "Apparently she's injured. Looks like she fell here, maybe laid here for a while, then went that way." She pointed to some heel prints.

Patrice and Jake followed the tracks over soft dirt for several yards, but then the ground became hard and the footprints disappeared. "Can't tell which direction she went," Jake said. He looked up at the sky; it was full of charcoal gray clouds. "Let's go back."

"She could be lying out there somewhere," Patrice said.

Carel directed the two uniformed officers to search the woods in the direction the footprints were heading. Jake took a plastic evidence bag and picked up the hammer. Before he returned, it began to rain. The steady drops quickly became a downpour. The drenched women were congregated in front of the cabin. The sky was almost completely black.

"You can go in the cabin," Carel told Candace and the other women, "through the back door. Stay in the kitchen and don't touch anything."

After telling Jake to go to the squad car and radio the Wisconsin State Police, Carel, too, went into the cabin.

Candace was staring anxiously out the window. "We should be out there looking for her," she said.

"There'll be an organized search," Carel responded.

Leslie was looking out the back door window. "Hey, you guys, there's something going on out there. There are a bunch of lights. Spotlights or something."

Carel opened the door.

"This is the police!" a tinny voice announced over a megaphone. "The cabin is surrounded!"

"They can't be here already," Carel said.

"The woods are crawling with cops," Leslie said, peering out the kitchen window.

"Come out with your hands up!" the amplified voice ordered.

"What the fuck is going on?" Patrice said.

"We better go outside," Leslie said. "I think they think there's a live criminal in here."

"Stay put," Carel said. "I'll go talk to them."

Carel took a few steps out the back doorway, her arms raised above her head. "I'm a Chicago police officer," she called.

There was a moment of silence. "Come forward slowly," a voice said.

As Carel began to walk, the rain suddenly stopped. Only a few drops now sprinkled her. Within seconds, daylight returned. Slivers of sunshine lit up the area. She could see a circle of uniformed Wisconsin police.

"Who else is in the cabin?" one of them said.

"Three women from Chicago," Carel answered. "Civilians."

"Keep your hands up, behind your head." One of the cops came and removed Carel's gun from her holster.

"You in the cabin, come out with your hands up in the air," the cop with the megaphone said. "One at a time."

Patrice turned to the others. "I guess they don't believe Lopez. Come on, let's go."

Patrice emerged first, her hands raised. Next came Candace, and then Leslie.

From behind a tree in the woods, Lyla watched with amazement. Then she was running.

Candace spotted her. "Lyla!" she screamed.

They ran toward each other, arms outstretched.

CHAPTER 35

After allowing a brief reunion, Carel took Lyla to her car to question her. The crime lab crew had arrived and was examining the corpse and the scene. Someone from the coroner's office was there.

When Carel was finished, Lyla went inside the cabin where the trio of women were waiting. Lyla sat in the same chair she'd used many times before as she told her story. She began with her conversation with Jenny Wocjak the Friday before, and the kidnapping that immediately followed. She talked about Jim Julian telling her with pride how he had contrived and committed the tattooings and murder. She told of his hatred for her, her captivity and fear, the building of the porch, her manipulation of his feelings but her ultimate failure to fully convince him that she was what he wanted her to be. Then she told of the hammer, of Jim lying unconscious on the floor, of her going for the gun in his belt . . .

". . . and then he grabbed my ankle. I struck at him again with the hammer, but it didn't stop him. He had the gun in his hand and I was sure I was a dead woman. I tried to make a run for it. I just got through the bedroom doorway when I heard a loud pop and then I was down on the floor. My leg was burning with pain."

"Oh, hon," Candace murmured. She looked at Lyla's blood-soaked pants leg.

"It's just a flesh wound," Lyla said. "Jeremy bandaged it for me."

"Who's Jeremy?" Leslie asked.

"I'll get to that."

"So you were on the floor, wounded, and then what?" Patrice said.

"He was standing over me with the gun. We were in the living room at that point. I don't exactly know how it happened, but somehow I got hold of the hammer . . . maybe I'd never let go of it . . . and I started swinging it wildly. I must have connected, because the next thing I knew, he was down on one knee and I was on my feet. I swung the hammer at him one last time and ran outside. I knew he was after me. I kept running through the woods and then . . . I don't know, maybe I tripped or maybe my leg gave out . . . I was down on the ground. I lay there trying to catch my breath. I heard sounds to my right. He was going past me. He didn't see me. He kept on going. I stayed there until I couldn't hear him anymore, and then I got up and ran in the other direction."

"And somehow you got to the police," Leslie said.

"That was much later," Lyla said. "I kept running and running. I had no idea what direction I was going or where the road was. There were only trees. At one point, I stopped by a stream and washed off my leg. The wound is in the calf. I could see that it wasn't deep but it was bleeding a lot and it hurt like hell. I ripped off part of my T-shirt and tied it around the wound. Then I kept going. My hope was to find a road or somebody to help me to safety before Jim found me."

"Jesus," Leslie whispered. "You were like a deer being hunted."

"Finally I came to a cabin. I banged on the door, but nobody was there. I was feeling very weak by then. Dizzy. I thought there might be a telephone in the cabin, so I broke a window and went inside. I looked all over for a phone and then . . . I must have passed out. The next thing I knew, a man was talking to me, offering me water. His name was Jeremy Clemmens. I told him what happened and he called the police. He cleaned out my wound and bandaged it. And then the police arrived and we came here."

"What a shock it must have been to see us," Leslie said.

"When I saw Carel come out of the cabin, I thought I was asleep and having a crazy dream. And then when I saw the three of you . . ." Lyla smiled broadly, her eyes brimming with tears. She looked lovingly at Candace.

"So Jim Julian must have given up his search for you," Patrice said, "and figured everything was over for him."

"I wonder why he put on the wig and stuff before he offed himself," Leslie said.

"He's a wacko," Candace said. "He was probably totally out of his mind by then."

"Carel thinks I might have shot him," Lyla said.

"What!" Candace was incredulous.

"She told me that if I killed Julian, there was no need to cover it up. That it was obviously self-defense and I'd be in no danger of prosecution."

"She actually said that to you?" Leslie said.

Lyla nodded. "She said she knows I don't trust the criminal justice system, but that the best thing to do would be to tell the complete truth. The crime lab people took scrapings from my hand, looking for gunpowder, I guess."

"What a bunch of assholes," Candace said.

"They're checking the suitcase where Julian kept the wig and clothes to see if my fingerprints are on it," Lyla said.

"I can't believe this," Candace hissed. "It's so stupid. It'll come to nothing. Oh, God, Lyla, you're back, you're safe. That's what's important."

"And the cops know who the real tattoo killer was," Leslie added.

Candace embraced her partner. "Can we go home now?"

CHAPTER 36

A month later, Lyla had just returned home from work when the phone rang. It was Reggie Hirtz.

"So how was Hawaii?" she asked.

"Beautiful," Lyla said coolly. "We had a good time."

"I bet you did. So everything's back to normal now, huh?"

"More or less."

"I'm glad it turned out how it did," Reggie said. "I guess I had the wrong impression of you, thinking you were more of a woman of action than you are. But no matter, the tattooing of those rapists ended up being a big boost to our cause anyway, even if some creep male did do the actions. You took care of him at least, Lyla. Good job."

"Reggie, I'm going to hang up now."

"That was smart to make it look like suicide. You must have done it well since I heard they're not prosecuting you. They ended up dropping all the charges on the LUSAR women, too. I suppose you've heard that. Anyway, we're thinking about the tattooing idea. It really does have potential. We're planning to —"

Click.

"Who was that?" Candace asked.

"No one," Lyla said. She gave her partner a warm hug.

"We got a postcard from Leslie," Candace said. "She and Jade are back from their camping trip in the Colorado San Juans. Looks like they're going to stay at Circle Edge for a while."

"I don't think Jade will last there too long," Lyla said.

"Do you miss her?"

Lyla looked askance at Candace. "I thought you weren't worried about that anymore."

"I'm not. Not really." Candace walked toward the kitchen. "I picked up some shrimp for dinner. You interested?"

"I'm interested," Lyla said warmly.

The following evening, Lyla finished with her last patient and went to the parking area behind the clinic to get her car. Carel Lopez was there.

"It's Wednesday," Carel said.

"So it is," Lyla replied.

"Got any plans tonight?"

"Dance class."

"Would you consider playing hooky?" Carel said, smiling seductively.

Lyla looked at the detective's perfect white teeth revealed by her sexy smile. She wondered if Carel had her handcuffs with her. She sighed softly. "No can do,

Detective. My dancing is very important to me. I can't neglect it again."

Carel nodded. "That's probably smart," she said. "Well, I just thought I'd check it out. Say hello to Candace for me."

"Will do," Lyla said. She got in her car and drove to her Wednesday night class, feeling just fine.

A few of the publications of
THE NAIAD PRESS, INC.
P.O. Box 10543 • Tallahassee, Florida 32302
Phone (904) 539-5965
Toll-Free Order Number: 1-800-533-1973
Mail orders welcome. Please include 15% postage.

FLASHPOINT by Katherine V. Forrest. 256 pp. Lesbian
blockbuster! ISBN 1-56280-043-4 $22.95

CROSSWORDS by Penny Sumner. 256 pp. 2nd VictoriaCross
Mystery. ISBN 1-56280-064-7 9.95

SWEET CHERRY WINE by Carol Schmidt. 240 pp. A novel of
suspense. ISBN 1-56280-063-9 9.95

CERTAIN SMILES by Dorothy Tell. 160 pp. Erotic short stories
ISBN 1-56280-066-3 9.95

EDITED OUT by Lisa Haddock. 224 pp. 1st Carmen Ramirez
Mystery. ISBN 1-56280-077-9 9.95

WEDNESDAY NIGHTS by Camarin Grae. 288 pp. Sexy
adventure. ISBN 1-56280-060-4 10.95

SMOKEY O by Celia Cohen. 176 pp. Relationships on the playing
field. ISBN 1-56280-057-4 9.95

KATHLEEN O'DONALD by Penny Hayes. 256 pp. Rose and
Kathleen find each other and employment in 1909 NYC.
ISBN 1-56280-070-1 9.95

STAYING HOME by Elisabeth Nonas. 256 pp. Molly and Alix
want a baby . . . or do they? ISBN 1-56280-076-0 10.95

TRUE LOVE by Jennifer Fulton. 240 pp. Six lesbians searching for
love in all the "right" places. ISBN 1-56280-035-3 9.95

GARDENIAS WHERE THERE ARE NONE by Molleen Zanger.
176 pp. Why is Melanie inextricably drawn to the old house?
ISBN 1-56280-056-6 9.95

MICHAELA by Sarah Aldridge. 256 pp. A "Sarah Aldridge"
romance. ISBN 1-56280-055-8 10.95

KEEPING SECRETS by Penny Mickelbury. 208 pp. A Gianna
Maglione Mystery. First in a series. ISBN 1-56280-052-3 9.95

THE ROMANTIC NAIAD edited by Katherine V. Forrest &
Barbara Grier. 336 pp. Love stories by Naiad Press authors.
ISBN 1-56280-054-X 14.95

UNDER MY SKIN by Jaye Maiman. 336 pp. A Robin Miller
mystery. 3rd in a series.   ISBN 1-56280-049-3.   10.95

STAY TOONED by Rhonda Dicksion. 144 pp. Cartoons — 1st
collection since *Lesbian Survival Manual*.   ISBN 1-56280-045-0   9.95

CAR POOL by Karin Kallmaker. 272pp. Lesbians on wheels
and then some!   ISBN 1-56280-048-5   9.95

NOT TELLING MOTHER: STORIES FROM A LIFE by Diane
Salvatore. 176 pp. Her 3rd novel.   ISBN 1-56280-044-2   9.95

GOBLIN MARKET by Lauren Wright Douglas. 240pp. A Caitlin
Reece Mystery. 5th in a series.   ISBN 1-56280-047-7   9.95

LONG GOODBYES by Nikki Baker. 256 pp. A Virginia Kelly
mystery. 3rd in a series.   ISBN 1-56280-042-6   9.95

FRIENDS AND LOVERS by Jackie Calhoun. 224 pp. Mid-western
Lesbian lives and loves.   ISBN 1-56280-041-8   9.95

THE CAT CAME BACK by Hilary Mullins. 208 pp. Highly praised
Lesbian novel.   ISBN 1-56280-040-X   9.95

BEHIND CLOSED DOORS by Robbi Sommers. 192 pp. Hot, erotic
short stories.   ISBN 1-56280-039-6   9.95

CLAIRE OF THE MOON by Nicole Conn. 192 pp. See the movie —
read the book!   ISBN 1-56280-038-8   10.95

SILENT HEART by Claire McNab. 192 pp. Exotic Lesbian
romance.   ISBN 1-56280-036-1   9.95

HAPPY ENDINGS by Kate Brandt. 272 pp. Intimate conversations
with Lesbian authors.   ISBN 1-56280-050-7   10.95

THE SPY IN QUESTION by Amanda Kyle Williams. 256 pp. 4th
Madison McGuire.   ISBN 1-56280-037-X   9.95

SAVING GRACE by Jennifer Fulton. 240 pp. Adventure and
romantic entanglement.   ISBN 1-56280-051-5   9.95

THE YEAR SEVEN by Molleen Zanger. 208 pp. Women surviving
in a new world.   ISBN 1-56280-034-5   9.95

CURIOUS WINE by Katherine V. Forrest. 176 pp. Tenth
Anniversary Edition. The most popular contemporary Lesbian
love story.   ISBN 1-56280-053-1   9.95

CHAUTAUQUA by Catherine Ennis. 192 pp. Exciting, romantic
adventure.   ISBN 1-56280-032-9   9.95

A PROPER BURIAL by Pat Welch. 192 pp. A Helen Black
mystery. 3rd in a series.   ISBN 1-56280-033-7   9.95

SILVERLAKE HEAT: A Novel of Suspense by Carol Schmidt.
240 pp. Rhonda is as hot as Laney's dreams.   ISBN 1-56280-031-0   9.95

LOVE, ZENA BETH by Diane Salvatore. 224 pp. The most talked
about lesbian novel of the nineties!   ISBN 1-56280-030-2   9.95

A DOORYARD FULL OF FLOWERS by Isabel Miller. 160 pp.
Stories incl. 2 sequels to *Patience and Sarah.*   ISBN 1-56280-029-9   9.95

MURDER BY TRADITION by Katherine V. Forrest. 288 pp. A
Kate Delafield Mystery. 4th in a series.   ISBN 1-56280-002-7   9.95

THE EROTIC NAIAD edited by Katherine V. Forrest & Barbara Grier.
224 pp. Love stories by Naiad Press authors.   ISBN 1-56280-026-4   12.95

DEAD CERTAIN by Claire McNab. 224 pp. A Carol Ashton
mystery. 5th in a series.   ISBN 1-56280-027-2   9.95

CRAZY FOR LOVING by Jaye Maiman. 320 pp. A Robin Miller
mystery. 2nd in a series.   ISBN 1-56280-025-6   9.95

STONEHURST by Barbara Johnson. 176 pp. Passionate regency
romance.   ISBN 1-56280-024-8   9.95

INTRODUCING AMANDA VALENTINE by Rose Beecham.
256 pp. An Amanda Valentine Mystery. First in a series.
                                           ISBN 1-56280-021-3   9.95

UNCERTAIN COMPANIONS by Robbi Sommers. 204 pp.
Steamy, erotic novel.   ISBN 1-56280-017-5   9.95

A TIGER'S HEART by Lauren W. Douglas. 240 pp. A Caitlin
Reece mystery. 4th in a series.   ISBN 1-56280-018-3   9.95

PAPERBACK ROMANCE by Karin Kallmaker. 256 pp. A
delicious romance.   ISBN 1-56280-019-1   9.95

MORTON RIVER VALLEY by Lee Lynch. 304 pp. Lee Lynch at
her best!   ISBN 1-56280-016-7   9.95

THE LAVENDER HOUSE MURDER by Nikki Baker. 224 pp. A
Virginia Kelly Mystery. 2nd in a series.   ISBN 1-56280-012-4   9.95

PASSION BAY by Jennifer Fulton. 224 pp. Passionate romance,
virgin beaches, tropical skies.   ISBN 1-56280-028-0   9.95

STICKS AND STONES by Jackie Calhoun. 208 pp. Contemporary
lesbian lives and loves.   ISBN 1-56280-020-5   9.95

DELIA IRONFOOT by Jeane Harris. 192 pp. Adventure for Delia
and Beth in the Utah mountains.   ISBN 1-56280-014-0   9.95

UNDER THE SOUTHERN CROSS by Claire McNab. 192 pp.
Romantic nights Down Under.   ISBN 1-56280-011-6   9.95

RIVERFINGER WOMEN by Elana Nachman/Dykewomon.
208 pp. Classic Lesbian/feminist novel.   ISBN 1-56280-013-2   8.95

A CERTAIN DISCONTENT by Cleve Boutell. 240 pp. A unique
coterie of women.   ISBN 1-56280-009-4   9.95

GRASSY FLATS by Penny Hayes. 256 pp. Lesbian romance in
the '30s.   ISBN 1-56280-010-8   9.95

A SINGULAR SPY by Amanda K. Williams. 192 pp. 3rd Madison
McGuire.   ISBN 1-56280-008-6   8.95

THE END OF APRIL by Penny Sumner. 240 pp. A Victoria Cross
Mystery. First in a series.   ISBN 1-56280-007-8   8.95

A FLIGHT OF ANGELS by Sarah Aldridge. 240 pp. Romance set at
the National Gallery of Art   ISBN 1-56280-001-9   9.95

HOUSTON TOWN by Deborah Powell. 208 pp. A Hollis Carpenter
mystery. Second in a series.   ISBN 1-56280-006-X   8.95

KISS AND TELL by Robbi Sommers. 192 pp. Scorching stories by
the author of *Pleasures*.   ISBN 1-56280-005-1   9.95

STILL WATERS by Pat Welch. 208 pp. A Helen Black mystery.
2nd in a series.   ISBN 0-941483-97-5   9.95

TO LOVE AGAIN by Evelyn Kennedy. 208 pp. Wildly
romantic love story.   ISBN 0-941483-85-1   9.95

IN THE GAME by Nikki Baker. 192 pp. A Virginia Kelly
mystery. First in a series.   ISBN 01-56280-004-3   9.95

AVALON by Mary Jane Jones. 256 pp. A Lesbian Arthurian
romance.   ISBN 0-941483-96-7   9.95

STRANDED by Camarin Grae. 320 pp. Entertaining, riveting
adventure.   ISBN 0-941483-99-1   9.95

THE DAUGHTERS OF ARTEMIS by Lauren Wright Douglas.
240 pp. A Caitlin Reece mystery. 3rd in a series.
                                               ISBN 0-941483-95-9   9.95

CLEARWATER by Catherine Ennis. 176 pp. Romantic secrets
of a small Louisiana town.   ISBN 0-941483-65-7   8.95

THE HALLELUJAH MURDERS by Dorothy Tell. 176 pp. A Poppy
Dillworth mystery. 2nd in a series.   ISBN 0-941483-88-6   8.95

ZETA BASE by Judith Alguire. 208 pp. Lesbian triangle
on a future Earth.   ISBN 0-941483-94-0   9.95

SECOND CHANCE by Jackie Calhoun. 256 pp. Contemporary
Lesbian lives and loves.   ISBN 0-941483-93-2   9.95

BENEDICTION by Diane Salvatore. 272 pp. Striking,
contemporary romantic novel.   ISBN 0-941483-90-8   9.95

CALLING RAIN by Karen Marie Christa Minns. 240 pp.
Spellbinding, erotic love story   ISBN 0-941483-87-8   9.95

BLACK IRIS by Jeane Harris. 192 pp. Caroline's hidden past . . .
                                               ISBN 0-941483-68-1   8.95

TOUCHWOOD by Karin Kallmaker. 240 pp. Loving, May/
December romance.   ISBN 0-941483-76-2   9.95

BAYOU CITY SECRETS by Deborah Powell. 224 pp. A Hollis
Carpenter mystery. First in a series.   ISBN 0-941483-91-6   9.95

COP OUT by Claire McNab. 208 pp. A Carol Ashton mystery.
4th in a series.   ISBN 0-941483-84-3   9.95

LODESTAR by Phyllis Horn. 224 pp. Romantic, fast-moving
adventure.   ISBN 0-941483-83-5   8.95

THE BEVERLY MALIBU by Katherine V. Forrest. 288 pp. A
Kate Delafield Mystery. 3rd in a series.   ISBN 0-941483-48-7   9.95

THAT OLD STUDEBAKER by Lee Lynch. 272 pp. Andy's affair
with Regina and her attachment to her beloved car.
                                    ISBN 0-941483-82-7   9.95

PASSION'S LEGACY by Lori Paige. 224 pp. Sarah is swept into
the arms of Augusta Pym in this delightful historical romance.
                                    ISBN 0-941483-81-9   8.95

THE PROVIDENCE FILE by Amanda Kyle Williams. 256 pp.
Second Madison McGuire   ISBN 0-941483-92-4   8.95

I LEFT MY HEART by Jaye Maiman. 320 pp. A Robin Miller
Mystery. First in a series.   ISBN 0-941483-72-X   9.95

THE PRICE OF SALT by Patricia Highsmith (writing as Claire
Morgan). 288 pp. Classic lesbian novel, first issued in 1952 . . .
acknowledged by its author under her own, very famous, name.
                                    ISBN 1-56280-003-5   9.95

SIDE BY SIDE by Isabel Miller. 256 pp. From beloved author of
Patience and Sarah.   ISBN 0-941483-77-0   9.95

STAYING POWER: LONG TERM LESBIAN COUPLES
by Susan E. Johnson. 352 pp. Joys of coupledom.
                                    ISBN 0-941-483-75-4   12.95

SLICK by Camarin Grae. 304 pp. Exotic, erotic adventure.
                                    ISBN 0-941483-74-6   9.95

NINTH LIFE by Lauren Wright Douglas. 256 pp. A Caitlin
Reece mystery. 2nd in a series.   ISBN 0-941483-50-9   8.95

PLAYERS by Robbi Sommers. 192 pp. Sizzling, erotic novel.
                                    ISBN 0-941483-73-8   9.95

MURDER AT RED ROOK RANCH by Dorothy Tell. 224 pp.
A Poppy Dillworth mystery. 1st in a series.   ISBN 0-941483-80-0   8.95

LESBIAN SURVIVAL MANUAL by Rhonda Dicksion.
112 pp. Cartoons!   ISBN 0-941483-71-1   8.95

A ROOM FULL OF WOMEN by Elisabeth Nonas. 256 pp.
Contemporary Lesbian lives.   ISBN 0-941483-69-X   9.95

PRIORITIES by Lynda Lyons 288 pp. Science fiction with
a twist.   ISBN 0-941483-66-5   8.95

THEME FOR DIVERSE INSTRUMENTS by Jane Rule. 208
pp. Powerful romantic lesbian stories.   ISBN 0-941483-63-0   8.95

LESBIAN QUERIES by Hertz & Ertman. 112 pp. The questions
you were too embarrassed to ask.   ISBN 0-941483-67-3   8.95

CLUB 12 by Amanda Kyle Williams. 288 pp. Espionage thriller
featuring a lesbian agent!   ISBN 0-941483-64-9   8.95

DEATH DOWN UNDER by Claire McNab. 240 pp. A Carol
Ashton mystery. 3rd in a series.   ISBN 0-941483-39-8   9.95

MONTANA FEATHERS by Penny Hayes. 256 pp. Vivian and
Elizabeth find love in frontier Montana.   ISBN 0-941483-61-4   8.95

CHESAPEAKE PROJECT by Phyllis Horn. 304 pp. Jessie &
Meredith in perilous adventure.   ISBN 0-941483-58-4   8.95

LIFESTYLES by Jackie Calhoun. 224 pp. Contemporary Lesbian
lives and loves.   ISBN 0-941483-57-6   9.95

VIRAGO by Karen Marie Christa Minns. 208 pp. Darsen has
chosen Ginny.   ISBN 0-941483-56-8   8.95

WILDERNESS TREK by Dorothy Tell. 192 pp. Six women on
vacation learning "new" skills.   ISBN 0-941483-60-6   8.95

MURDER BY THE BOOK by Pat Welch. 256 pp. A Helen
Black Mystery. First in a series.   ISBN 0-941483-59-2   9.95

LESBIANS IN GERMANY by Lillian Faderman & B. Eriksson.
128 pp. Fiction, poetry, essays.   ISBN 0-941483-62-2   8.95

THERE'S SOMETHING I'VE BEEN MEANING TO TELL
YOU Ed. by Loralee MacPike. 288 pp. Gay men and lesbians
coming out to their children.   ISBN 0-941483-44-4   9.95

LIFTING BELLY by Gertrude Stein. Ed. by Rebecca Mark. 104
pp. Erotic poetry.   ISBN 0-941483-51-7   8.95

ROSE PENSKI by Roz Perry. 192 pp. Adult lovers in a long-term
relationship.   ISBN 0-941483-37-1   8.95

AFTER THE FIRE by Jane Rule. 256 pp. Warm, human novel
by this incomparable author.   ISBN 0-941483-45-2   8.95

SUE SLATE, PRIVATE EYE by Lee Lynch. 176 pp. The gay
folk of Peacock Alley are *all cats*.   ISBN 0-941483-52-5   8.95

CHRIS by Randy Salem. 224 pp. Golden oldie. Handsome Chris
and her adventures.   ISBN 0-941483-42-8   8.95

THREE WOMEN by March Hastings. 232 pp. Golden oldie. A
triangle among wealthy sophisticates.   ISBN 0-941483-43-6   8.95

RICE AND BEANS by Valeria Taylor. 232 pp. Love and
romance on poverty row.   ISBN 0-941483-41-X   8.95

PLEASURES by Robbi Sommers. 204 pp. Unprecedented
eroticism.   ISBN 0-941483-49-5   8.95

EDGEWISE by Camarin Grae. 372 pp. Spellbinding
adventure.   ISBN 0-941483-19-3   9.95

FATAL REUNION by Claire McNab. 224 pp. A Carol Ashton
mystery. 2nd in a series.   ISBN 0-941483-40-1   8.95

KEEP TO ME STRANGER by Sarah Aldridge. 372 pp. Romance
set in a department store dynasty.   ISBN 0-941483-38-X   9.95

IN THE BLOOD by Lauren Wright Douglas. 252 pp. Lesbian
science fiction adventure fantasy ISBN 0-941483-22-3   8.95

THE BEE'S KISS by Shirley Verel. 216 pp. Delicate, delicious
romance. ISBN 0-941483-36-3   8.95

RAGING MOTHER MOUNTAIN by Pat Emmerson. 264 pp.
Furosa Firechild's adventures in Wonderland. ISBN 0-941483-35-5   8.95

IN EVERY PORT by Karin Kallmaker. 228 pp. Jessica's sexy,
adventuresome travels. ISBN 0-941483-37-7   9.95

OF LOVE AND GLORY by Evelyn Kennedy. 192 pp. Exciting
WWII romance. ISBN 0-941483-32-0   8.95

CLICKING STONES by Nancy Tyler Glenn. 288 pp. Love
transcending time. ISBN 0-941483-31-2   9.95

SURVIVING SISTERS by Gail Pass. 252 pp. Powerful love
story. ISBN 0-941483-16-9   8.95

SOUTH OF THE LINE by Catherine Ennis. 216 pp. Civil War
adventure. ISBN 0-941483-29-0   8.95

WOMAN PLUS WOMAN by Dolores Klaich. 300 pp. Supurb
Lesbian overview. ISBN 0-941483-28-2   9.95

HEAVY GILT by Delores Klaich. 192 pp. Lesbian detective/
disappearing homophobes/upper class gay society.
ISBN 0-941483-25-8   8.95

THE FINER GRAIN by Denise Ohio. 216 pp. Brilliant young
college lesbian novel. ISBN 0-941483-11-8   8.95

HIGH CONTRAST by Jessie Lattimore. 264 pp. Women of the
Crystal Palace. ISBN 0-941483-17-7   8.95

OCTOBER OBSESSION by Meredith More. Josie's rich, secret
Lesbian life. ISBN 0-941483-18-5   8.95

BEFORE STONEWALL: THE MAKING OF A GAY AND
LESBIAN COMMUNITY by Andrea Weiss & Greta Schiller.
96 pp., 25 illus. ISBN 0-941483-20-7   7.95

WE WALK THE BACK OF THE TIGER by Patricia A. Murphy.
192 pp. Romantic Lesbian novel/beginning women's movement.
ISBN 0-941483-13-4   8.95

SUNDAY'S CHILD by Joyce Bright. 216 pp. Lesbian athletics, at
last the novel about sports. ISBN 0-941483-12-6   8.95

These are just a few of the many Naiad Press titles — we are the oldest and
largest lesbian/feminist publishing company in the world. Please request a
complete catalog. We offer personal service; we encourage and welcome direct
mail orders from individuals who have limited access to bookstores carrying
our publications.